Praise for

To Brew or Not to Brew

"Joyce Tremel's debut novel is cleverly developed, infused with fascinating details of craft brewing plus the very real flavor of Pittsburgh, and distilled into a unique and charming mystery. A delicious blend of strong characters and smooth delivery, *To Brew or Not to Brew* is sure to appeal to mystery readers and beer aficionados alike."

—Jennie Bentley, *New York Times* bestselling author of the Do-It-Yourself Mysteries

"A heartwarming blend of suds and suspense, featuring a determined heroine and her big Irish family. Tremel knows and loves her Pittsburgh setting, making the mystery all the more real and enjoyable."

—Cleo Coyle, *New York Times* bestselling author of the Coffeehouse Mysteries

"This charming debut novel stands out with a brewery setting that offers a unique twist on typical books within the genre. An assorted mix of characters provides a diverting dose of humor, flirtation, and heart. Between the peek into the brewing industry and the mouthwatering food descriptions, readers may find themselves scurrying to their nearest pub even while the baffling case compels them to devour just one more chapter!"

—*RT Book Reviews* (top pick)

Berkley Prime Crime titles by Joyce Tremel

TO BREW OR NOT TO BREW

TANGLED
UP IN
Brew

JOYCE TREMEL

BERKLEY PRIME CRIME
New York

BERKLEY PRIME CRIME
Published by Berkley
An imprint of Penguin Random House LLC
375 Hudson Street, New York, New York 10014

ISBN: 9780425277706

First Edition: October 2016

Printed in the United States of America
1   3   5   7   9   10   8   6   4   2

Book design by Kristin del Rosario

ACKNOWLEDGMENTS

Whew! I can hardly believe that a second book has hit the shelves (or e-reader in some cases). It never would have happened without a lot of help.

The two people I want to thank first are my agent, Myrsini Stephanides at the Carol Mann Agency, and my editor, Kristine Swartz. Myrsini has been a great champion of my writing and is truly awesome to work with. Kristine has an amazing editorial eye, and it's due to her that the timeline works in this book because, frankly, it was a mess. She has the ability to see everything I miss and to help me make sense of it.

I also want to thank everyone at Penguin Random House for giving me the opportunity to write this series. They employ the most wonderful editors, copy editors, and cover artists who all work hard to make each and every book a success. And I can't forget publicist Danielle Dill. She is great to work with and always quick to answer my questions.

Thanks also to the reviewers, book bloggers, librarians, booksellers, and all the cozy mystery groups and readers for being so supportive of the Brewing Trouble series. Special thanks to everyone in the Pittsburgh chapter of Sisters in Crime and booksellers Natalie Sacco and Trevor Thomas at Mystery Lovers Bookshop.

Once again, thank you to Scott Smith at East End Brewing, who is still willing to answer my dumb questions. If you're ever in Pittsburgh, be sure to stop at his place. Tell him I sent you. On second thought, maybe it's better not to mention me.

Last, but not least, thank you to my husband and sons for being so supportive. It means everything to me. I love you guys!

CHAPTER ONE

𝔍 looked at the printout in my hand one more time, then checked the number spray-painted on the gravel in the formerly empty lot in Pittsburgh's Strip District. "Thirty-eight. This is it," I said to Jake Lambert, my assistant and chef—and, more importantly, my boyfriend. Sometimes I couldn't get used to the fact that we were a couple. Sort of, anyway. Jake was my older brother Mike's best friend and I'd known him almost all my life. He'd been the object of my huge teenage crush, even though I had been only Mike's baby sister to him. When he moved back to Pittsburgh after retiring from hockey, I hired him as my chef and I realized that crush had never gone away. It also finally sank in that I wasn't just Mike's sister to him anymore. We had decided to take things slowly, though. He'd just gotten out of a bad relationship and we didn't want to jump into anything and ruin a good friendship.

Jake dropped the poles and tent parts he'd lugged from his truck. "Thank goodness. I was starting to think they skipped us." He swiped at his forehead with the back of his hand. It was only nine in the morning and already the temperature had hit eighty. Not unusual for a mid-July day, and we'd dressed for the heat. Jake wore khaki shorts and a white tank top, while I'd opted for my ancient denim cutoffs and a teal tank.

It had taken us twenty minutes to find the designated spot where we were to set up our tent for the inaugural Three Rivers Brews and Burgers Festival, which would take place over the course of this weekend and next weekend. It was Friday, and while the festival didn't officially begin until tomorrow, most of the participants would be setting up today. It was kind of like a soft opening. It would give everyone a chance to meet the other brewers, and the judges the chance to sample our brews if they wanted. My brewpub, the Allegheny Brew House, was one of the fifty breweries and brewpubs invited to participate in what everyone hoped would be an annual event. There would be prizes for the best beers and for the best burger creation. I was entering three beers in the competition—a chocolate stout, an IPA, and my newly developed citrus ale.

So far, Jake was keeping his burger recipe top secret. Even my friend Candy Sczypinski, who owned the Cupcakes N'at bakery next door to the brewpub, couldn't get it out of him. And Candy had an uncanny knack for learning everyone's secrets. Her information network rivaled the

NSA's. Maybe it was the fact she looked like Mrs. Claus— if Mrs. Claus were a devout Steelers fan, that is. In any case, she'd never failed to get the scoop on anything going on in our Lawrenceville neighborhood—until now.

Jake stuck his hands into the front pockets of his shorts. "Do you want me to start setting up?"

Before I answered, a model-thin woman with an auburn ponytail and carrying a clipboard came up to us. She was dressed less casually than we were, in white capris and a navy-and-white cotton blouse. She reached out her hand. "Ginger Alvarado. You must be Maxine O'Hara. We spoke on the phone."

I shook her outstretched hand. "Call me Max. It's nice to finally meet you in person." I introduced her to Jake.

"The hockey player, right?" she said.

"Retired." Jake smiled, although I was sure he knew the inevitable question was coming.

"Aren't you a little young for that?"

"It just leaves me more time for my second career." It had become his standard answer, even though it wasn't the reason he'd had to quit a few years early.

"I'm looking forward to tasting whatever masterpiece you've come up with." Ginger turned to me. "And tasting your beer. I've heard a lot of good things about your pub."

"Thank you," I said. "I'm happy to hear that."

Ginger slid a paper from her clipboard and passed it to me. "These are some general suggestions on getting your tent up and situated today. You can pull your vehicle up to unload, but move it to the lot next door when you're finished. If you're going to tap your kegs today, I don't recommend leaving them here overnight. We've hired some off-duty Pittsburgh police officers, but only for the festival itself. Definitely don't leave anything valuable in your tent." She pointed to an area behind us. "Most of the temporary electric you'll need is set up, and by the end of the day we should have all of it in place.

"Jake, the kitchen is over there." She pointed to a large white tent at the far end of the lot. "There are twenty-five chefs registered for the contest, so you'll all be sharing the prep space under the tent. There are plenty of both charcoal and propane grills surrounding the tent, thanks to some generous donors. The burger tasting will begin tomorrow afternoon, and the field will be whittled down to ten finalists by four o'clock. Those ten will compete next weekend in the final, where it will be whittled down to five—a winner and four runners-up. Your time slot is on that paper I just gave you two."

She reminded us that the festival hours would be this Saturday from eleven a.m. to nine p.m. and Sunday from noon to five p.m. The second week would be the same, with the addition of official Friday hours of eleven to eight.

"The beer judging will be ongoing, since there are so many brewers," she continued, "and everyone attending the festival will get a scorecard to mark their favorites so they can vote online in addition to scoring by our three judges. Winners will be revealed next weekend at the festival's conclusion."

Ginger glanced at her clipboard. "Feel free to roam around and meet the other vendors. I know you probably know some of them, but there are quite a few from out of town. Give them a real Pittsburgh welcome. If you need anything, my cell phone number is at the bottom of the page."

After she moved on to the next brewer who had arrived, Jake turned to me. "I'm a little nervous about the competition."

"Maybe if you tell me about your burger, I can help you decide whether or not to back out."

Jake grinned, showing the dimple I liked so much. "Oh no, you don't. I know what you're trying to do."

I gave him my most innocent look. "I'm not trying to do anything. I just want to help my most trusted employee make the proper decision."

"Right." He laughed and a curl of Irish-stout-colored hair slipped onto his forehead, and I reached up and pushed it back. Not an easy feat, since at six foot three, he was a foot taller than me. He rested his hands on my shoulders. "I thought Nicole was your most trusted employee," he said.

Nicole was my part-time hostess-waitress-bartender, recently promoted to manager. I was leaving the pub in her capable hands while we were at the festival. "She is. But you're a close second," I teased. "So. About this burger . . ."

Jake ruffled my hair just like he'd done when we were kids, and took a step back. "I'm not falling for it, O'Hara. You'll have to wait to be awed by my creation like everyone else."

I finger-combed my short black pixie into place. "Did anyone ever tell you how mean you are?"

"All the time." He leaned over and picked up one of the metal tent poles. "Any idea how we put this thing together?"

An hour later we had the ten-by-ten-foot canopy tent up and Jake's truck unloaded. We had a banquet-size folding table, which I covered with a white paper tablecloth. We weren't bringing the kegs until tomorrow—the first official day of the festival—but I'd brought several large coolers filled with ice and growlers. We'd have plenty of beer for the other brewers, any festival workers, and the judges without having to lug the heavy kegs. With everything in order, I opened a package of plastic cups and placed them on top of the table.

I stood back to admire my handiwork. Many of the other vendors had arrived by that time, and the previously empty lot looked like a sea of colorful canopies against the backdrop of the Pittsburgh skyline and the bright yellow David McCullough Bridge (which everyone still called the Sixteenth Street Bridge). My booth was bright enough, but I needed to find something to make it stand out. I wasn't sure what it would be, though. I had brought a printed list of my beers with me, but that wasn't enough—everyone probably had one of those. Maybe I could make a colorful poster board with the list and put it in front of the tent.

Jake had already gone to check out the kitchen, so I decided to make the rounds and talk to the other brewers before the judges came around. I'd waved to a few friends while we were setting up, and I really looked forward to talking shop with them. Since the brewpub opened two months ago, I'd been too busy to do much else but run it. Not that I was complaining. I was thrilled the pub was a hit so far.

No one had set up in the space beside us yet, so I strolled over to the next one, where Dave Shipley was having a tug-of-war with the canopy as he tried to slip it over the metal corner. As I reached him, the opposite side of his tent swayed and I grabbed it and pulled. The tension was just enough for Dave to attach his end.

"Thanks, Max," he said. "When the directions said pop-up, I didn't think I'd need help putting it up."

"Are you here by yourself?" I held the pole while he secured it with a stake.

"Yep. I couldn't spare anyone today. The Pirates play tonight." Dave owned Fourth Base, a popular brewpub on the North Shore, situated between PNC Park and Heinz Field. It was a prime location—he got baseball fans in the summer and football fans in the winter. He brewed pretty good beer, too. He was one of the first brewers I'd met when I moved back to town, and he'd been a big help when I had questions on starting up the brewery and the pub.

"What about tomorrow?" I said.

"Cindy and Tommy will be here." Cindy was his wife and Tommy his eighteen-year-old son. "Tommy's gonna enter that burger thing."

"That's great. I didn't know Tommy could cook."

Dave's grin lit up his bearded face. "The kid's never cooked a thing in his life, but he's spent the last two weeks trying out different hamburgers on us. They're not bad, either. Except for the one he stuffed with hot jalapeños and pepper jack cheese, then topped with hot sauce. My mouth didn't cool off for days."

I laughed. "I can imagine."

He snapped open the legs on a folding table. "So, what's Jake come up with for the competition?"

"I wish I knew. He's keeping it top secret."

"Must be something pretty good, then."

"I don't doubt it. I just can't stand not knowing," I said. "He knows it's driving me crazy, too."

"You don't have that much longer to wait."

"Good thing."

We talked for a few more minutes until a white cargo van pulled up to the empty space between our tents. I fought the urge to groan aloud when the driver got out of the vehicle. Dave mumbled an expletive.

Dwayne Tunstall was the last person I'd expected to see here. On second thought, maybe I wasn't all that surprised. Dwayne had a habit of turning up where no one wanted him, which was pretty much everywhere he went. The man was a leech. He was well-known in the brewing community, and not in a good way.

Dwayne walked over to where we stood. "Well, if it isn't my two favorite brewers."

"I wish I could say the same," Dave said, ignoring the hand Dwayne had extended.

Twelve years of Catholic school had taught me if I couldn't say something nice to not say anything at all, so I stayed silent.

"I must say, I'm surprised to see you here, Maxine," Dwayne said.

I gritted my teeth at his use of my given name. "It's Max. Only my grandmother called me Maxine." And the nuns, but he didn't need to know that. "Why are you surprised? This is a brews and burgers event. Where else would I be?"

Dwayne ran a hand through his sandy-colored mullet. Between the hairstyle and the jeans and muscle shirt he wore, he looked like a wannabe Billy Ray Cyrus. Somehow he'd managed to find a barber who was stuck in the eighties. I was tempted to ask him who did his hair. He or she was someone to be avoided at all costs.

"I figured you'd be keeping an eye on your pub," Dwayne said. "Not to mention that you're new to this whole brewing gig. Not like me. And Dave here. You don't have a snowball's chance of winning anything."

"Max has a better shot than you do," Dave said.

Dwayne laughed. "For the record, I'm going to be the one taking home that Golden Stein and the thousand buckaroos."

"Who'd you steal the recipe from this time?" Dave put a stack of plastic cups down on the table a little harder than necessary. "I know it wasn't mine. I learned my lesson the hard way."

"I never stole anything. Not from you and not from anyone else. It was a coincidence."

Dave straightened and put his hands on his hips. "You're a real piece of work. You expect me to believe you just happened to come up with the same beer I'd been brewing for months. It's no coincidence. You helped me brew it. You knew exactly what went into it."

I braced myself to break up a fight, but instead Dave shook his head and turned away.

Dwayne looked at me. "I suppose you'll take his side."

I didn't say anything. I didn't have to.

"Fine. You just wait and see who wins the competition. Everyone will come flocking to my place. I guarantee it." He strode to the back of his van, yanked open the door, and started unloading.

I wasn't about to let Dwayne or anyone else ruin my weekend. Hopefully I'd be so busy serving up samples I wouldn't even know he was here. I told Dave I'd see him later and moved on to visit some of the other brewers.

An hour later, Jake and I were sitting on folding chairs back in our booth taking a short break. We had been busier than I'd thought we'd be pouring samples for other vendors and some of the festival workers.

Dwayne Tunstall had stopped at our booth several times and tried to engage me in conversation, asking questions about my brews. I'd tried my best to ignore him without success. I finally ended up answering his questions curtly without telling him much of anything.

Jake had watched the exchange in silence, then finally said, "Maybe he wants to try a sample."

"No, he doesn't," I said.

Dwayne raised his hands in the air. "I know when I'm not wanted." He spun on his heel, then turned back. "You're wrong about me, you know."

I didn't say anything and he walked away.

"What was that all about?" Jake said. "Other than the guy's a little weird. He seemed harmless."

"It's a long story."

Jake reached into a cooler and lifted out two bottles of water. "I'm not going anywhere."

I opened the bottle he passed to me and took a swig. "Dwayne has a bad reputation. Some of the brewers have had problems with him in the past."

"What kinds of problems?"

"Stealing," I said. "Several years ago, Dwayne worked part-time for Dave, as well as part-time for Cory Dixon over at South Side Brew Works. Neither one of them knew it at the time, but Dwayne was filching the beer recipes. As soon as he got what he needed, he quit. The whole time he worked for Dave and Cory, he was in the process of starting up his own place. Dwayne didn't even bother to put his own spin on the brews."

"What did Dwayne mean when he said you were wrong about him?"

I recapped my bottle and put it on the ground beside me. "He insists it's a coincidence that his beer just happens to taste exactly like the others. If they were merely similar, maybe I could buy it. But identical? No way. Every ingredient would have to be the same, and in exactly the same proportions—not to mention the brewing times and the fermentation."

Jake finished his water and tossed the bottle into the crate I'd brought for recycling. "Kind of makes you wonder why he's here."

"What do you mean?"

"If he's a pariah in the brewing scene," he said, "why would he want to be where no one wants to have anything to do with him?"

"Good point." I thought about what Dwayne had said earlier. "He's here for the competition. He told Dave and me he's going to win the Golden Stein. He sounded sure it was going to be him."

"Sounds more like he's delusional."

I shook my head. "No. I don't think so. But I wouldn't put it past him to do something underhanded to make sure he walks away with that trophy."

CHAPTER TWO

$\mathcal{J}$ ake and I stood as two men carrying clipboards and a woman holding a tablet computer headed our way. I recognized Leonard Wilson, food critic for the *Pittsburgh Free Paper*. He'd written a wonderful review of my brew house a month ago. Leonard was one of those people with a constant smile on his face. He wasn't particularly good-looking, but his cheerfulness more than made up for anything he lacked in the looks department. He was tall and skeletal, which was surprising for a food critic. He was balding and I gave him extra credit for not resorting to a comb-over. He shook my hand, and then Jake's. "I'm so happy to see you both here," he said, then introduced his companions.

Phoebe Atwell was a columnist for *Midwest Cuisine*. Pittsburgh wasn't exactly the Midwest, but somehow was included in the regional coverage of the magazine. She was taller than me—maybe five foot six or so. I'd guess her age to be midthirties. Her dark blond highlighted hair was cut in a chin-length bob and she was dressed for the heat in a floral shift.

Marshall Babcock looked more like how I pictured someone who made his living eating and drinking all the time. Ruddy-faced and portly, he appeared older than his forty years. Marshall was a prominent freelance restaurant critic. A Pittsburgh native, he wrote articles published in numerous newspapers and magazines throughout the country. I was impressed Ginger Alvarado had the pull to get someone of his caliber to participate. I doubted there was much money in it for him, but maybe the fact Ginger was married to a city councilman had something to do with it. Rumor had it Edward Alvarado would be running for Allegheny County Executive in the next election. I once tried to explain the local political setup to a friend who had just moved here. She didn't understand why the city of Pittsburgh had a mayor and a council, and was separate from the county council and executive. I didn't quite get it, either.

"It's very nice to meet you," Marshall Babcock said after the introductions had been made. "I'm looking forward to sampling your brews."

"Would you like to try some now?"

Marshall shook his head. "We'll have plenty of time for that. Right now we're just introducing ourselves to everyone and making notes on what you'll be serving."

As Leonard and Marshall made those notes, Phoebe Atwell was sizing Jake up like he was a lobster on a plate. "I've heard all about you," she purred, ignoring me altogether.

"All good, I hope," Jake said.

"Down, Phoebe," Leonard said. "I believe the young man is taken."

"What a shame," she said, not taking her gaze off Jake.

Women flirted with Jake all the time, especially when they found out he had been a professional hockey player. The fact that he'd played with the New York Rangers and not the Pittsburgh Penguins didn't seem to deter many of them. I was getting used to it. When he put his arm around my shoulders, I resisted the urge to stick my tongue out at her. I smiled instead.

"We don't want to take up too much of your time," Marshall said, looking up from his clipboard. "But we do want to go over how the judging will take place."

Ginger had already gone over most of this, but Jake and I listened closely in case there was something new. It seemed pretty cut-and-dried to me. They would taste the beers and check off qualities on their score sheets. Near the end of the festival, the scores would be tallied and added together with the online votes from festival attendees. The online voting was a smart idea. I couldn't imagine how many volunteers they would have needed to count paper votes. The judging for the chefs would proceed differently. It wasn't possible to make enough burgers for all the festivalgoers, so only Leonard, Phoebe, and Marshall would be involved in the tasting.

We chatted for a few more minutes and they moved on to the next tent. It was one in the afternoon by this time, and I suggested to Jake we go back to the brew house, grab a bite to eat, and return after lunch. We needed to refresh the ice in the coolers anyway. A few of the other brewers had mini-refrigeration systems set up, but I didn't have anything like that. I'd be keeping my beer cold the old-fashioned way.

The Allegheny Brew House was situated in a single-story, redbrick building that had once housed the offices for the long-closed Steel City Brewing Company. The large windows faced Butler Street, the main street that ran through Lawrenceville.

Nicole Clark, my newly promoted manager, had everything under control inside the pub. Not that I was worried, but it was the first time I'd left her in charge. Nicole was a graduate student at the University of Pittsburgh. We'd become fast friends since I'd hired her. Her major was chemistry—the same as mine had been. It was fun to talk about the chemistry of the brewing process with someone who really understood it. Jake was learning brewing as well, but when Nicole and I talked, we might as well be speaking another language as far as he was concerned.

The lunch crowd had waned and only two tables were occupied at the moment. Nicole was behind the bar, stocking glasses for the evening rush. Jake headed to the kitchen to check on things there and grab us a bite, while I slid onto one of the oak stools at the bar.

"How is it going so far?" Nicole asked.

"Not bad. It should be an interesting weekend." I told her a little about the setup, the brewers, and the judges. When I finished, I said, "Are you sure you don't mind keeping things going here?"

"Not at all. Besides, I'll get to the festival on Sunday."

I'd chosen to keep the brew house closed on Sundays. More for family reasons than religious ones. I was the youngest of six—and the only girl—in an Irish Catholic family. My oldest brother, Sean, was a priest and he made sure I didn't neglect my weekly obligation to attend Mass. Dinner on Sundays at my parents' house was an event, and Mom expected us to be there. Three of my brothers lived out of town, so they got an exemption. The only other one who got a pass was my dad. He was a homicide detective with the Pittsburgh Bureau of Police, so if he got a call, there wasn't much Mom could do about it.

Despite my complaints at times, I loved the family get-togethers. I'd missed them terribly during my years in Germany learning brewing. Sometimes Mom would call and put everyone on the phone, but it wasn't the same. You couldn't play backyard football long-distance. Since I'd be at the festival this weekend, Mom and Dad, and my brother Mike and his family, were planning on spending the afternoon there, too.

"Any problems so far today?" I asked.

"None at all," Nicole said. "Lunch was busy, but not crazy like it is sometimes."

Jake returned from the kitchen just then with two club sandwiches. He placed one of the plates on the bar in front of me, then took a seat beside me. I noticed his mound of fries was twice the size of mine. I reached over and lifted several from the pile.

"Hey!" He slid his plate out of my reach. "Hands off the lunch."

"You have more than me." I stuffed a fry into my mouth.

"Do not."

I gave him the same look my mother used to give us.

"Okay. You caught me. I didn't think you'd notice."

I laughed. "Don't do it again, Lambert."

Jake grinned. "Yes, boss."

Nicole shook her head. "You two crack me up."

"Happy to oblige," Jake said.

The battle of the French fries had been settled, so I ate quickly, then headed into the brewery to check on the lager in one of the fermentation tanks. I brewed more ale than I did lager, mainly because it took only about two weeks for an ale to be ready to serve. Lagers fermented for four to six weeks, and at a lower temperature. But I did like to serve a variety of brews, including some seasonal ones. The summery citrus ale I'd developed had turned out to be very popular. It was the first time I'd used Citra hops, which gave the beer a strong citrus aroma. It was a wheat ale, so the slight sweetness balanced out the stronger hops. It was one of the beers I hoped would do well in the competition.

The temperature gauge on the tank where the lager was fermenting read forty-eight degrees, which was perfect. It had only another week or two to go, so I didn't want to mess it up now. It would be a month of work down the drain. Literally. I checked the other tanks one by one and found no problems. I remembered I wanted to dress up our booth a little, so I grabbed one of our black dry-erase menu boards and some neon markers. While I did that, Jake loaded up the coolers with ice; then we headed back to the festival.

"Oh, this is terrible!" Ginger Alvarado said.

She'd dashed by our tent twice while talking into her cell phone and waving her free hand frantically in the air. The third time she passed by, she'd just shoved her phone into her pocket. I called her name.

"This is terrible," she said again. "What am I going to do?"

"What happened?" I said, thinking there had been some kind of catastrophe.

Ginger tucked a strand of hair that had come loose from her ponytail behind her ear. "We lost one of our judges."

"Lost?" Surely she didn't mean one of them had died.

She let out a big sigh. "Phoebe just let me know she's been called away on a family emergency."

"Is there anything we can do?" Jake asked.

"I don't think so," she said. "Thank you for asking, though." Her phone rang again and she reached into her pocket. She took a few steps away and in less than a minute she was smiling again. When she finished the call, she said, "I'm so relieved. There's nothing to worry about after all. That was Phoebe. She has arranged a replacement for us."

Before I could ask her who it was, she hurried away. I turned to Jake. "I guess we'll find out who it is soon enough."

It didn't take long. The news began with a murmur on the far side of the festival grounds and swelled to a crescendo of groans and obscenities by the time it reached Dave

Shipley, two booths over from us. He stormed past Dwayne Tunstall's tent.

"Did you hear the news?" he asked when he reached us.

Judging by his expression, it couldn't be good.

"We heard that Phoebe had to bow out, but that's it," Jake said. "What's going on?"

Dave jammed his hands into his pockets. "We've gone from a man-eater judge to a business-ruining one."

Oh no. If he meant who I thought he did, it was definitely bad news. "Not—"

Dave didn't let me finish. "The one and only. I may as well just pack it up now."

"Crap," I said. "Maybe he'll be fair for a change."

Dave snorted. "You don't really believe that."

"Not for a minute."

Jake looked from me to Dave, and back again. "Who are you talking about?"

"You tell him," Dave said.

"Reginald Mobley, the food and beverage critic for the *Pittsburgh Times*," I said. "As far as I know, he's never given a good review for as long as he's been with the paper."

"And I know for a fact," Dave chimed in, "that he's driven more than one restaurant out of business."

Jake was skeptical. "One person couldn't possibly be that powerful."

"He shouldn't be, but he is." I went on to explain how a former restaurant in my own neighborhood of Lawrenceville had closed up overnight because of Mobley's scathing review. "Somehow he manages to not only attack the food, but the owner's family and friends as well."

"He's a mean SOB," Dave said. "I won't let him near the Fourth Base. He came in wearing a disguise once and I tossed him out. His piece in the paper wasn't much of a review, but he ranted on about me having something to hide and dropped hints about cockroaches and rats. Fortunately, I have a reputation for cleanliness and lots of customers came to my defense in the online comments section and refuted everything he said. Others aren't so lucky."

Jake shook his head. "How does he get away with it? You'd think the paper would fire him."

"Not if it gets them more readers," I said. "People eat up the bad stuff and it doesn't have to be true. He's the local dining scene's equivalent to that guy on national talk radio."

"So what can we do about it?" Jake asked.

"Not a damn thing, bro." Dave slapped Jake on the back and turned to me. "You might want to tell your brother to start a new novena. We could use all the help we can get."

I watched Dave return to his tent, then plopped down into my folding chair. I'd been so looking forward to this festival and having a good chance to win the Golden Stein, and now all my hopes were down the toilet. "Great. Just great."

Jake took the seat beside me. "Maybe it won't be that bad."

"That's like telling someone a root canal isn't so bad."

"I've had a root canal. It's not all that painful."

"Yeah, but you played hockey. You're used to getting whacked in the face with a puck or a stick. Take my word for it—Mobley is going to ruin the festival and probably a few careers as well."

"You don't know that for sure."

I treated him to my best glare.

He laughed. "You can't scare me, O'Hara." He took my hand. "It will be fine. So what if the guy's a jerk? Everyone here seems to be onto him. We can deal with anything he dishes out."

Jake was right. We were all here to showcase our products and have a good time. We shouldn't let one person ruin the entire festival. There were two other judges who could surely balance out anything bad Mobley came up with. I certainly hoped so, anyway.

Dwayne Tunstall left his booth and strolled over to ours. "I don't get what everyone's so worked up about," he said. "Reggie is perfect for this gig."

Reggie? I'd heard the hated critic called lots of names, but never Reggie.

"I'm happy they replaced that witch with someone of his caliber. It'll bring a whole new dimension to this festival. It's a dream come true."

"A nightmare is more like it," I said.

Dwayne waved his hand. "I, for one, don't have anything to worry about. I expect to awe all three judges. I will definitely be taking home that trophy."

"How do you figure that?" Jake asked.

Instead of answering, Dwayne leaned over the counter. "How about a sample of what you got in those coolers? I'm parched."

I was tempted to hand him a bottle of water. I didn't want to give him anything I'd brewed, but I didn't have a good reason to deny him again. I knew he didn't have the ability or the ambition to figure out the ingredients by taking a taste. It wasn't his style, and he didn't have the background to do so. It was more the principle of the thing. I decided to pour him a few ounces of the IPA—the India pale ale—I'd brought. More than half the brewers here were entering IPAs in the competition and I didn't think mine would win. I had a much better chance with my citrus ale or chocolate stout.

Dwayne sipped the IPA and rolled it around his mouth before swallowing. He held the clear plastic cup up in the air, pretending he knew what he was doing. "Interesting," he said. "Nice and clear, but not hoppy enough for my taste." He downed the rest of it and smiled like the Cheshire Cat. "No competition for mine, of course."

"Oh, of course."

He turned and went back to his booth.

Jake shook his head. "What a jackass."

I opened the cooler and placed the growler back in the ice. "That's the general consensus. I can't wait for Reginald Mobley to knock him off his self-imposed pedestal. That alone might be worth having to deal with Mobley."

"It almost makes you feel sorry for the guy."

"I wouldn't go that far." I picked up the dry-erase board and a fluorescent pink marker and wrote WELCOME near the top of the board. I then used a lime green marker to fill in the rest with ALLEGHENY BREW HOUSE and a list of the brews I'd brought. For a finishing touch, I added a few curlicues in a hot orange. I placed it in front of our booth and stood back to check out my handiwork.

"Looks good," Jake said.

"It's a little extra color, anyway."

I looked down the row of tents as I went back to my own and spotted Reginald Mobley at the booth on the far side of Dave Shipley's. I'd only seen photographs of the critic, but I would have recognized him anywhere. I was sure no one else could possibly look the same. His snow-white hair was styled in a curly perm similar to an Afro. His stature resembled Danny DeVito's and he wore khaki pants and a white polo shirt that stretched so tightly across his gut the seams could burst at any time. Unlike the other judges, he didn't seem to be bothering with any preliminary introductions. He took the sample offered to him. I pointed him out to Jake and we both watched as Mobley took a sip. He then poured the rest out and threw the plastic cup onto the ground. I couldn't hear the comment he made, but I was sure it wasn't complimentary.

When Mobley reached Dave's booth, he stopped for a moment, then moved on. Either Dave refused to serve him, or Mobley decided to pass because of what had happened when he wrote his scathing review of Fourth Base. Next up was Dwayne Tunstall.

"Mr. Mobley," Dwayne said loudly, like he wanted everyone to hear him. "I am so thrilled that you are one of the judges—the only one who matters, in my opinion." While he groveled, he placed three plastic cups on the counter and poured an inch of beer in each. "I'm entering all three of these in the competition. I just know you'll love them."

Mobley smiled at Dwayne. "I'm sure I will." He raised the first cup into the air and made a show of studying it. "Nice color." He then sniffed it. "A pilsner?"

Dwayne nodded like a bobblehead.

Mobley took a sip, rolled it around his mouth, and swallowed. "Ah. Dry, but not too dry. Good mouthfeel. And a wonderful hop bitterness at the finish. Very nice. Very nice indeed."

I couldn't help but wonder whose recipe it was that Dwayne had used. I doubted it could be one he'd developed himself. I hadn't actually tried any of Dwayne's brews, but I'd heard about them from those who had. If the one the critic tasted was from a recipe belonging to another brewer, I sincerely hoped Dwayne didn't get the credit for it.

While Mobley tasted Dwayne's other samples—with much the same reaction—Jake helped me get mine ready. I hadn't been nervous up until now, but my hands shook as I poured the citrus ale.

Jake squeezed my shoulder. "Don't worry. He's going to love it."

I didn't believe him and neither did the butterflies in my stomach.

As Mobley approached, I wiped my sweating palms on the front of my shorts and pasted a smile on my face when he reached the booth.

"Allegheny Brew House." His gaze moved from the dry-erase board to me. "You're the lady brewer."

"Yes, I am," I said. "I'm happy to finally meet you."

"We'll see about that." He looked at Jake. "And you're the hockey player who thinks he can cook."

"I do a pretty good job," Jake said.

Mobley snorted. "I'm not counting on it." He turned his attention to the three samples on the counter. He picked up the IPA and sniffed it. "Smells too hoppy."

Too hoppy? If anything, my IPA had fewer hops than most.

He took a sip and made a face. "This is terrible." He picked up the chocolate stout.

He was going out of order. Just like with wine, it was best to taste from lightest to darkest. "Mr. Mobley, you should try the middle one before the stout."

He glared at me. "I know what I'm doing, young lady. I'll taste them any way I want to." He didn't bother sipping this one. He downed it in one gulp and shuddered. "I realize a stout is supposed to have a roasted taste, but I can't help but wonder what you roasted your barley with. My guess is Mr. Hockey's old, smelly socks."

I clenched my hands into fists and somehow managed to keep the smile on my face.

Mobley then picked up the cup with the citrus ale. He took the time to study it. "Interesting color."

That sounded promising. Maybe he'd like it.

"Reminds me of the sample I left in a cup at the doctor's office last week," he said.

Jake took a step forward. I put my hand on his arm and shook my head. Mobley would like nothing better than for someone to hit him. He probably had his attorney on speed dial.

Mobley sniffed the cup. "Ugh. This stinks. Smells like grapefruit. It figures a girl would make a beer that smells like fruit."

I widened my artificial smile. My cheeks were beginning to hurt.

He tilted his head back and poured the contents into his

mouth. Instead of swirling it around or swallowing, he suddenly straightened and spit the beer out, spraying it all over my dry-erase board.

"What swill! This is the worst thing I've ever tasted," he bellowed, smashing the plastic cup onto the ground.

Shocked, I watched the colors run together on my marker board. Jake swore, then rounded the table and went after Mobley, who was already moving on to his next victim across the aisle. I ran after him, hoping Jake wouldn't do anything stupid.

Jake grabbed Mobley's arm and spun him around.

"Get your hands off me," Mobley said.

"Not until you apologize to Miss O'Hara."

"Jake, let him go," I said. "He's not worth it."

He loosened his grip but didn't let him go. "You still owe her an apology."

I saw Dave Shipley and Dwayne Tunstall heading our way.

Mobley sniffed. "If anyone owes an apology, it's the person who made that slop." He glared up at Jake. "And if you don't release me at once, you will be hearing from my attorney, as well as the police. I will not be manhandled."

"Is there a problem here?" Dave asked.

"Nothing I can't handle," Jake said.

Several other brewers arrived and Dwayne went to stand beside Mobley, looking very smug. "I think what we have here is a sore loser, Mr. Mobley."

"No one's lost anything yet, Tunstall," Dave said. "If you need an assist, Jake, I wouldn't mind taking a shot at him myself."

"That's enough," I said. I stepped between Jake and Mobley. "This is ridiculous. Let him go. I don't need an apology."

Jake released him.

Mobley rubbed his wrist, then shook his fist at the three of us. "You will all be sorry. No one messes with Reginald Mobley. I've ruined better people than you. You just wait."

"Don't pull anything with us," Dave said, "or you'll be the one who's sorry."

"Are you threatening me, Shipley?" Mobley said.

Dave shrugged. "I'd call it more of a promise."

"It sounds like a threat to me, Mr. Mobley," Dwayne said. "I'll be happy to escort you out of here."

"Don't bother." Mobley's gaze rested on me. "I should have known a woman brewing beer could only mean trouble." He grinned suddenly. "In the long run, though, this may be fun. Be sure to read the paper tomorrow."

He strode away and Randy Gregory, owner of Butler Brewing, shook his head. "I'm not sure what he meant by that, but it doesn't sound good."

I was a little concerned, but I wasn't about to show it. "It doesn't matter what he says or even what he does. I'm not going to let that big windbag put a damper on this festival."

Jake put his arm around me. "I agree. We're all here for the same reason—to show off our stuff and have a good time."

"Speak for yourself," Dwayne said. "The only reason I'm here is to take home that trophy."

"Good luck with that," Brandon Long said. Brandon owned a microbrewery just over the border in Ohio. He'd been an assistant brewer at Cory Dixon's South Side Brew

Works until he decided to branch out on his own. "I can't wait to read Mobley's review when he finds out you steal your stuff from everyone else." Unlike Dwayne's, Brandon's brews were all original.

Dwayne sniffed. "Sour grapes. You're just mad that he loved mine and hated yours. I'm going to win. I can promise you that." He stalked back to his booth.

"Any idea what we can do about Mobley before he ruins this festival?" Cory Dixon asked.

"I don't think there's much we can do," I said. "We can talk to Ginger, but at this point I don't know what good it will do. It was probably hard to get a replacement for Phoebe Atwell at the last minute. We're just going to have to make the best of it and hope the other two judges can put Mobley in his place."

"I'd sure like to put him somewhere," Cory Dixon said.

Dave made a face. "You and everyone else. I'd say it's a matter of time until a certain critic gets what's coming to him."

CHAPTER THREE

Despite Reginald Mobley's actions, we made the most of the rest of the day. By the time all the brewers packed up to leave later that afternoon, everyone was in better spirits. I was determined to not let him get to me. If he hated my beer, I was no worse off than anyone else.

The next morning, I arrived at the brew house early. The festival didn't begin until eleven, but I still had my other duties to take care of before then. Besides, early mornings in the brewery were my favorite. I still got a thrill when I unlocked the front door and entered my pub. Sometimes I couldn't quite believe I actually owned the place. I stood inside the door for a moment to take it all in. The pine plank floors that I'd discovered under fifty-year-old linoleum shone with a satin luster, and the dark oak bar gleamed. I gave a lot of credit for this to my staff. All of them took great pride in the place and put as much effort into cleaning up as they did into serving customers. And as soon as I could afford it, every one of them would be getting a raise.

After I dropped my purse and keys onto the old desk in my office, I headed for the brewery. I checked the fermentation tanks, then went to the supply room to inventory what I needed to order for the next couple of months. Although it was July, I'd already begun brewing some fall varieties. One was a dunkel, which is a dark lager, and my very own version of an Oktoberfest. I was planning a celebration in September to coincide with Germany's Oktoberfest. There was nothing like the real thing, but I'd try my best to do it justice. But first, I had the Three Rivers Brews and Burgers Festival to get through.

When we'd left the festival yesterday, I thought I had myself convinced that Mobley's reaction to my brews didn't bother me, but after I got home, it was all I could think about. It didn't matter that he hated everyone's else's beer, too. Except for Dwayne Tunstall's, of course. That surely didn't make me feel any better about it. I looked at the clock—seven a.m. I decided a visit to Cupcakes N'at was in order. I could talk to Candy to see if she knew anything about Mobley and at the same time fix my growling stomach. Even though I was only going to the bakery next door, I locked the pub and set the alarm. I was a bit of a fanatic about it after everything that had happened two months ago. It didn't matter that there had been no way I could have known how someone was getting into the pub without setting off the alarm. I wasn't going to let anything like that happen ever again. I glanced over at the empty storefronts and hoped they'd be filled soon. Maybe then I'd stop being reminded of the best friend I'd lost.

It seemed like everyone in Lawrenceville had a sweet tooth this morning. The line reached to the bakery door. Candy and her assistant, Mary Louise, were behind the glass cases waiting on customers with their usual good humor. Mary Louise was a new addition to Cupcakes N'at. When I'd first suggested to Candy that she needed a full-time assistant at the bakery, she hadn't been keen on the idea. Although Candy was a healthy and active seventy-two-year old, working twelve-hour days operating a busy bakery with only a couple of part-timers was running her ragged. She finally relented and hired Mary Louise, who was fifteen years younger and knew the bakery business almost as well as Candy. They got along like sisters.

Candy spotted me and waved. Today she was decked out in a yellow apron over gold slacks and a black jersey that I was sure had a picture of one of her beloved Steelers on the front. She'd recently gotten new wire-rimmed glasses that made her look more like Mrs. Claus than ever. Mary Louise, on the other hand, was the spitting image of Olive Oyl from the old *Popeye* cartoons except she wore a pale pink apron with ruffles over a pair of worn blue jeans and a white blouse.

The line moved quickly and in less than five minutes I was at the counter.

"Good morning, Max," Mary Louise said with a smile. "How is our favorite brewer today?"

I returned her greeting and ordered two apple cinnamon

muffins. I usually had a hard time deciding between the apple muffins and the double-chocolate ones. Today, however, the aroma of cinnamon filled the air, so it made my choice easy. I didn't even have to think about it.

"Are you all ready for the big festival?" Candy said. "I just know both you and Jake are going to take away the big prize."

"You have a lot more confidence than I do," I said. I told them about what happened the day before.

Mary Louise's eyes grew wide when I got to the part where Reginald Mobley spit all over my display. "That's horrible!" she said. "I don't understand how anyone could be that mean."

"It doesn't surprise me," Candy said. "I've met the man. He's a beast."

"So he's always like that?" I asked.

"As far as I know," she said. "I haven't heard of anyone who's had a good experience with him—except for that one brewer you just mentioned."

She passed the waxed bag containing my muffins over the top of the counter and I paid for my order. "That's the really weird thing," I said. "I understand how the guy is a jerk and doesn't like anyone's stuff. What I don't get is how he could possibly rave about Dwayne's beer, especially when it's most likely not even his own recipe."

"Maybe they're friends," Mary Louise said.

I almost laughed. "No way. I seriously doubt whether either one them has any friends at all."

Candy drummed her fingers on the glass case. "That might not be so far off base."

"What? That neither one of them has any friends?"

"No, that maybe they are friends," Candy said. "Stranger things have happened. Two outcasts nobody likes, so they kind of bond."

I shook my head. "I don't buy it. Mobley may have been complimentary about Dwayne's beer, but the way he looked at him was anything but. If Dwayne had been a bug, Mobley would have squashed him."

Candy smiled at me as another customer came in. "Looks like you have another mystery to solve, Max."

That was the last thing I needed, I thought as I walked back next door. I spotted Jake's truck parked a few car lengths up the street and a little thrill went through me. "I brought breakfast," I called out as I entered the pub.

Jake stood behind the bar with the morning newspaper spread out in front of him. "Great. I'm starving. I'll get the coffee." He folded the paper, stuck it under his arm, and started for the kitchen.

"Leave the paper," I said.

He kept walking. "I'll be right back."

I pulled the muffins out of the bag and placed each of them on napkins. Some streusel topping fell off the muffins and I picked up a piece of it and popped it into my mouth as Jake returned, carrying two mugs. "Here you go. Nice and sweet. Just like you." He leaned over and kissed me on the cheek.

"I bet you say that to all the girls."

He grinned. "Nah. Only the ones who like to ruin their coffee by putting sugar in it."

"Ha. Very funny."

We sat side by side at the oak bar. I was halfway through my muffin when I noticed he hadn't brought the newspaper back with him. "Where's the paper? I want to take a look at it."

"No, you don't."

"Of course I do."

Jake shook his head. "No. You don't."

"Yes . . ." I suddenly remembered Mobley's comment from yesterday. I slipped from my seat. "What did he say?"

"You don't want to know. Really. Take my word for it."

My blood pressure shot up a notch. "I need to see it, Jake. Good or bad. Stop trying to protect me."

He stood. "I threw it out. There's no point in you reading what that jerk wrote. No one's going to believe it anyway."

"I'm going to read it." I stomped to the kitchen and retrieved the paper from the recycling bin. I didn't go back into the pub. Instead I spread the paper on the stainless steel prep counter and flipped through until I found Reginald Mobley's article. The title in big black letters read SWILL EVEN A SWINE WOULD HATE.

The article was more or less a repeat of everything he'd said yesterday. He ripped apart every brewer at the festival with the exception of Dwayne, who got a rave review. I wasn't mentioned until the last paragraph.

Last but not least, there's the girl brewer who wouldn't know a good beer if she fell into one of her beer tanks. Oops. I believe someone did exactly that. Maybe that's what gives Ms. O'Hara's brews that distinctive flavor of Eau de Corpse.

My stomach crashed to my knees. I read it again to be sure I'd read it right. The words didn't change. No wonder Jake had tried to keep it from me. I slammed my fist down on the counter as Jake came through the swinging door. "I can't believe he wrote that." I felt tears forming in my eyes. "He has no right to bring that up. It's over and done with. He makes it sound like Kurt's death was my fault."

"I warned you it was bad." Jake put his arm around me. "I didn't want you to see that."

I blinked the tears away and forced myself to read on. *If the beers aren't bad enough, the food would make a starving person think twice about eating it. On my visit to the Allegheny Brew House on Sunday* . . . I stopped reading and looked at Jake. "Wait a minute. We're not even open on Sundays."

"I know."

"He's making all this up. That jerk!" I read more. *The oh-so-typical pub fare should be called sub fare, as in substandard.* He went on to describe two dishes we didn't even have on the menu. But would anyone else know that? The critic continued in the same vein and finished up by warning the public to avoid the festival. I couldn't believe the *Pittsburgh Times* let him get away with blatantly lying to their readership. I'd gone from teary-eyed to livid in record time. I tossed the paper back into the recycle bin and turned to Jake. "I suppose the great Reginald Mobley will expect me to be in tears today, groveling at his feet."

"He obviously doesn't know you very well."

"If he thinks he can bully me, he's wrong. I don't have to take this from anyone."

* * *

We arrived at the festival grounds at ten thirty to set up and tap the kegs so the three judges could officially sample the beverages before the gates opened to the public at eleven. I wasn't looking forward to seeing Mobley again. It was going to be hard not to pour his samples over his head. Jake and I weren't the only ones who felt that way.

The article in the paper had been the talk of all the brewers so far. Dave had been livid. He had arrived before us and hustled over as soon as Jake pulled his truck up to our booth.

"Did you see the paper this morning?" he asked as soon as I'd opened my door. "What a piece of sh—"

"I saw it," I said, cutting him off.

"He'd better not come anywhere near me today," Dave said. "I'll be tempted to wrap my hands around his throat."

"You'll have to get in line." Jake climbed into the back of the truck and rolled a keg to the edge.

Dave lifted it like it was nothing. "Where do you want this?"

I showed him where I wanted the barrels set up. As soon as they were in place, I iced and tapped them. While Jake moved the truck to the parking area, Cory and Randy wandered over. I tried to tune out their conversation with Dave. It wasn't going to do any of us any good to dwell on Mobley's vitriol, especially when their words were just as nasty against the critic. Finally I had enough. "Can we just forget about Mobley for a while? I don't know about you, but I'm here to show off my beers and have a good time. Are we really going to let one person spoil this event for us?"

The three of them stared at me. Randy shook his head. "Think what you want, Max, but he's already ruined this and a lot more. He'll get what's coming to him one of these days."

Just then Ginger's voice came over the loudspeaker requesting that all brewers return to their respective areas because the judges would be around shortly. Thankfully that ended any more talk about Mobley. For now, anyway.

When Marshall Babcock and Leonard Wilson made the rounds, Reginald Mobley wasn't with them. Instead they were accompanied by Ginger Alvarado.

"Before you ask," she said, "Mr. Mobley has decided he tasted enough beer yesterday, and he won't be coming until later today for the burger competition." Her hand shook when she placed the clipboard she'd been carrying down on the table beside a stack of plastic cups.

Leonard patted her hand. "Ginger's afraid no one will show up because of the article in the paper."

"We've told her that no one will believe anything he wrote and not to worry about it," Marshall said. "I predict there will be large crowds."

"I hope you're right," I said.

Jake added, "Frankly, I think we're better off without him."

Ginger smiled slightly. "I appreciate everyone's support. If I had known what he was like, I never would have let him come aboard." She picked up her clipboard. "Enough about that."

She recited the procedure and the rules again without looking at her clipboard. With fifty brewers to inform, she had them memorized. Any beer that the judges tasted yesterday—if any—was only to familiarize them with what each brewer had to offer. It wouldn't be counted in the official judging.

After what happened the day before, I was thankful for that. Mobley's opinion wouldn't be considered.

Ginger went on to explain that the judges would be tasting the beer at various intervals throughout both weekends of the festival. One of the things they'd be judging would be the consistency of the products by sampling them more than once. The results would be tabulated along with the votes of festival attendees. The winner and the runners-up would be announced at a ceremony next Sunday near the end of the festival.

I poured my three offerings—the citrus ale, the IPA, and the chocolate stout—into cups for Leonard and Marshall. Jake put his arm around me while we watched them sip. Unlike Mobley the day before, each of them took his time sipping.

"Very nice aroma on the citrus ale," Marshall said.

"And the stout is exceptional," Leonard said. "You can really taste the chocolate character of the roasted malt."

Neither one of them said anything about the IPA, which I took to mean it wasn't the best they'd tasted. I was okay with that. IPAs weren't my specialty.

After I'd thanked them and they moved on, Jake pulled me into a hug. "I knew you'd wow them, O'Hara."

If he was right, maybe I had a chance to win the Golden Stein after all.

Despite Reginald Mobley's false criticism in the paper and his recommendation that people skip going to the Three Rivers Brews and Burgers Festival, by three o'clock that afternoon it appeared the festival was a rousing success. The crowds were unbelievable and I had to call my brother Mike to stop at the pub and get another keg of each brew I was serving. Mike was going to cover for me later that afternoon so I could watch Jake's portion of the burger competition. I hoped Mobley would go easier on the chefs than he had on the brewers, but I wasn't counting on it.

Jake had just left for the area set aside for the chefs to prepare their entries when Mike arrived with the three extra kegs and more ice. I wheeled a dolly over to his truck. He exited the driver's side and kissed me on the cheek. "Big brother to the rescue once again," he said.

"And I appreciate it." He opened the tailgate and I hopped up into the bed. I rolled a keg to the edge, then got down, and together we lifted it down and onto the dolly. We repeated this for the remaining kegs, and put them on ice. When we finished, I rewarded him with a sample.

Mike picked up a paper napkin, wiped the sweat from his face, then ran a hand through his red hair. We chatted for a few minutes and I gave him some instructions on serving the samples—like making sure to ask to see ID and not serving anyone visibly intoxicated. He helped out in the brewpub on occasion—he knew the drill. He assured me he'd be fine, so I headed to the burger competition.

The contest would be in two parts. Today's was a preliminary elimination that took the twenty-five entrants down to ten. Then the last ten would be whittled down to five next weekend when the winner would be chosen and receive a check for a thousand dollars. Jake wasn't interested in the money. He'd entered because he thought it would be a chance to prove to everyone that he was as serious about his new career as he'd been about his old one in the NHL. If he won, he planned to donate the money to the Mario Lemieux Foundation, which did a lot of good for sick kids in Children's Hospital.

When I reached the roped-off section, I showed my lanyard ID to the off-duty police officer working security, and he let me into the area designated for special guests. There was a large white canopy over three rows of banquet tables where the twenty-five chefs had been preparing their entries. The twenty-five had been broken into groups of five. Jake had been assigned to the last group of five. The chefs in the group before his were at the grills and the air was filled with the aroma of what they were cooking.

The judges had taken a short break, but now Marshall Babcock and Leonard Wilson were seated at the judging table waiting for Reginald Mobley to return. Just as I crossed my fingers that maybe he'd left for the day, I heard him. As a matter of fact, everyone heard him, even though he wasn't all that close.

"Leave me alone, Linda," Mobley bellowed. A woman grabbed hold of his arm. "Let me go, you witch." He yanked his arm from her grip and walked away. He went only a few feet before she caught up with him. He spun on her. "Crawl back into that hole you crawled out of. You're not getting another penny from me."

They were closer now and I got a better look at the woman. She had chin-length gray hair and was slightly overweight. She wore beige capris and a coral T-shirt. She grabbed his arm again. "The hell I'm not, you weasel," she said. "I'll take you to court."

Mobley let out a vicious laugh. "You tried that once, remember? It's not going to work again."

"You'll give me my due, or—"

"Or what? You'll kill me like you've threatened to do any number of times?" He started walking again. "Good luck with that."

"You'll be sorry. You will be very sorry." She stood clenching and unclenching her fists for a moment, then stalked off in the opposite direction, mumbling to herself. I watched her duck under the rope and she was gone, leaving me wondering who she was.

I looked around for anyone I knew and spotted Dave Shipley in the crowd near the grills and headed in his direction. When I got closer, I noticed his son was at one of the grills. He looked calm and relaxed for a teen in his first cooking competition. I noticed Dwayne Tunstall coming toward me and pretended not to see him. I picked up my pace, hoping Dwayne would go away. Gloating over his glowing review was the last thing I wanted to hear.

Dave was intent on watching his son and barely gave me a look when I said hello. "How is he doing?" I asked.

"So far, so good. I think I'm more nervous than he is."

"He'll be fine."

"I warned him about our favorite judge. He says he can handle it." Dave grimaced. "I'm not sure I can, though."

Apparently Dwayne didn't take my hint and took that moment to join us. "I, for one, have been hanging on every word that comes out of Reggie's mouth."

Reggie. Like they were best friends.

"I'm sure you are," Dave said. "By the way, how much did you pay him to write that article in this morning's paper? I hear he doesn't come cheap."

Dwayne pursed his lips. "Not a thing." He turned to me. "I feel bad he was so harsh to you, Maxine. I know the truth hurts, but—"

I'd sworn I wasn't going to get into it with him, but I couldn't help myself. "Truth? Mobley wouldn't know the truth if it slapped him in the face. There were so many inconsistencies in that piece it was ridiculous."

"I guess you didn't notice that, did you, Dwayne?" Dave said.

"You're both just jealous," Dwayne said. "There was nothing wrong with that article."

Dave snorted. "Right." He turned to me. "What was that commotion before? Any idea who the woman was giving Mobley a piece of her mind? I'd kind of like to shake her hand."

I started to tell him I didn't, but Dwayne butted in.

"She's Reggie's second ex-wife. A very bitter woman,

from what I hear. She's trying to get more money from him. She claims she needs it desperately and what he's giving her now isn't enough. I say she should get a better job."

I was still back on the fact the woman was his second ex-wife. I couldn't imagine even one woman marrying him. "He's been married twice?"

"Three times, actually," Dwayne said. "The first wife was Catherine. She remarried and lives in Ohio. Then there's Linda—the one today. His current wife is Melody. She's here someplace."

"How do you know so much about him?" Dave asked.

Dwayne's smile was like the Cheshire Cat's. "I have my ways."

The cooks at the grills were plating their wares and Dave excused himself to cheer on his son. I pulled my phone from my pocket, and pretending I had a call, I wandered away from Dwayne. I'd heard quite enough about his idol.

The judging up until that point had gone as I expected. Mobley's comments about the food were cruel and malicious. Marshall Babcock and Len Wilson tried their best to balance it out. Dave's son took the comments in stride, since he'd been warned by his dad what to expect.

Jake looked up and winked at me as he plated his burger. I still wasn't sure exactly what he had done with it, but I spied mushrooms, green peppers, and onions, and it was on a pretzel bun. It looked like he might have gone with a more traditional take, unlike some of the others, who went overboard to be different.

The five contestants lined up their plates on a table in front of the three food critics. They were graded first on presentation, then one by one they cut samples for each judge. Jake was the last to go in his group. Mobley had been the first in line to taste everyone's offerings—on his insistence, I was sure. I was also sure that Leonard and Marshall were more complimentary than they would have been if Mobley hadn't eviscerated every contestant.

My heart was in my throat as Jake put a plate in front of Mobley. Mobley held the plate under his nose and sniffed dramatically. He coughed and waved his hand in front of his face. "I hope it tastes better than it smells." He placed it back on the table and looked around. "Where is my water?" he roared. "Who took my water?"

Ginger rushed over and picked up a water bottle that was sitting on the ground beside his chair and handed it to him.

He snatched it from her hand. "I don't know what kind of a thing you're running here. This bottle should have been on the table and readily available." He twisted off the cap. "And it should have been opened for me already. And a cup of ice would have been nice."

"I'll remember that for next year," Ginger said.

Mobley snorted. "I seriously doubt that there will be a next year. Not if I have anything to say about it. And I will have plenty to say."

Jake stood there calmly as Mobley poked at the burger with his fork and popped the top of the pretzel bun off. "Hmm. Peppers, onions." He let out an exaggerated sigh. "And what is this? Common white mushrooms? How very ordinary. I should have expected that from you. You wouldn't know a chanterelle from a shiitake."

"I like to keep things simple," Jake said.

"You're simple, all right." Mobley scraped the mushrooms off the sandwich, then forked a chunk of the hamburger and placed it in his mouth. He chewed slowly, almost like he was really evaluating it. After he swallowed that bite, he took a drink of his water. "That was the absolute worst thing I ever tasted. What did you marinate that in?"

"A brown ale," Jake said.

"I suggest you don't do it again," Mobley said. While he spoke, beads of sweat formed on his face. "Somebody get me some ice. It's sweltering hot here." He lifted his water bottle and drank. His whole face reddened and the sweat that had formed there dripped onto his chest. He took another drink and some of the water dribbled from his lips. "Something's wrong." He tried to stand, but he didn't seem to have the strength to push himself up. "Somebody help me." His voice was weak and shaky. Nothing like the bombastic tone he'd been using.

As Marshall and Leonard rose from their seats, the water bottle dropped from Mobley's hand. He clutched at his throat and pulled at the neckline of his shirt. As he tried to stand again, he tipped his chair over and toppled to the ground.

•

CHAPTER FOUR

𝕴 was frozen in place, not sure what happened. A woman screamed. Several people hollered to call 911. Others started clicking away with their cell phone cameras. I snapped out of my stupor and ducked under the barrier, making my way to the judges' table, where Jake was on his knees beside the critic, feeling his neck for a pulse. One of the off-duty police officers who was working security pushed his way through the bystanders while talking into his portable radio. My stomach lurched when I reached the fallen man. His face had been red before, but now it was a dark cherry color and his lips had turned a sickening bluish purple. Jake was already doing chest compressions, but I didn't think it would help.

Within minutes, paramedics arrived along with several

police units. The medics took over from Jake and we moved out of the way. They worked on him for what seemed like forever, but in the end Reginald Mobley was pronounced dead.

Despite the heat, I shivered. Jake already had his arm around me and now he pulled me close.

"Are you okay?" he asked.

"I just can't believe it. He was fine one minute, then boom. No warning at all."

"It happens like that sometimes."

Randy Gregory and Cory Dixon wove through the crowd to where we stood. "Is it true?" Randy said. "Mobley's dead?"

"See for yourself." Jake pointed to where medics and police officers stood.

"Oh man," Cory said. "That's great news."

"I bet you're glad, Max," Randy said.

"Glad?" I felt a flash of heat in my cheeks. "How can you say that? A man is dead. I didn't like him much. As a matter of fact I didn't like him at all, but I'd never wish anyone dead. No, I'm not glad."

Randy shrugged. "I'll be happy for both of us, then. I have no sympathy for that jerk."

Cory stared at his feet. "I only meant it's great we don't have to deal with him anymore."

Jake nudged me. "Look."

Two of the officers on scene were stringing crime scene tape around the area of the judging table. I wasn't surprised. It was standard procedure. They'd want to keep the area clear until someone from the medical examiner's office arrived to take the body away. There would also be an autopsy, since the death was so sudden.

Another officer came over and ordered everyone who'd been watching the competition to move to the open tent where the kitchen had been set up so they could get statements. I wondered why the uniforms didn't just take everyone's name and phone number and let everyone go. They could get statements later. Maybe they were being extra careful because of who the dead man was.

"I can't stay," one woman complained. "I have to be at work in half an hour."

"Call your boss," the officer said. "You're gonna be late."

"How long do we have to stay there?" a man asked.

The cop's answer was "As long as it takes."

The complaints continued long after all fifty of us were stuffed under a tent that had room for only thirty at most. And the fact that there were only half a dozen chairs made things worse. Randy and Cory told the officer they had arrived after Mobley died and hadn't seen a thing. We backed them up, so they were permitted to leave.

Jake and I stayed near the edge of the tent, not only because it was cooler there, but so we could see what was going on. I called Mike to tell him what had happened, but the word had already reached him. I asked him to close up the booth and take any remaining beer back to the pub. We'd start fresh tomorrow. If we were out of here by then, that was.

I saw my dad arrive with a detective I didn't recognize. It wasn't unusual for detectives to investigate when someone died suddenly, but I was beginning to think there was more to Mobley's death than we thought. First we'd been sequestered, then crime scene tape went up, and now detectives were here. Individually, it didn't mean anything, but all three together was a little out of the norm. I told the officer who was babysitting us that my dad was one of the investigators. He either didn't believe me or didn't care, because he wouldn't let me leave. At one point I spotted Ginger Alvarado standing with her arm around a tall woman with long platinum hair wearing a hot pink sundress. Every once in a while the woman dabbed at her eyes with a tissue. I wondered if this was the current wife. What did Dwayne say her name was? Melanie? No, it was Melody. Marshall Babcock and Leonard Wilson were nearby, too, and already talking to my dad and the other detective.

Tired of standing, I found a tiny patch of grass in the gravel just outside the tent and sat down. The officer gave me a look, but didn't say anything. I guess as long as I was sitting, I couldn't escape. I'd been seated for only five or ten minutes when Marshall pointed in this direction, and my dad and the other detective headed our way. Thank goodness. I got to my feet and motioned for Jake to join me.

Dad bussed me on the cheek and shook hands with Jake. "Are you all right, sweetie?" he said to me.

"I'm okay," I said. "It's just such a shock."

The other detective cleared his throat.

"Sorry," Dad said. "This is Vincent Falk."

Vincent Falk was the epitome of the perfect TV detective, or at the very least, a model for *GQ*. His charcoal suit looked expensive, as did the gold cuff links attached to a shirt that was the whitest I'd ever seen. He wore a red patterned tie that had to be silk. I wasn't an expert in these things, but I did have five brothers. His blond hair was cut and styled so perfectly it made me wonder how many cans of hair spray he used in a week.

"Vince is new to the department and I'm showing him the ropes."

Dad smiled. Vince did not.

"Nice to meet you," I said.

He didn't reply—only nodded, then looked at Jake. "I understand the victim was eating your hamburger when he collapsed."

"Yes, he was," Jake said.

"I'll need to see where you prepared your food."

I noticed he said *I* and not *we*. "Why?" I asked.

Vince ignored me. "Show me where."

I looked at my father. His face was a blank, but his jaw was clenched, which told me he wasn't happy about something. My guess would be his new partner.

Jake led the detective and my dad through the over-crowded tent to the table where he'd been working. Two teenage girls sat cross-legged on top of the plastic banquet table.

Vince approached them, giving the two a dazzling smile. "Would you young ladies mind sitting somewhere else? We need to work here."

The girls blushed and jumped to their feet.

"Thank you very much," he said. "I appreciate it." He smiled again and they giggled as they walked away.

So, Vince could be charming when he wanted to be. Just not with us. As soon as the girls were out of sight, he turned back to Jake. "Where is everything you used today?"

"Right there in the cooler."

Vince pulled a pair of latex gloves from his pocket and began slipping them on.

My dad finally spoke up. "Vince, I don't think that's necessary."

"I'm following protocol. I'm not bending the rules because you know these people."

"They're not just people."

"That's my point." Vince snapped the wrist of the glove as he finished putting it on. He pawed through the contents of the cooler, which took all of about five seconds. There was only plastic wrap that had held ground beef, some empty containers where the vegetables had been, and a couple of jars of assorted spices. "That's all there is?"

"That's it," Jake said.

"I'm going to take this for processing," Vince said.

I expected Dad to say something. When he didn't, I spoke up. "What exactly is going on here? Why do you need our cooler? What does any of this have to do with Mobley having a heart attack?"

Vince looked at me with a smug smile on his face. "Because it wasn't just a heart attack."

"Vince." Dad's voice was sharp. "That's enough. Take the cooler and I'll meet you at the car."

The detective clamped his mouth shut, snatched up the cooler, and stalked out of the tent. He reminded me of one of my nieces when they didn't get their way.

Jake shook his head. "That guy's got issues."

I was angry. "Where does he get off treating us like that?"

"I'm sorry about that," my dad said. "Vince is a little intense."

"You think?" He needed to do better than that.

"Let's go back out where we can talk." He didn't need to add "without anyone eavesdropping."

Jake and I followed him out of the tent. There were now two vehicles from the medical examiner's office and half a dozen techs where Mobley had collapsed. "Why so much activity for a heart attack?" Jake asked.

"We won't know for certain yet," Dad said, "but it appears the victim didn't die of natural causes. He may have been poisoned."

I can't say I was surprised. Not only because of Vince's last statement, but there was way too much activity for a medical issue. Mobley had been murdered. The image of his cherry red face and blue lips came to mind. I tried to recall what poison or poisons would cause that. I had a master's degree in chemistry, but it had been more than a few years since I'd used the knowledge for anything other than brewing beer.

Dad continued. "He may have ingested cyanide."

I did a mental head slap. Of course. Cyanide.

All of a sudden it hit me why Dad's new partner was so cold to us. He considered us suspects. Mobley collapsed while eating Jake's contest entry. And I had a chemistry background. "That explains Vinnie the Viper's attitude, then."

Dad kept a straight face, but there was a twinkle in his eyes. "Don't let him hear you call him that."

"How did you get saddled with him?" Jake said.

"It's a long story, which we don't really have time for right now." He glanced over to where Vince stood talking to one of the crime scene techs. "He's a good cop. This will be his first homicide, so he's a little too gung ho. He'll settle down eventually. I hope."

"Let me get this straight," Candy said. "That poor excuse for a food critic died while he was eating Jake's hamburger."

It was late in the evening and we were sitting in Jump, Jive & Java, the coffee shop across the street from the brew house. The festival was supposed to end at nine, but given what had happened and the police presence, Ginger decided to close down earlier. After Jake and I packed up, we returned to the brewery. The events of the day had taken a toll on us and by the time we filled our staff in on what had happened, we were both exhausted. When Jake dropped me off at my loft, he reminded me we had planned to trade vehicles. I had totally forgotten about it. His parents were coming in from Florida for a two-week-long visit, so he took my Corolla to pick them up at the airport in the morning. It worked out perfectly, since I needed the truck anyway to haul the kegs to the festival.

I thought about going straight to bed after I fed my kitten, Hops—a gray tabby that I'd adopted two months ago. Despite being tired, I couldn't settle down, and I ended up pacing the floor in my living room for half an hour. When Hops pounced and attached herself to my leg for the third time, I peeled her off and took a walk. By the time I reached Butler Street, Candy was just locking up the bakery and together we headed across the street.

The coffee shop was owned by my good friend Kristie Brinkley, who, by the way, had nothing in common with the supermodel other than they were both gorgeous. Kristie "with a *K*," as she liked to say, looked more like Halle Berry—if the actress wore dreadlocks. Kristie changed the color of her hair more often than some people changed socks. Today's color was a deep purple. I liked it, but there's no way I'd have the nerve to wear it myself. I'd keep my black pixie, thank you very much.

"That's not the worst of it," I said. "Someone poisoned him."

Kristie shook her head, making her braids sway back and forth. "That's not good."

"Anyone ever tell you you're a real Einstein?" my ninety-two-year-old friend Elmer Fairbanks said. He didn't mince words about anything or anybody. He had made himself part of our book group at the library, and since then he'd been a permanent fixture at either the bakery, the pub, or here.

"We know you're not," Candy said to Elmer. The two of them were always at odds. Most of the time it was good-natured. I think they just liked to argue.

"What happened next?" Kristie asked.

I filled them in, including the part where Vince Falk took our cooler.

It was Elmer's turn to shake his head. "I don't like it.

That detective—your pop's new partner—reminds me of a CO I had once." Elmer was a World War II vet who had served with the 101st Airborne. "Tried to railroad one of my buddies for something he didn't do."

"There are much better suspects," I said.

"Maybe," Elmer said. "But I'd bet the victim wasn't eating any of their food when he keeled over."

"Who are the other suspects?" Candy asked.

I sipped my mocha. "His ex-wife for starters. She actually threatened to kill him."

Candy tapped her Steeler-decaled fingernails on the table. "Who all heard the threat?"

"Half the festivalgoers," I said. "Mobley was heading for the table where the judges were sitting and his ex had latched onto his arm. He shook her off and told her she wasn't going to get any more money from him. He laughed and asked if she was going to threaten to kill him again."

Kristie leaned forward. "What did she say?"

"That he'd be very sorry."

"That's not a death threat," Elmer said.

"Maybe not," I said. "It was more the way she said it. Apparently she threatened him before. And money is always a good motive."

"Who else do you suspect?" Candy wanted to know.

I ticked off a list that included half the brewers and restaurateurs in town. It was a long list.

Elmer finished his decaf. "Looks like you got your work cut out for you, missy."

"And time is of the essence," Candy said.

I reached for one of the caramel pecan brownies Candy

had brought. "What do you mean?" I bit into the brownie and stifled a groan. It was heavenly—dense, moist chocolate drizzled with gooey caramel and sprinkled with chopped pecans. The perfect combination of chocolate and caramel. And the pecans were a nice addition. I hadn't realized how hungry I was. With everything that had gone on, neither Jake nor I had thought about eating dinner. I licked my fingers and took another brownie.

Elmer and Candy talked at the same time. Candy rolled her eyes and Elmer said, "Go on, ladies first. No one can say I'm not a gentleman." He looked at me with a twinkle in his eyes. "Of course, I know she would've kept talking anyway."

Candy ignored his remark. "Here are the facts. Reginald Mobley collapsed eating the hamburger Jake made. Mobley gave you and Jake a hard time yesterday and wrote that terrible thing in the paper this morning."

"Yeah, but it wasn't all about me. He criticized several of us."

"Let me finish," Candy said. "That detective took your cooler. The one that Jake had all his cooking stuff in."

"Plus the ones from the other four chefs who prepared their food at the same time as Jake."

Candy gave me a look for interrupting her again. "I'm just saying that we need to find who did this before either you or Jake ends up in the hoosegow."

I laughed at her choice of words. "I seriously doubt either one of us is going to jail. When they test everything, they'll see we had nothing to do with it."

"Maybe so," Candy said. "But I'm not leaving it up to

chance, and neither should you. I'll ask around and see what I can find out about Mobley, his ex-wife, and some of the others you mentioned."

By morning, she'd probably have a dossier on all of them. I'd attempted numerous times to discover how Candy was able to ferret out so much information all the time. She could find out anything on anybody—and I was sure it wasn't only from gossiping with the neighbors. Every time I asked what kind of work she'd done before she became a baker, her answer was always "Oh, a little of this and a little of that." I'd dreamed up a scenario that she'd been a spy or a secret agent. Part of me hoped it was true. I'd be disappointed if I was wrong.

"Are they going to cancel the festival now?" Kristie asked.

I shook my head. "I thought they would, but Ginger Alvarado—the woman who organized it—made an announcement that even though we closed early tonight, the rest of the weekend would continue on schedule. Her city councilman husband convinced the mayor that the city would lose a lot of revenue if they shut it down."

Elmer pushed himself to his feet. "I bet your pop wasn't happy about that."

"I haven't talked to him tonight, but I'm sure he's not going to like a couple thousand people tramping all over a crime scene." I didn't say it, but his new by-the-book partner would hate it even more. The thought made me smile.

CHAPTER FIVE

incent Falk stood on the sidewalk outside the brew house peering into one of the front windows when I arrived at five thirty the next morning. He turned when he heard me approach. His white shirt and navy pants looked freshly starched and his blue paisley tie was so tight I didn't know how he could even breathe. "I was told you were always here early," he said. His tone made me feel like he didn't think I was early enough. It was well before I usually arrived, but I wanted to brew a batch before the festival.

"I'm here by seven or eight. Most days, anyway." I unlocked the door and the detective followed me inside, where I punched in the alarm code and switched on some lights. "There's a lot to do in the brewery even when the pub is closed."

"I have a few questions for you."

"Of course," I said, although I couldn't imagine what he needed to ask. Anything he needed to know about me he could just ask my dad. I'd given more than a full report yesterday and I was sure I hadn't left anything out. I put my purse and keys on top of the bar. "I'm going to make some coffee. Would you like some?"

"That would be great."

I led the way across the pub and through the swinging door into the kitchen. I pointed to a metal stool beside the stainless steel counter. "Have a seat." I watched the detective out of the corner of my eye while I measured coffee grounds into the paper filter. His gaze seemed to take in everything in the room. After I poured the water into the machine and turned it on, I took the seat next to him. "Coffee shouldn't take long."

Vincent Falk retrieved a small notebook and a silver pen from his shirt pocket and opened the pad to a blank page. "Tell me again what happened yesterday."

I went through the events exactly as I'd told my dad the day before. By the time I finished, the coffee was done and I poured us each a cup. I added cream and sugar to mine. Vince took his black.

He sipped his coffee, then set the mug down and picked up his pen again. "How long have you known Jake Lambert?"

"Almost my entire life. I was three or four years old when he and my brother Mike became friends."

"And what is your relationship now?"

I wasn't sure that was any of his business. "Why do you need to know that?"

"For the investigation," he said. "What is your current relationship with Lambert?"

"We're friends and he works for me." I didn't add *which you already know*.

"Just friends?"

For some reason the scene from the movie *Young Frankenstein* where Frau Blücher dramatically declared Victor was her boyfriend flashed through my mind. Although I thought of him as my boyfriend, to say the word aloud sounded juvenile to me. When I introduced Jake to anyone, I didn't use the word. I just said *This is Jake*. "We're . . . dating," I told the detective. Even that sounded juvenile to me.

"I see."

"What does that mean?"

He took another drink before he answered. "It means I can't believe anything you tell me about him."

I didn't like his attitude. "I don't lie, Detective."

Vince gave me a half smile. "Everyone lies, Miss O'Hara."

"I don't."

"If I had a quarter for every time someone said they were telling the truth when it was a blatant lie, I'd be a very rich man. I expect to be lied to."

"That's a very cynical thing to say."

"More like realistic."

"Not in my experience." I drained my mug and pushed it aside. He'd decided I was a liar when he didn't know a thing about me, and most likely didn't want to know anything that might change his mind. This whole line of questioning was ridiculous. I got to my feet. "Are we finished here? I have a busy day ahead."

"Almost." The detective stood and flipped his notebook closed. "I have one last question. How far would you go to protect your boyfriend?"

My jaw about dropped to the floor. I couldn't believe he'd just asked me that. "Are you serious?"

"I wouldn't have asked if I wasn't."

"You can't possibly think Jake had anything to do with this."

Vince slipped his notebook and pen back into his pocket. "Oh, I'm sure of it. It's not a coincidence the victim died while eating Lambert's food the day after you both had a run-in with him, and the same day he published that article about this place."

I jammed my hands into the front pockets of my shorts so I wouldn't be tempted to slug him. "Have you even bothered to check how many others had run-ins with him? Or would that be too much work for you?" My face grew hot with anger. "Jake did CPR on Mobley, for heaven's sake. Do you really think if Jake wanted him dead, he'd try to revive him?" I had a sneaking suspicion my dad had no idea his new partner was here and making accusations. "Have you talked to my father about your theory?"

"You haven't answered my question."

"And I'm not going to," I snapped. "If you want to know anything else, talk to my father. I highly suggest you mention this little talk to him before I do, because he's not going to be happy with you going behind his back." I stalked to the swinging door to the pub and held it open. He took the hint.

At the front door of the brew house, Vince turned around. "I should have figured you'd go running to Daddy. Don't think that just because he's a homicide detective, he can protect you from justice. You and your boyfriend aren't going to get away with murder. I plan on making sure of that."

I hauled the fifty-pound bags of Munich two-row barley malt up the steel steps to the mash tun in record time. My anger at Vincent Falk had tempered a bit by the time I dumped the contents into the tank and switched it on. The rake in the bottom cut into the grain and I breathed deeply at the aroma rising from the mixture of malt and hot water. Just being in the brewery improved my mood. The sight of the five gleaming stainless steel fermentation tanks always made me feel better.

While I worked, I tried not to jump to conclusions about my dad's new partner, although he certainly was jumping to conclusions about Jake. It was obvious he hadn't talked to Dad about his theory—if you could even call it that. Wild speculation was more like it. I knew enough about police work from my father to know he was going about it all wrong. No wonder the department had Dad showing him the ropes.

After an hour had passed, I drained the liquid from the tank and recirculated it back to the top, where it filtered through the grain again. Then I added more heated water to be sure all of the sugars were removed, and transferred the liquid to the brew kettle. I was brewing a German Oktoberfest, so I added Hallertau Mittelfrüh and Tettnanger hops at the appropriate intervals.

I thought about my assistant Kurt—who had died right here two months ago—every time I brewed, but this batch had a special significance. He had really looked forward to this particular brew. The fact that it was Kurt's recipe made it all the more special to me. I'd have to find a way to commemorate it during our celebration in September, although I was sure he would have complained about my making a big fuss.

While the wort boiled, I pulled out the hose and began the cleaning process. Most people don't realize that a good part of a brewer's day is spent cleaning. The tanks and hoses must be immaculate. A batch of beer will quickly be ruined by contaminated equipment. By the time I finished with the mash tun, the wort was ready to move to the fermentation tank, where I added the yeast. Since Oktoberfest was a lager, I'd let it ferment about six to eight weeks.

I made one last check of all the tanks, then headed back home to shower. I'd have just enough time to make it to Mass before the festival, which would make my brother Sean happy.

When I drove up to our festival booth in Jake's truck, I noticed the crime scene tape still surrounded the area around the judging table. I shivered at the sight. It was a reminder a man had died here and no matter how despicable he was, someone had taken his life. And Detective Vincent Falk thought Jake and I had something to do with it. Last night when Kristie, Candy, and Elmer tried to tell me I had something to worry about, I hadn't really believed them. Now I wasn't so sure. I hadn't had a chance to talk to my dad yet about Vincent's little visit this morning.

I hadn't spoken to Jake yet, either. He was probably on the way to the airport to pick up his parents. Although they'd made the move to Florida last year, they kept their house here. It was where Jake was living now. A win-win situation for all of them. Jake planned on bringing them down to the festival later today to meet up with my family; then when the festival was over at five, we would all meet for dinner at my parents' house.

In the meantime, I was on my own.

When I got out of the truck, the other brewers were in varying stages of preparation for the crowds that hopefully would descend on us today. I climbed into the truck bed and rolled one of the stainless steel half barrels to the edge. This was when it came in handy to have some muscle around. Fortunately, I was stronger than I looked. By the time Dave Shipley noticed I was lugging kegs by myself, I had just lifted the last one to the ground.

"I didn't realize you were by yourself," Dave said. "Where's Jake?"

I filled him in.

"Well, let me help you get these on ice, then."

Dave retrieved the tubs and ice from the back of the truck. While we worked, he asked, "Have you heard any more about what happened yesterday?"

I dumped some ice around one of the barrels. "Nothing, other than my dad's new partner asking me a bunch of questions this morning."

"What kind of questions? Like who do you think killed the guy?"

I shook my head. "Not exactly. He seems to think Jake and I did it."

"He can't be serious," Dave said. "You and Jake. Your dad's a cop for crying out loud."

"He was serious all right, although he did stop short of telling me not to leave town."

Dave put a barrel in place behind the table in my tent. "What did your dad say about it?"

"I haven't talked to him yet." I poured ice over another keg. "I expect he'll be here today. There will be people he'll want to question—plus my whole family is coming down later. When Vinnie the Viper left this morning—"

"Vinnie the Viper?"

"That's my name for Detective Falk."

Dave laughed heartily. "I like that." He put the next barrel in place. "Your dad will straighten him out."

"That's the thing," I said. "My first thought was to tell my dad, but now I'm not so sure. He has to work with the guy and I don't want to cause trouble between the two of them. I got the feeling there's enough tension there already. Vinnie's attitude might just be because he's inexperienced."

"Or maybe he's just a jackass." Dave lifted the last barrel into place. "I hope you don't mind a little advice, 'cause I'm gonna give it to you anyway. I've seen guys like Falk before. He thinks he's better than everyone else. You were right with the viper description. He's got higher aspirations than being a junior detective. I'll bet you anything he thinks this case is his ticket to a promotion and he'll step on anyone and everyone to get what he wants."

"Maybe. Maybe not." I let out a sigh. "I have to give him the benefit of the doubt, though, because of my dad. Even if he's sure we had something to do with Mobley's murder, the truth will come out and he'll see he's wrong."

"I hope you're right and I'm wrong about the guy." He gave my arm a quick squeeze. "In the meantime, watch your step with him."

"I plan on it."

"Plan on what?" Dwayne Tunstall's voice came from behind me. I hadn't seen him walk up.

"Crawl back in your hole, Tunstall," Dave said.

Dwayne wasn't deterred. "You're talking about Reggie, aren't you?"

"This is a private conversation," Dave said. "It's none of your business." He looked at me. "You okay now?"

I could tell he was itching to get away from Dwayne. I nodded. "Thanks for the help."

As Dave walked back to his tent, Dwayne turned to me. "Were you talking about Reggie?"

"No, it was somebody else," I said, and left it at that. I certainly wasn't going to tell him about the visit from the detective this morning. It would be all over the festival grounds in a matter of minutes.

"Well, you should be," he said. "Everyone should be talking about Reggie. He was such a wonderful person and the best food critic that ever walked the face of the earth.

At the very least, he was the best we ever had in Pittsburgh. The others can't hold a candle to him."

I couldn't help myself. I had to ask. "Why are you so enamored with the man? I don't understand. From what I saw, he wasn't a nice person."

Dwayne sniffed. "He was nice to me."

I said the first thing that popped into my head. "Why?"

"What do you mean by that?"

I opened one of the cardboard cartons I'd tucked under the table and took out a stack of small plastic cups. "He seemed like an equal-opportunity hater. Why would he treat you differently than everyone else?"

"Maybe because I deserve it. He saw the genius in me."

Genius? Oh, brother.

"The rest of you are just jealous. You can't stand the fact that I'm the best and Reggie recognized that. And now he's gone and I don't know what I'm going to do without him." He actually wiped a tear from his eye. "I'll never get a fair shake now."

I might have felt sorry for him if I hadn't known his history. "You'll have the same chance as everyone else here. A fair chance."

He snorted. "Right. All you brewers are out to get me. I wouldn't be surprised if all of yinz paid off those other two critics to make sure I don't win. Come to think of it, I wouldn't be surprised if one of you poisoned Reggie."

"That's ridiculous."

"It's not. It makes perfect sense. It's the only way any of you—especially you—could win." He pointed a finger at me. "Don't think you'll get away with it, either. I heard all those threats. I'm going to have a talk with those detectives." With that, he turned and marched off.

Great. Detective Falk was going to love that. I finished setting up, all the while thinking about the strange conversation I'd just engaged in. Dwayne had to be wrong that Reginald Mobley had truly liked his brews, not to mention liking Dwayne himself. I'd seen the way Mobley looked at him yesterday—like he wanted to squash him like a bug. Mobley's words didn't match what I'd seen in his eyes. He'd felt the same about Dwayne as everyone else. So why had he offered such effusive praise about Dwayne? It didn't make sense.

Unless Dwayne had something on him. That was a possibility. But what could it be? When Mobley had that run-in with one of his ex-wives, Dwayne knew all about her and their divorce. So either Dwayne was right and Mobley really was close to him, or Dwayne had somehow discovered something that Mobley didn't want revealed. I was betting on the latter.

CHAPTER SIX

During the first hour of the festival I barely had time to breathe, let alone think much about what Dwayne might have had on Reginald Mobley. The crowds were much heavier than the previous day. I hoped it was because word got around about the great beer and not because everyone wanted to see where a man was murdered.

I talked to Jake briefly when he called to say he was on his way after getting his mom and dad settled at home. His parents were tired, so instead of Jake bringing them to the festival, they were going to rest for a while and join us at my parents' house later. Nicole called me right after that to see if I needed her to pick anything up. I told her we had plenty of beer at the moment, but we were running short on plastic cups for the samples. She really was a gem and once again I felt extremely lucky to have her working for me.

As busy as I was, I was enjoying myself. It was fun to interact with the public and teach them a bit about craft beer. Everyone seemed happy to be there and I'd gotten many compliments on my offerings—especially my citrus ale. Maybe it was because of the hot sunny day, but it was the number one beer everyone who stopped at my booth wanted to sample. I'd run into only one surly person so far. He was underage and loudly voiced his displeasure when I refused to serve him. He didn't understand why he couldn't have "just a little." When I mentioned that maybe one of the off-duty officers might be able to explain it to him, he stalked off.

I was tapping another keg of citrus ale when Jake arrived at two. He kissed me on the cheek and said, "Hi, beautiful."

He needed to have his eyes examined. "I bet you say that to all the girls."

Jake grinned. "How did you guess?" He held up a paper bag. "But I don't bring any of them a sandwich."

I hadn't even thought about eating, but now my stomach growled as I peeked into the bag. Turkey on whole wheat. Yum.

"It looks like it's been busy," Jake said.

"And this is a lull. For a while, the lines were three deep." At the moment there were only a few people sipping their samples.

"I'll take over for a while," he said. "Why don't you take a break? Go find a nice quiet spot to eat your lunch."

I took him up on his offer. He'd learned a lot about brewing in the last two months, so he'd be fine explaining the brews. I made sure all my staff—Jake included—knew enough about our offerings that they could answer any questions customers threw at them. I did want to tell him about my visitor at the pub that morning, but now wasn't the time. It wasn't exactly a good idea to mention we were suspects in a poisoning when we were pouring beer samples and might be overheard. It could wait until later.

I grabbed a bottle of water from our cooler, then wove through the crowd searching for a place to sit. Although some picnic tables and benches had been set up here and there, all of them were occupied. I finally settled for a concrete barrier at the edge of the parking lot. Not exactly comfy, but at least it was somewhat quiet. I could still hear the murmur of the crowd and the traffic on Penn Avenue, with the occasional honking horn. While I ate, I thought more about what Dwayne could possibly have had on Mobley. I discarded every idea I came up with. None of them seemed to fit. It had to be something big—otherwise the critic would have told Dwayne to go stick it. It had to be something big enough to ruin him. I just couldn't figure out what.

After I finished my sandwich, I walked around the festival grounds and spotted Ginger Alvarado stuffing the last of the crime scene tape into the pocket of her turquoise slacks. I said hello and she jumped.

"Oh!" She spun around. "I didn't see you there."

"I didn't mean to startle you."

"No problem." She reached up and smoothed her already perfect ponytail. "Did you need something?"

"No. I was just stretching my legs and ended up here. I take it the police released the scene."

Ginger crossed her arms. "More or less. I told that young detective if the tape wasn't down this afternoon, I was taking it down."

Uh-oh. Vinnie the Viper wasn't going to like that.

"He even wanted me to cancel the festival," she said. "Can you believe that?" It must have been a rhetorical question, because she didn't wait for an answer. "I explained that a number of people had invested a lot of time and money in this event and it would go on. He didn't like that much. I told him my husband was on the city council and do you know what he said to me?"

I shook my head. "What did he say?"

"He said, 'I don't care if your husband is president of the United States.' When I told my husband about that last night, he was not happy. At all."

Score one for the Alvarados. "What happened after the detective told you that?"

"Nothing. He strutted away. I haven't seen him since."

Lucky for her.

Ginger was quiet for a moment, then said, "This is going to sound horrible, but I'm glad that awful man is gone."

I wasn't quite sure how to respond. There were many others here who felt the same way.

She blushed. "Not that I wanted him dead. I just wanted him gone. I made a huge mistake listening to Phoebe Atwell when she said I needed a third judge and he'd be a great replacement for her. It's just that . . . I was desperate. I didn't have anyone else."

"I understand," I said. "You were in a bind and did what you thought was best."

"Exactly," she said. "I—oh crap."

Her eyes widened at something she saw over my shoulder. I turned around. Vincent Falk was marching our way. *Oh crap* was right. I was about to make a hasty exit, but Ginger grabbed my arm.

"Stay here and back me up," she said. "Please?"

It would have been hard to leave with the grip she had on my wrist. For all her talk, Ginger was chicken.

By the time she released me, Vincent had reached us. He was as stiffly starched as he had been this morning. I didn't know how he managed it in this heat. If my dad had been working today, he'd have had his tie loosened and his sleeves rolled up.

"Mrs. Alvarado, I could have you arrested," Vince said. "That tape was to stay up until I said it could come down."

Ginger took a deep breath, then straightened and lifted her chin. It gave her a regal appearance, like she was gazing down her nose at an undeserving subject. She might have been quaking inside, but she sure didn't show it. "I will not have you disrupting this festival, Detective," she said. "There was no reason for you to keep this roped off."

"That is not for you to decide."

"Yes, it is. Mine and my husband's."

They stared at each other for what seemed like five minutes although in reality it was more like ten or fifteen seconds. Vincent must have realized he wasn't going to win that round, so he turned to me. "I should have known you two would be in cahoots. You haven't heard the last of this.

Neither one of you." With that, he turned on his expensive Italian leather heel and strode off.

When he was out of sight, Ginger said, "What does he mean 'in cahoots'?"

Did I really want to tell her Jake and I were at the top of the detective's suspect list? I decided it was best not to mention that. "He doesn't like me."

"Why?"

"You know the older detective who was here yesterday?"

Ginger nodded. "Detective O'Hara." The lightbulb went on. "Your name's O'Hara, isn't it? Is he a relative?"

"He's my father. Detective Falk is his partner."

She smiled and clapped her hands together. "That's wonderful news! I won't have to talk to that twit anymore. I can go straight to your father." Her cell phone rang just then. She squeezed my arm before she answered. "If you need anything—anything at all—you come right to me. I'll take care of it."

I watched her walk away. If Edward Alvarado decided to run for county executive and won the election, Ginger was going to make a great politician's wife.

Jake had been joined by Nicole by the time I returned to our tent. The line for tasting was three deep again and she was helping him draw samples. "I didn't expect you to work today," I said to her. I reached under the table for the plastic bottle of hand sanitizer and squirted a dollop onto my palm.

"I don't mind. Our esteemed chef here looked like he needed some help. I was here, so . . ." She shrugged.

Jake passed a sample across the table to the next person in line. "I didn't need any help. At least not until a couple guys asked me to sign their cups."

Nicole grinned. "Don't forget the five women holding up the line because they were sipping their beer too slowly so they could gawk at you."

"What can I say?" Jake said, winking at me. "I'm eye candy."

I laughed. "Maybe I should have you cook in the window of the brew house. Although then I'd probably get cited for blocking the sidewalk because of the throngs of admirers."

"Maybe even shirtless," Nicole chimed in.

Jake shook his head, laughing. "No can do. I think cooking without a shirt is some kind of health code violation."

"Ooh, Jake's cooking without a shirt." Kristie's voice came from beside our tent. "Sign me up."

He looked at me. "See what you started?"

Candy stood beside Kristie, and I did a double take when I saw her. Candy wore black pants with a metallic gold stripe down the leg, her favorite Steelers shirt with letters sewn in gold sequins, and a large handbag with a Steelers logo. None of that was out of the ordinary for her. What she had on her head was another story altogether. The tall hat she sported was black and gold (of course), but it was made of felt sewn into the shape of a beer mug. The top of the hat—where the foam would be on an actual beer—was some kind of cream-colored fuzzy material. When Kristie reached up and grabbed the handle on the side, I lost it. Jake and Nicole followed and by the time our laughter subsided, we were all wiping tears from our eyes. Candy took a bow and everyone waiting in line applauded. Several people wanted to know where they could buy one of the hats and were disappointed to learn they weren't for sale at the festival. I made a mental note to mention it to Ginger for next year. Judging by everyone's reaction, they'd be very popular.

Once the excitement abated, we chatted for a few minutes; then Candy asked, "Any news about the murder victim?"

"Nothing." Which was true. Other than Jake and me being Vincent Falk's prime suspects, there was nothing new, and even that really wasn't new. It did remind me that I still needed to talk to Jake about it, but I didn't see that happening until the festival was over for the day.

"We're going to take a stroll and see what we can find out," Candy said.

I pointed to her hat. "Wearing that?"

"Of course. It's a conversation piece. It will get people talking."

"It'll get them talking all right," Jake said.

Candy stuck her tongue out at Jake and turned to Kristie. "Let's go, Watson. There's no time to lose. We have a crime to solve."

I emptied the last keg about fifteen minutes before the five o'clock close of the festival. We took down the tent and packed everything up. Then Jake loaded the empty barrels onto his truck and headed back to the brewery. After that, he was going home to shower, then take his mom and dad over to my parents' house. Mom, along with Mike and his family, had stopped at our booth earlier, but it was too busy to do more than say hi. Dad had been called out on another case and I hoped that meant his partner would have someone new to harass.

Before I left, I headed across the makeshift aisle to Cory Dixon's tent, where he was packing up and loading things onto his truck.

"Hey, Max," he said. "How'd you make out today? You looked pretty busy over there."

"Good, I think. I guess we'll find out next week when the winner is revealed. How about you?"

"Same here. I didn't expect so many people after yesterday. I thought they'd be spooked and stay away."

"I did, too," I said. "I'm glad I was wrong."

"The scuttlebutt is Mobley was poisoned."

He looked to me for confirmation, but at this point, I wasn't sure what information had been released to the public. I hadn't had a chance to listen to any news reports or read the paper. "Where did you hear that?" I asked.

Cory shrugged. "That's what everyone is saying."

"Everyone?"

"And that detective—what's his name. Falk. Asked me if cyanide was used in brewing beer. If that's not a clue, I don't know what is."

Vinnie the Viper strikes again.

"He asked a lot of questions about you. And Jake." He

lifted one of his empty barrels onto his truck bed. "It kind of rubbed me the wrong way."

I let out a sigh. "Detective Falk thinks Jake and I killed Mobley."

Cory laughed. "You? You're the last person who'd off anyone. And isn't your dad the guy's partner?"

"Yep." I passed a stack of plastic cups to Cory and he tossed them into his truck. "That doesn't seem to matter to him."

"What's your dad think?"

"I'm not sure he knows. Hopefully I'll get to talk to Dad tonight and find out what's going on."

"Well, good luck. Personally, I think it's a tragedy they're even investigating. Whoever killed Mobley did the world a favor."

I bade Cory good-bye and invited him to stop by the pub when he got a chance. As I walked to where Jake had parked my car, I couldn't help thinking about what Cory had said. That whoever killed Mobley had done the world a favor. Dave felt the same way, and probably Randy Gregory and Brandon Long did, too. Maybe I was just naive, but that mind-set didn't sit well with me. As despicable as he'd been, it wasn't right his life was taken from him. I didn't like the next thing that went through my mind. They'd all voiced what could be considered threats against the dead critic. Had one of them taken that a step further?

I'd reached my car by this time. I unlocked my door, tossed my bag inside, then stood beside the open door to let some of the hot air out. I looked around the almost empty lot and stopped when I spotted Dwayne Tunstall's van three rows over. It wasn't the van that halted my gaze, though. It was another sight altogether. Dwayne stood beside it, but he wasn't alone. He had his arms around a tall blonde in a red dress. Just then she lifted her head and I was able to see her face. It was Melody Mobley—the brand-new widow.

CHAPTER SEVEN

I'd gotten only a brief look at Melody yesterday, but I was sure it was her. And she was with Dwayne. I was thankful I was short and most likely couldn't be seen by either one of them. As I peered over the roof of my car, I tried to decide whether to approach them. I took too long to make up my mind. Dwayne stepped back, squeezed Melody's shoulder, and got into his van. Melody entered a red Miata that was parked beside the van and sped away. Dwayne left seconds later. I got in my Corolla, started it, and rolled down the window until the air-conditioning kicked in, thinking about what I just saw.

Was it possible they were lovers? I didn't understand what she could possibly see in Dwayne, but then again, she had married a guy who looked like a cross between Danny De-

Vito and Albert Einstein. And now her husband was conveniently out of the way. In my mind, this meant there was a good chance that one or both of them had killed Reginald Mobley. The way Dwayne had fawned over the critic and sang his praises was all a big act. Given his reputation, it shouldn't have surprised me.

What if I was thinking wrong, though? Dwayne's embracing the widow might have been perfectly innocent. It was possible he had just been consoling her. There had to be more to it than that, though. It didn't explain why Melody would have come to the very place—the parking lot beside it, anyway—where her husband had been killed the day before. She should have been home mourning her loss, not embracing another man in a parking lot. I drove home mentally kicking myself for not crossing the lot to talk to them. I'd have to come up with a way to see one or both of them before the festival resumed on Friday.

When I unlocked the door to my loft apartment, Hops greeted me with a meow that told me she was none too pleased she had been left alone all day. I scooped her up and scratched the white spot under her chin. "I'll make it up to you," I said.

"Murp." Hops swatted my arm.

I laughed. "You really are mad, aren't you?" I placed her back on the floor. "How about some dinner and a couple of treats for dessert?" She purred and coiled herself around my ankle. I quickly washed up and changed while she ate, then loaded Hops into her carrier and headed to my parents' house in Highland Park.

Mom and Dad's house was an eighty-year-old white

brick two-story house on a double lot, not too far from the Pittsburgh Zoo. On occasion, if it was quiet enough, you could hear the lions roar. My four-year-old niece Maira charged out the front screen door when she saw me pull up in front of the house. Seconds later, she was followed by her two-year-old sister, Fiona, who was always trying to keep up with her. Both girls were spitting images of their mother, Kate, although Maira's white blond hair was beginning to darken a little and take on some red highlights. I didn't think it would ever be as red as Mike's, though.

"You brought Hops!" Maira jumped up and down beside the car as I reached in for the carrier secured in the backseat.

"Hops!" Fiona bounced beside her sister.

I laughed at their excitement. "Hops will be glad to have playmates." The girls walked beside me as I headed up the front walk. "Just remember to be gentle with her."

"Is her leg still getting better?" Maira asked.

One of the kitten's front legs had been broken when I'd taken her in. "It's all healed now, but she's a lot smaller than you, so you have to be careful."

"Not a toy," Fiona piped up, repeating what she'd been told when I first introduced her to the kitten.

I patted her on the head. "Exactly."

Inside the house, I opened the carrier and Hops leaped out. She immediately gave Maira a head butt on the leg. A minute later, the three were happily playing with a toy mouse, so I headed down the hallway to the kitchen at the back of the house. Mom and Kate were standing at the island in the center of the room putting a salad together. My mother was coming up on her sixtieth birthday, but to me she looked younger than ever. Her salt-and-pepper hair was cut in a short bob, which was a new style for her. She wore white capris and a royal blue sleeveless blouse that went really well with her hair. Kate wore her hair much like her young daughters—straight and halfway down her back. She was dressed for the heat in a brightly colored flowered sundress. For once, I wasn't underdressed. I knew Jake's parents were coming and even though I'd met them several times growing up, I wanted to make a good impression. I had donned a long, white gauzelike skirt and a mint green peasant top.

I greeted my sister-in-law, then kissed Mom on the cheek and asked if I could help.

"Definitely not," she said. "You must be exhausted."

"Not really," I said. "I kind of got my second wind after a shower."

Just then, Mike barged into the kitchen, carrying a football. His face fell when he saw me. "I guess that getup means you're not my running back tonight."

"Michael," Mom said before I had a chance to open my mouth. "The last thing your sister wants to do is play football. She's been working all day."

"Sorry, brother," I said. "You'll have to play without me."

Kate squeezed her husband's arm. "You could skip the game for once, you know."

Mike gave Kate a quick kiss. "Michael O'Hara has never missed a pickup game, and I'm not going to start now. I'll just have to find someone else to fill in. Maybe I can talk Dad into it." With that, he headed back out to the yard.

I had half expected Dad to still be working. I was glad he was home, because I wanted to talk to him. I was up in the air about what—or even if—I should tell him about his partner's visit that morning. It was apparent there was some friction between them and I didn't want to make it worse, or cause my dad to be any more overprotective than he already was. I'd play it by ear and see where things stood with the investigation.

Mom put the salad in the fridge and the three of us made our way to the patio that overlooked the large backyard. Dad was at the grill, and Mike and Sean were tossing the football back and forth. Mike wouldn't have to worry about losing me as a teammate if no one else showed up to play. Tonight's get-together was later than usual because of the festival. The football portion of Sunday—when there wasn't a Steelers game on TV, that is—occurred in the afternoon. Any neighbor who would have participated was at home relaxing or eating dinner by now.

While Mom and Kate took seats on the patio, I made my way over to the grill. "Mmm, something smells good."

"Tomato-basil chicken. At least that's what I think your mother said it was." Dad gave me a one-armed hug, since his other one was occupied with turning the chicken. "She warned me not to burn it."

Although Dad was the master of the grill, he had a tendency to overcook things a bit. "I'll help you keep an eye on it." I reached over and turned the heat down to low on the gas grill. "That should help."

"Thanks, sweetie." He finished turning the chicken and closed the lid on the grill. "How did it go today? Sorry I didn't make it down there."

"We were busy. After what happened yesterday, we

weren't sure if anyone would show up. There was a much bigger turnout than anyone expected." I paused for a moment, hoping Dad would volunteer a little information, since I'd more or less brought up the murder, but he didn't. I guessed I hadn't been specific enough, so I came right out and asked him how the investigation was going.

"It's a little too early to tell. We're still interviewing witnesses and haven't gotten all the lab work back."

"Do you have any suspects yet?" I knew his partner sure did.

Dad gave me the same look he did when I was a kid and asked him a question that was none of my business. "I can't tell you that."

"What about the lab work? You said you got some of that back."

"Yes." Dad drew out the word to three syllables.

"Well? What did you find out?"

"It was cyanide, but I'm sure you figured that out already."

"And?"

"And that's all I can tell you," he said. "I can't discuss it."

Maybe I should have expected that's what he'd say. There were always certain things he couldn't talk about. That didn't mean I had to like it. Besides, this case was different. Jake and I were involved—no matter how indirectly—and I thought we had a right to know what was going on. "Why can't you discuss it?" I asked. "If Jake and I are suspects—"

Dad put a hand up. "Stop right there. What in the world gave you that idea?"

Just then I heard Jake's voice as he came out the sliding door, followed by his parents.

"We'll talk about this later," Dad told me.

Mom was already greeting our guests by the time I reached them. I hadn't seen Jake's parents for years—since well before I went to Germany after grad school. I shouldn't have been, but I was surprised at how much they'd aged. Jake—their only child—had been what everyone called a "change of life" baby. They were both in their late seventies now. Jake's mother was smaller than I remembered, but she was still taller than me. She was dressed in pastel pink slacks and a white short-sleeved blouse. Her white hair was short and wavy. His dad still looked the same—just older. He still had a thick head of steel gray hair that was the same color as his pants.

"You remember Max, don't you?" Jake said to them.

"Of course we do," Mrs. Lambert said as she hugged me. "You're even prettier than I remember."

"And no skinned knees," her husband chimed in. "I remember you had a lot of them."

I laughed. "It was hard keeping up with my brothers and your son."

"Looks like you caught him now," Mr. Lambert said with a wink.

I felt my cheeks redden.

Mrs. Lambert smacked her husband on the arm. "Bob, stop teasing her." She turned to me. "Don't pay him any mind. I don't. We always knew our boy would come to his senses."

I wasn't sure if she was referring to Jake's ex-fiancée, Victoria, or just that he was seeing me.

Jake put his arm around me. "Sheesh. Keep talking like I'm not here."

91

"Get used to it, son." Bob Lambert looked around. "So, where's this beer we keep hearing so much about? I'm parched."

Jake led his dad to get a drink and I took a seat on the patio with his mom and my mother. We chatted for a few minutes until Dad took the chicken off the grill and it was time to eat.

All in all, it had been an enjoyable evening. Mike, Kate, and the girls headed out shortly after dinner to get Maira and Fiona into bed at a reasonable hour. Hops was worn-out from playing with my nieces and she was curled up in a corner of the kitchen. I was disappointed I hadn't had much of a chance to talk to my oldest brother. One of Sean's parishioners had passed away and he left to go comfort the family. After Jake and his parents left, I helped Mom clean up, then put a sleepy Hops in her carrier.

"I'll walk you out," Dad said. He helped me buckle the kitten's carrier in the backseat, then closed the door and turned to me. "I'm sorry if I was short with you before."

"You weren't," I said. "Not really, anyway. I would like to know what's going on, though."

"I know you would." He let out a sigh. "I'd like to tell you more, but I can't."

"When Kurt died, you didn't have a problem filling me in."

"Things are different now."

"I don't see how. Jake and I were there. The man died right in front of us—eating Jake's food."

"Is that why you think you and Jake are suspects?"

I hesitated before I said, "More or less."

"What does that mean?"

"Nothing."

Dad crossed his arms over his chest. "You're not telling me something."

Drat. I should have realized I wouldn't be able to keep Vince's visit from my dad. It didn't help that he was used to questioning suspects and could see right through the smallest of fibs. "It's nothing. Really."

"Let me be the judge of that," he said. "If it has something to do with Mobley's death, I need to know."

"It doesn't. At least not directly."

He gave me his tough-detective look and I caved.

"Detective Falk came to see me at the pub this morning."

"He what?"

I'd been right. He hadn't known about his partner's visit. "He made it plain that Jake was his number one suspect and I was guilty by association."

Dad rarely swore, but by the set of his jaw I knew he was holding back a string of words that would have turned the air blue.

"I figured he hadn't told you and I didn't want to rat out your partner. That's why I didn't say anything."

"I'm glad you finally did." He put his arm around me. "Don't ever feel like you have to keep things from me. Especially something like this. I knew Vince was a little gung ho, but I didn't think he'd go this far. What else did he say?"

"That's about it. Other than he plans to prove we did it."

"Well, that's going to be a little hard, since there was no cyanide in what Jake served to Mobley."

I knew there hadn't been, but it was a relief to hear it.

"I shouldn't have told you that, but this whole situation has gotten way out of hand."

I was about to ask him why he wasn't supposed to tell me when Hops meowed loudly from inside the car.

Dad smiled. "I think someone wants to get going." He opened my car door for me and I gave him a hug. "Go home and forget about it," he said. "Don't worry about anything. I'll take care of it."

"I'm sorry if any of this caused you problems."

"It's nothing I can't handle."

I hoped he was right. Despite what Dad said, I had a feeling Vincent Falk wasn't through with us.

CHAPTER EIGHT

I slept so soundly it took both alarms on my clock and Hops batting me in the face to wake me up. I had a lot to catch up on at the brew house, or I'd have gone back to bed after feeding the cat. Although the pub had been in Nicole's capable hands and I had stopped in yesterday morning, there were still things that only I could take care of. I'd been teaching both Nicole and Jake about brewing, but neither one was ready to go it alone. I also wanted to talk to Jake before anyone else arrived and fill him in on everything. I'd considered calling him when I got home last night, but I hadn't wanted to interrupt his time with his parents. It had become a nightly ritual that one of us would call the other, and it felt off to not say good night to him. We exchanged text messages, but it wasn't the same.

I arrived at the pub around seven and once I got settled, I headed into the brewery and checked all the tanks. The gauges showed the beer was fermenting nicely. A traditional Irish stout and an IPA would be ready to keg by the end of the week. Satisfied, I headed to the storage room at the far end of the brewery, where I did another quick inventory in case I forgot to order anything for next week's scheduled brewing.

Back in my office I made a note of the ingredients that were getting low. After that, I went through some invoices and put them in the order I wanted to pay them. All of this took less than an hour and when I finished, I found myself thinking about something Dad had said last night. I hadn't paid much attention to it at the time, but now I was curious. He'd said he "shouldn't have told" me there was no cyanide in the food Jake had made. There were always aspects about a case he couldn't discuss, but this time it sounded like he wasn't to discuss it with me in particular. I wasn't sure what to make of that. Did his new partner have something to do with it? That didn't make sense to me, either. Dad was the senior partner, not the other way around.

I rose from my chair. I had some time to spare—Jake wasn't due in for another hour. Maybe Candy could help me figure it out. I also wanted to know what she thought about me seeing Dwayne with the brand-new widow. Besides, I hadn't eaten breakfast and a cheese Danish was sounding pretty good about now. I locked up and headed next door.

Candy was behind the counter and Mary Louise was in front cleaning the glass display case. Both of them looked up when the bell on the door jingled. The Monday morning rush was over and I was the only customer at the moment.

Mary Louise stopped wiping and smiled. "Good morning."

"Good morning, ladies," I said.

"I thought you'd be sleeping in after this weekend," Candy said.

"I did, too," Mary Louise said. "And to think you'll have to do it all again next weekend. Minus that terrible tragedy, of course. Candy told me what happened, and it was all over the news."

"I almost did sleep in," I said. "I hit the snooze alarm twice, but fortunately Hops made sure I got up."

"That kitten of yours is so adorable," Mary Louise said. "I'm going to have to take a trip to Animal Friends and see about adopting one. Maybe one of the older cats for me. I never thought I'd want another cat after my Nellie passed last year, but I think I'm ready."

"You should do that. Taking Hops in was one of the best things I've ever done." I smiled. "And you won't need an alarm clock."

I made my purchase, then asked Candy if she had a minute. She followed me outside.

"I thought you'd never ask," she said once we reached the sidewalk. "I could tell you had something you wanted to talk about."

The street was too busy for carrying on a conversation, especially one about murder, so Candy and I went into the pub, where we settled at one of the tables.

"What's up?" she asked. "Where do we stand with our investigation?"

"Our investigation?"

"You know what I mean," she said. "I know you're snooping around and you have a theory or two. So unless you have some enticing tidbit to share about that hunk of burning love of yours—"

"You sound like Kristie. My romantic life is not your concern."

"At least you have one now. That's an improvement."

"Can we get back on track here?"

Candy gave me a look she normally reserved for Elmer. "You're the one who interrupted me. I'll ask you again. Where do we stand?"

I should have known better than to argue with her. Although *argue* wasn't exactly the right word. *Spar* was more like it. "Fine. Where do you want me to start?"

"How about at the beginning?" she said. "With the visitor you had yesterday morning."

"How did you . . ." I didn't bother finishing the sentence. It didn't matter how—she always seemed to know everything. One of these days I was going to press her on it, but right now I wasn't going to let it sidetrack me again. I told her about my conversation with Vincent Falk.

Candy was shaking her head by the time I finished. "So he really does think you and Jake killed the critic."

"He does," I said. "I talked to my dad last night and he didn't know anything about his partner's visit. He was pretty angry about it. Dad told me there was no cyanide in the food

Jake served, but when I tried to get more information from him, he wouldn't tell me anything."

"Is that unusual?"

"Kind of. There are always things pertaining to his cases that he can't talk about, but this seemed different. I got the feeling he wanted to say more, but couldn't. He said he wasn't even supposed to tell me that much. I think maybe he was told not to."

"Hmm." Candy tapped her index finger on her lips. "What's your dad's relationship like with his bosses?"

"Great," I said. "He's been there a long time. They respect him. Why?"

Candy was silent for a moment. "You're probably not going to like what I have to say."

I waited.

"I've seen it before. Up close and personal. A young hotshot comes in and even though he's a little too big for his britches, the higher-ups see that he's the future and your dad's the past."

She was right about one thing. I didn't like it. "If that's the case, why do they have my dad training him? My dad is a decorated, dedicated officer. He's got commendations galore. He's the mayor's friend, for goodness' sake."

Candy put her hand on my arm. "I know. But you have to face the facts. Your dad has been eligible for retirement for a few years now. Falk is what? Thirty-five or so? He's got twenty years to go."

"Vinnie the Viper is not going to force my dad out. I won't let that happen. And even if you're right, which I don't think you are, it doesn't tell me why Dad's clammed up all of a sudden."

Candy looked thoughtful. "It could be he just doesn't want it to get back to Falk that he told you anything."

"Dad's the senior partner. Why would he care if Vince knew that?"

Candy shrugged. "Maybe Detective Falk is like those kids in school we used to call *brownnoses*. You know—those kids who'd ingratiate themselves to the teachers and tattle on everyone."

That almost made sense to me. "In other words, Vince is trying to make himself look good by making my dad look bad. Dad has to watch his step or his partner tattles on him. But wouldn't that work the other way, too? Why wouldn't Dad just turn the tables on his partner, especially if he's supposed to be training Vince?"

"Because your dad is an honorable man, my dear," Candy said.

She was right about that. Dad wouldn't think of tattling on his partner. He preferred to lead by example. He would correct Vince and deal with him directly. From what I'd seen so far of Detective Falk, I wasn't sure that approach would work. I'd have to tread lightly when dealing with him. I wouldn't want to give him any ammunition to use against my father. I'd already blundered by telling Dad that Vince had stopped in to see me. I'd have to be more careful in the future.

I filled Candy in on everything else that had happened the day before, including Vince catching Ginger Alvarado taking down the crime scene tape and accusing us of being in cahoots. I finished up with my sighting of Dwayne Tunstall with his arms around Melody Mobley.

"You're sure it was her?" Candy said.

"Positive. What do you make of it?"

She rolled her eyes. "I'd say it's pretty obvious."

"It could be perfectly innocent," I said. "He could have been comforting the widow. It wasn't like they were trying to hide anything. It was a public parking lot."

Candy shook her head. "It doesn't smell right. Why would she return to the place her husband was murdered—the very next day, no less? There's something going on there." She grinned. "I think we may have our suspects, Max. All we have to do is prove it."

I was sitting at the bar reading Reginald Mobley's obituary in the paper when Jake came in. He squeezed my shoulder and slid onto the adjacent stool. "A little light reading, I see."

I pushed the paper aside, leaned over, and kissed him on the cheek. His hair was still damp from the shower and he smelled like Irish Spring soap. A winning combination. "I was just checking to see when Mobley's viewing would be. How are your mom and dad?"

"They're fine. They're spending the day with some of their old friends. They said to tell you they had a great time last night." Jake pointed at the paper. "You're not actually thinking about going to the funeral home, are you?"

"Well . . . maybe."

"That's not a good idea."

"Why not?" I asked, even though I'd told Candy the same thing when she'd suggested it half an hour ago. She had decided that going to the funeral home was the best way to get to talk to Melody Mobley. The widow had no idea who we were and if she asked, we'd tell her we knew her husband. I hadn't been thrilled with the idea, but Candy was persuasive and finally talked me into it. I was even beginning to like the idea.

Jake said, "Given the fact I'm on the suspect list, it might be awkward."

"You're in the clear as far as my dad's concerned." I told him about my conversation with Dad last night.

"That's good," Jake said. "Not that I was really worried. I knew they wouldn't find anything. What about your dad's new partner, though? He seems like the type who'd want the facts to bend to his theory."

"You're right about that. Detective Falk stopped here yesterday morning."

"He did? Why didn't you tell me?"

"I haven't had the chance. This is the first time we've been alone and I didn't want to get into it with all those people around. Yesterday was so busy, and last night we were at my parents'."

"Tell me what happened."

"He asked some questions about you and our relationship."

"Our relationship is none of his business."

"That's what I told him, but he thinks, because we're seeing each other, that anything I tell him is a lie."

"That's crazy," Jake said.

"Yep. I told him that I don't lie, but he didn't believe me.

He seems to think that everyone lies and I told him that was a very cynical way to view things. Then he said he planned to prove that you killed Mobley."

"That will be tricky, since your dad said there was no cyanide in what I served."

"It doesn't mean he won't keep trying, though," I said. "That's what has me worried. I have a feeling that whatever they discover the poison in, he'll accuse you of putting it there."

"He can accuse me all he wants. It won't make it so."

"The good news is that I've come up with much better suspects." I told him about Dwayne and Melody.

"So that's why you want to go to the funeral home. You're playing detective again."

"I'm not playing anything. I just want to see the widow and give her my condolences."

Jake grinned. "And see if you can catch her in a clinch with Dwayne."

I smiled back at him. "That would definitely be a bonus."

Jake slid off his stool and wrapped his arms around me. "Speaking of clinches . . ."

CHAPTER NINE

Mondays at the pub were generally a little slow, but today hadn't been one of them. We were busy all day long. I worked the taps most of the day with help from Nicole—when she wasn't assisting the servers. There were many new faces among the customers, and several mentioned they had sampled our offerings at the festival and wanted to try the food. That was great news, especially if we kept them coming back.

I finally got a breather around seven o'clock when the dinner rush was over. Only three tables were occupied, so I headed back to my office to put my feet up. I hadn't been resting for long when Nicole knocked on the door.

"Sorry to bother you," she said, "but there's someone out here asking for you and Jake."

I swung my legs down from my desk, wondering who it could be. "Did they give you a name?"

"I didn't ask."

"Probably someone from the festival," I said, hoping it wasn't Detective Falk. I wouldn't put it past him to show up during pub hours and expect me to speak to him. I followed Nicole out of my office and down the hallway to the pub. I was pleasantly surprised to see who was standing by the entrance.

"Mr. and Mrs. Lambert! Welcome to the Allegheny Brew House," I said, giving them both a hug.

"Mrs. Lambert is much too formal," Jake's mother said. "Call me Dot. Or Dorothy if you must, but I prefer Dot."

They had both told me the same thing last evening, but it was going to take me a while to get used to. It had been ingrained in me since childhood to never call my friends' parents by their first names.

"And you can call me Bob, or anything you want," Jake's dad said. "Just don't call me late for supper."

It was an old joke, but I laughed anyway. I introduced them to Nicole, who then went to tell Jake his parents were here.

I asked them if they had eaten dinner yet. They hadn't, so I led them to a table by the window and told them their meal was on the house. Dot wanted only water to drink, but I went over the brews we served with Bob. We had four beers on tap year-round—a lager, a stout, a hefeweizen, and an IPA. We had two more taps that we used for other brews. Right now we were serving the citrus ale I'd developed, plus a brown ale. I had plans to add two more taps in the next couple of months.

Bob couldn't decide which beer he wanted, so I suggested the Allegheny Sampler, which was a selection of four beers in five-ounce glasses and served on a wooden paddle. He liked that idea and I headed to the bar. By the time I returned to the table, Jake had joined them.

"I see you're sitting down on the job again," I said, placing the sampler on the table in front of Bob and a glass of water at Dot's place.

Jake grinned. "She's a tough boss," he said to his parents. "Max thinks a man's place is in the kitchen."

I took the seat beside him. "And don't you forget it."

"That a girl," Bob said. He tapped Jake on the arm. "The secret to happiness is to remember the woman is always right. Even if she's wrong."

"Robert!" Dot nudged him with her elbow. "That's terrible."

We all laughed and Bob winked at me. He liked to get a rise out of his wife and it seemed like he succeeded. Although Jake's sense of humor was a little bit like his dad's, it was tempered by his mother's common sense. Thank goodness.

After they'd eaten, I asked them if they'd like a tour of the brewery.

"I'd love it," Bob said. "I don't think I've ever seen the inner workings of one."

Dot said, "Are you sure it's not too much trouble? I know how busy you must be."

I assured them it was no trouble at all. Jake told them he'd show them the kitchen when we were finished. He returned to the kitchen; then I led his mom and dad across the pub and through the swinging door to the brewing area.

"Oh my," Dot said. "It looks so clean. It must take a lot of work to keep those tanks that shiny."

"I've got it down to a routine." I explained how important cleanliness was in the brewing process. We crossed the room to the steel stairs leading to the mash tun. "This is where the process begins. There's a rake at the bottom that mixes the grain with hot water. Eventually this liquid is transferred to the brew kettle."

Bob went up the stairs to check out the mash tun, but Dot was afraid of the steps. I tensed up when he leaned over to look into the opening. I pushed the thought of Kurt out of my mind, wondering if I'd ever stop thinking of him. I was relieved when Bob came back down.

I showed them the fermentation tanks and answered Bob's many questions. When we were finished, Dot said she was very impressed. She hadn't known there was so much involved and it gave her a new appreciation for the beverage.

Next, I took them to the kitchen and Jake showed them around. I could tell Dot was happy with Jake's change of career. Bob didn't say so, but I had the feeling he was more comfortable saying his son was a professional hockey player instead of a chef.

Dot had as many questions about the kitchen as Bob had about the brewery. While Jake answered her questions, Bob pulled me aside. "I've been wanting to ask this since I got here and this might be my only chance. What's this I hear about a murder at that festival? Jake's been mum about it, but I saw it on the news. Dot doesn't watch the news and I didn't want to ask in front of her. She'd be upset."

I told him what had happened, but I left out the part that Jake had been a suspect. He didn't need to know that at this point.

When I finished, he said, "You said the dead guy's name was Reginald Mobley?"

I nodded.

Bob rubbed his chin. "This might sound strange, but when I saw his picture on TV, I thought I recognized him. I knew a guy years ago who looked like him—just younger—but his name wasn't Mobley. And he didn't write for a newspaper."

"What are you two talking about?" Dot asked as she and Jake crossed the room.

"We're just shooting the breeze," Bob said. "This is really quite a place you've got here, Max. You should be proud. You, too, son."

Jake and I thanked them. The four of us chatted a few more minutes; then they bade us good-bye.

"What were you and Dad talking about?" Jake asked as soon as they were gone.

"He asked about me about the murder."

Jake made a face. "I've been avoiding saying anything to him about it. It would only worry Mom, so I kept my mouth shut."

I nodded. "That's why he pulled me aside while she was talking to you." I told him what his dad said about thinking he recognized the dead critic. "But he said the man he knew wasn't named Mobley and he didn't write for a newspaper."

Jake laughed and shook his head. "One time he was sure a cashier at Giant Eagle was someone he went to high school with. Turned out she wasn't. I wouldn't put much stock in that."

The funeral home where Reginald Mobley was *laid out* (as we say in Pittsburgh) was located on the South Side. I didn't have too much trouble finding it. It was a couple of blocks off East Carson Street, the main thoroughfare. The only time I got confused was when my GPS wanted me to turn the wrong way on a one-way street. It was Tuesday evening and I had been running late, so I was meeting Candy in the parking lot. Jake had opted to stay at the pub, since one of his cooks had called off. I think he was glad to have an excuse to stay back, even though I'd told him a couple of times he didn't have to come along.

When I pulled into the lot, Candy was standing beside her gold sedan and Elmer was with her. I groaned inwardly. I had hoped we'd be able to be discreet with any questions I wanted to ask, but with outspoken Elmer along, that wouldn't be possible. He would interrogate the widow like she was a World War II German spy. I was going to have to find a way to keep him occupied and out of my hair.

"I decided you needed some backup," Elmer said when

I got out of my car. "Can't have you ladies questioning suspects by yourselves."

"And who told you that's what we were doing?" I glanced at Candy, who was looking everywhere but at me. "We're here to pay our respects. Nothing more. Aren't we, Candy?"

"Pay your respects, my foot," Elmer said.

Candy finally spoke up. "He wouldn't take no for an answer. I told him we needed to do this alone, but he had to butt in."

"If you didn't want my help, you should have kept your yap shut."

I held my hands up. "Can we not argue in the middle of the parking lot?" I had an idea. I turned to Elmer. "I appreciate that you want to help, and I do have something important for you to do."

"But—"

I nudged Candy before she could say any more.

"Think of it as a critical mission. I need you to be on the lookout for Detective Falk." It was actually a pretty good idea. If Vince decided to pay a visit to the funeral home—which wasn't unheard-of—and he spotted us, we'd probably have some explaining to do. Not to mention it would cement the theory in his mind that Jake and I had killed Mobley.

"What's this Falk guy look like?" Elmer asked.

I gave him a brief description.

Elmer saluted. "You can count on me. What's our code word?"

"Code word?"

"Yeah," Elmer said. "If that detective shows up, we need a code word."

"Oh, for goodness' sake," Candy said. "Just come in and get us."

"No can do. A paratrooper doesn't leave his post. We didn't do it in Bastogne and I'm not gonna do it here. We have to have a code word."

Candy rolled her eyes. "How do you propose to let us know that the detective is here with your code word? Smoke signals?"

Elmer grinned and pulled a cell phone from his pocket and waved it in Candy's face. "You girls do know how to text, don't you?"

After some discussion, we settled on a word. Elmer proposed we use the same code the Airborne had on D-Day. He wanted to text *flash*, then have us respond *thunder*. I finally convinced him it would take too long to text back. Candy and I would just leave if we got his message. With much grumbling, he agreed and we settled on *flash* alone.

Candy and I made our way inside, where we found a black message board with Reginald Mobley's name in white plastic letters and an arrow pointing to the left. The place was eerily quiet, even for a funeral home. The dark red floral carpeting muffled any sounds our footsteps would have made as we walked down the hallway. I hadn't expected a crowd, but I surely thought there would be more than the half dozen people who looked our way when we entered the room. The only one I recognized was the widow. Melody Mobley had ditched the red dress she'd worn on Sunday and was now more appropriately attired in a black sleeveless shift dress.

As she came our way, I began having second thoughts about being here, but apparently Candy didn't. She rushed forward and pulled Melody into a hug like she was a long-lost relative.

"I am so sorry for your loss," Candy said. "You poor dear."

Melody disentangled herself from Candy's arms and dabbed a tissue at her eyes. "Thank you for coming."

"When we heard Reginald passed on, we just had to come." She nudged me.

"Yes, we had to," I said.

I could tell that Melody was trying to place who we were and if she should know us. She must have decided it didn't matter, because seconds later she offered to walk us over to the casket. I hadn't considered the fact that we'd actually have to see the deceased. My Catholic upbringing kicked in and I said three Hail Marys while we stood at the casket. After a few long minutes we stepped to the side.

"How did the two of you know Reggie?" Melody asked.

I had wondered if she'd get around to that question. Candy and I had decided it was best not to let anyone know who I really was. She had come up with a good story, so I let her answer.

She took both of Melody's hands in hers. "Your dear husband was a frequent visitor to my bakery—Cupcakes N'at. I'm sure he must have told you all about it. He was such a dear man."

Candy was really laying it on thick. Maybe too thick—especially with the "dear man" comment.

"Really?" Melody sounded surprised. "He never said a word. He really shouldn't have been going to a bakery."

"Why not?" I asked.

"His doctor told him he had to lose weight. He was borderline diabetic. He wasn't supposed to have sweets."

Candy didn't miss a beat. "I know, dear," she said. "That's why I'd only let him buy my sugar-free goodies. He wasn't happy about it at all. Sometimes he would beg me for something with real sugar in it, but I wouldn't give in."

The widow nodded. "Thank you for that. He wasn't always easy to get along with."

That was an understatement if I ever heard one.

Someone else came in just then and Melody excused herself. I took Candy by the arm and pulled her to the far side of the room. "We should go," I said. "We're not going to learn anything from her—especially not here."

"How dare you!" Melody screeched.

For a second I thought she was yelling at us, but I turned just in time to see her shove the woman who'd entered moments ago. The woman flew backward into a flower display and both crashed to the ground.

"You have no right to be here," Melody said. Her face was as red as the dress she'd worn on Sunday. "He's my husband now. Not yours."

I put two and two together, and when I got a closer look at the woman attempting to stand, I realized she was the ex-wife who'd caused the disturbance at the festival. I tried to recall her name. Linda. That was it. The others in the room who had been talking quietly were now silent. Candy and I exchanged glances.

Linda made it to her feet, brushing carnations and rose petals from her white blouse. "I have more right to be here than you. I'm the mother of his child. We were married for ten years. You've been his wife for what? Six months?"

"Eight," Melody said. "But that doesn't matter. We were very much in love."

"Love?" Linda said, rolling her eyes. "Give me a break."

"We had our whole lives to look forward to—until you did this." Melody pointed to the casket.

"Me?" Linda said. "Why would I kill him?"

"Because you hated him. You wanted our money—"

"It's not your money, you witch." Linda took a step forward. "Maybe that's why you killed him—to get his money. Well, it's not going to work. I'm not going to let you get away with it."

"Out!" Melody jabbed her finger toward the door. "Out. Get out before I call the police."

The undertaker stepped into the room. "Is there a problem here?" He'd sure taken his good old time to show up.

"I want this woman removed," Melody said.

Linda brushed a stray petal from her navy skirt. "Don't bother. I'm leaving. But you haven't seen the last of me. I want what's rightfully mine."

I motioned to Candy that I was going to follow Linda and she nodded. By the time I got outside, Linda was halfway across the parking lot. I called her name and she stopped and turned around.

When I reached her, she said, "Who are you and what do you want? If you're a reporter, I have nothing to say."

"I'm not a reporter."

Linda crossed her arms over her chest. "So who are you, then?"

I told her, including how I knew her ex-husband. She was smiling by the time I finished.

"Welcome to the Reggie Hates Everyone Club," she said. "You're in good company."

"So I hear. If you have a minute, I'd like to talk to you."

"I have nothing but time right now. There's a little coffee shop a few blocks up." She gave me directions. "I'll meet you there in fifteen minutes."

I found the coffee shop with no problem. It had been more of an issue getting away without Elmer tagging along. I stood my ground and told him he had to wait for Candy in case she needed help. His nosiness almost won out until I brought up what he'd said earlier about a paratrooper never leaving his post.

Linda was already seated at a battered wooden table near a window when I entered. This coffee shop was nothing like Kristie's Jump, Jive & Java. The ancient black-and-white linoleum floor was scuffed and pitted. The tables and chairs were also remnants of another era. I generally liked vintage, but this was just old stuff thrown together. The only thing going for the place was that it was clean. The glass case holding a few baked goods sparkled. I told Linda I was buying. All she wanted was black coffee, which I ordered along with an iced latte for myself.

Linda watched as I put two packets of sugar in my glass. "How can you do that to your coffee?"

I smiled. "I've actually cut down. I used to use three."

She shook her head, took a sip of her drink, then put the cup down. "What did you want to talk to me about? I assume it's something to do with my ex and his murder."

"Yes," I said.

"I didn't do it, if that's what you're looking for. That bimbo witch did him in. There's no doubt in my mind."

"Why are you so sure?" I didn't disagree that it was possible Melody killed him, but Linda could have as well. After all, she'd been the one who had threatened him.

"She married him for his money. Despite the fact he wrote for a newspaper, Reggie had money. I always assumed he inherited it. It wasn't something we talked about."

"You didn't find it odd that he didn't tell you?" I sure would have.

Linda shrugged. "A little, I guess. It should have been a warning sign that he wasn't the man I thought he was. Believe it or not, Reggie could be very charming when it suited him. He wasn't good-looking, but there was something about him I fell in love with. That changed over time. His reviews weren't all that got nastier and nastier. He became a bitter, unlikable man." She took a sip of her coffee. "I don't know why I'm telling you all this."

"I'm glad you are."

"I guess I just needed someone to talk to. Don't get me wrong—I have friends, but they've heard it all before. They kind of zone out when I mention Reggie's name. And my son . . . well . . . I don't want him to know what a jerk his father was. Although he probably has a pretty good idea. He's a smart kid."

She went on to tell me her son was ten and had some health problems, which was one reason why she needed her ex to help out. I hated to think it, but it was no wonder someone killed him. As much as I'd have liked Melody and Dwayne to have committed the murder, the fact that Linda and her son needed some financial help moved her up on the suspect list. Surely even someone as despicable as Reginald Mobley wouldn't write his ten-year-old child out of his will. I didn't want Linda to be the killer, though. I liked her.

"Anyway. Back to your original question. That woman wanted his money and I'm sure she's the reason why Reggie refused to increase his child support. He never had an issue with it until he married her. Even though we were divorced for a few years and he didn't see Stevie much, he always paid the medical bills I sent him. After the wedding they all came back to me marked 'Return to Sender.'"

I pushed my empty glass aside. "That doesn't mean she killed him. It could have been any number of people."

Linda shook her head. "It was her. I'm sure of it. I just wish I could prove it." She seemed as sure of her theory as Vincent Falk was about his. "I don't care what it takes, but she and that brother of hers won't get another dime of Stevie's inheritance."

"Brother?" I didn't know anything about a brother.

"Melody's brother was Reggie's new best friend and business partner."

I had a funny feeling in my stomach. It couldn't be. Could it? "I wasn't aware she had a brother."

"You might even know him," Linda said. "He was at that festival over the weekend. A weird-looking guy by the name of Dwayne."

CHAPTER TEN

"Dwayne? Dwayne Tunstall?" I said. That explained a lot—Dwayne's great review, him acting like Reggie was his best friend, and the hug he'd given Melody in the parking lot. Candy would be disappointed that they weren't lovers.

Linda nodded. "Yep. Do you know him?"

"Unfortunately, yes," I answered. "He calls himself a brewer, but he has a lousy reputation." I told Linda about his history with Dave and Cory.

"I knew he was a little creepy, but I didn't realize he was a thief, too." Linda leaned back in her chair. "If he's underhanded enough to steal those recipes . . ."

She didn't need to finish the sentence. I was thinking the same thing. I'd been wrong about the nature of Dwayne and

Melody's relationship, but the fact they were brother and sister didn't change the notion that they could have planned Mobley's murder together. The good reviews hadn't been enough for Dwayne. He wanted his brother-in-law's fortune as well. If Mobley was eliminated as his business partner, he'd have it all to himself. And Melody would have the house, the bank accounts, and who knew what else.

Before we parted, Linda and I exchanged phone numbers and she promised to call if she thought of anything else. I considered asking her to call Vincent Falk—if she hadn't talked to him already—but if he found out she'd spoken to me, he'd think we were in cahoots like he had when he saw me with Ginger. I'd call my dad later and he could talk to Linda.

My phone buzzed as I got into my car. I barely had time to say hello when Candy's voice barked, "Where are you? What's going on?"

I suggested she meet me at my apartment and we could fill each other in. When I got there, she was standing in the parking lot tapping her foot and looking at her watch.

"What took you so long?" she asked.

It hadn't been long at all and I told her so. Hops greeted us with a very dissatisfied meow as soon as I unlocked the door. She strutted directly to her empty dish in the kitchen and gave me her equivalent of the evil eye. I couldn't help laughing.

"Someone is hungry," Candy said. "You'd better take care of her first or we'll never have any peace."

"We may not anyway." I opened the kitchen cupboard where I kept the cat food. "I have some iced tea in the fridge, if you want some." I fed Hops and refreshed her water, and

Candy found two glasses and poured us both some tea. While the kitten ate, we headed to the living room area and took seats on my hand-me-down sofa from Grandma O'Hara. I knew Candy was itching to hear what I'd found out and I was dying to tell her, but I wanted to hear her story first. "What happened at the funeral home after I left?"

"You first," she said.

I shook my head. "Nope."

"Your mother didn't do a very good job at teaching you to respect your elders."

"I'll be sure to tell her," I said with a laugh. "Now spill." Hops meandered into the living area, ignored me, and jumped onto Candy's lap, where she proceeded to knead her thighs before circling and settling down. "See? Hops wants to hear it, too."

"You are no fun at all."

"So I've been told."

She put her glass down on the coffee table. "After you were gone, Melody ranted about how that woman was trying to ruin her life. She yelled at the poor funeral director for several minutes, wanting to know what kind of a place he was running where anyone could just walk in. The poor man was almost in tears when he left the room. I heard a few words I hadn't heard in years in the process, too. She swears like a trucker."

I could only imagine.

"After that spectacle, the few people who were still in the room made a hasty exit. When she calmed down enough to be coherent, I asked her who the woman was. She told me she was Mobley's ex-wife and she was after his money."

"That's interesting," I said. "Linda accused Melody of the same thing."

Candy picked up her glass and drank some of her iced tea. "She told me the ex was faking her son's illness to get more child support."

"That's pretty despicable."

"I agree. What kind of a mother would do something like that?"

"No, I meant what Melody said was despicable. I don't believe it's true." I told her Linda's side of the story.

"Let me get this straight," Candy said. "According to this Linda, she sent her child's hospital bills to Mobley and he paid them?"

"Yep. But after he married Melody, the bills kept getting sent back."

Candy thought for a moment. "Maybe Reginald Mobley never saw those bills. Melody may have been the one returning them. When Linda came around asking for more money, he thought she was just being greedy. He had no idea the bills were being sent back."

"I don't know," I said. "Maybe. I think there could be more to it. Wouldn't he wonder why all of a sudden he stopped getting those bills?" I wished I had asked Linda what kind of medical issues her son had. Was it something that could have been fixed or cured, so that Mobley would think all was well? Or was it a chronic condition? Maybe it didn't really matter. Even though it was possible that money was the reason Mobley was killed, I told Candy I didn't think it had anything to do with Linda's son's illness.

"Why not?"

"Linda told me something else. I found out why Dwayne was hugging Melody."

"An affair?"

"Nope. It turns out Dwayne is Melody's brother."

"That's quite a surprise," Candy said. "Are you sure?"

"According to Linda, they are definitely brother and sister. She said Mobley was also Dwayne's new business partner."

"That would explain why Dwayne was the only one who got a positive review. Don't you think it odd, though, that Dwayne wasn't at the funeral home? You would think he'd want to be there to support his sister."

I nodded. "Unless for some reason they don't want anyone to know they're related."

"I can think of one good reason for that."

"I can, too," I said. "They could have planned and carried out the murder together."

"Exactly."

I was still thinking about it after she left. I didn't want to make the same mistake I'd made two months ago and have my mind so set on someone I was sure was a killer only to find out it was someone else. I'd even gone so far as to tell a couple of people I thought they were guilty of murder. Not exactly a brilliant move on my part. Dwayne and Melody were the most likely suspects, but I wasn't going to rule anyone out at this point.

Linda had a strong motive, too—money and protecting her son. The fact that I liked her wasn't a good reason to think she couldn't have killed her ex-husband.

There were others who hated Mobley, too. There were

numerous other restaurant and pub owners who had received scathing reviews and lost business. I also had to consider some of the other brewers. Dave, Randy, Cory, and Brandon had all voiced their loathing of the man. Even if they hadn't exactly wished him dead, they had certainly rejoiced in his death. It wasn't much of a stretch to think one of them could have taken that a step further. I didn't like the idea, but I had to keep it in mind. I hadn't planned on attending the monthly Tri-State Brewers Association meeting tomorrow night, since it was sandwiched between the two weekends of the festival, but I changed my mind. Dave and Randy rarely missed a meeting. I knew for sure that Dave would be there since he was hosting, and I hoped Randy, Cory, and Brandon would attend as well. It would be a chance for me to question them before the weekend.

When Jake called to say good night, I filled him in on the events of the evening. Then we talked about his parents and other things, and soon I'd pushed all thoughts of murder out of my mind. By the time we ended our thirty-minute call, I was smiling and felt like all was right with the world.

As usual, I was the first to arrive at the brew house on Wednesday morning. After I finished checking the fermentation tanks, I parked myself in my office to do some paperwork. I paid some bills and prepared next month's schedule for the waitstaff. I wanted to get it to them as soon as possible so there would be time to make changes if necessary. Once that was out of the way, I concentrated on the report I had to fill out for the state every month. Or tried to concentrate. It wasn't a coincidence that my mind wandered about a third of the way through the report.

My thoughts went back to something Linda had said about her ex-husband that I had forgotten to tell Candy. Mobley had been well-off when Linda married him, but she hadn't known how or where the money came from. She thought he might have inherited it. Why wouldn't he have discussed this with his wife? It might not matter where he got his money, but I wanted to know anyway. If he'd somehow gained his fortune illegally instead of inheriting or earning it, it would be worth looking into as a possible motive. I just had to figure out how to do that. I was sure his widow wouldn't tell me. If she even knew, that is. If Linda hadn't known, maybe Melody didn't, either.

But there was someone who did—Dwayne. I didn't for a minute buy Mobley tolerating Dwayne just because he was his wife's brother. I'd previously thought that Dwayne had to have something on the critic and that made even more sense now. I'd seen firsthand the way Mobley looked at his brother-in-law. It didn't match up with he'd said or what he'd written in his review.

Dwayne knew something no one else did. And I meant to find out exactly what it was.

I didn't have to wait long to see Dwayne. After the lunch rush, Jake and I were behind the bar in the pub, replacing an empty keg with a fresh one of lager. Usually Nicole and

I did this, but she was working the evening shift, so I had enlisted Jake. He was more than happy to oblige. Work duties seemed to be the only way we had been able to see each other so far this week. Not that I was complaining. Things would settle down again.

I had just finished telling Jake the theory I'd come up with that morning about Dwayne when he strolled into the pub. Jake spotted him first and he nudged me. "Speak of the devil," he said.

"That could be an accurate description." I rinsed my sticky hands in the bar sink and dried them on a paper towel. I greeted Dwayne politely instead of saying "Look what the cat dragged in," which was one of Grandma O'Hara's favorite expressions.

Dwayne wasn't nearly as polite. He didn't bother with a greeting. "This place is nicer than I thought it would be," he said. Coming from him, that could almost be construed as a compliment.

"What brings you here?" Jake asked. "I'm sorry. I forgot your name."

It took everything in me not to laugh.

Dwayne looked at Jake like he was a complete idiot. "Dwayne Tunstall."

Jake slapped himself on the forehead. "That's right. You were friends with the dead guy."

"Yes, very good friends," Dwayne said. "The best." He slid onto one of the barstools and studied the taps. "I think I'll have one of the lagers. It won't be as good as mine, though."

"I'm sure you'll let me know." I handed Jake a glass.

Jake drew the beer and placed it in front of Dwayne. "That'll be four bucks. Or do you want to run a tab?"

Dwayne's eyes widened. "You're making me pay for this?"

"Of course," I said. "This is a place of business, you know."

"You don't give freebies to fellow brewers?"

"Do you?" I figured he didn't and it likely wouldn't cross his mind. If it had been Dave or one of the other brewers, I would have comped his drink. If I did that for Dwayne, I had a feeling he'd expect it all the time.

"Not usually," he said. "I would have made an exception for you, but don't expect it now. Sheesh." He took out his wallet and slapped four ones down on the bar.

I guessed I wasn't getting a tip.

He sipped his lager. "This really isn't bad."

Wow. Two almost-compliments. That was high praise coming from him. I couldn't help but think he wanted something.

Dwayne took another drink and set down his glass. "I guess you're wondering why I'm here."

I knew there had to be a reason he was being so nice. I waited.

"I've been trying to join the Brewers Association for three years and keep getting turned down. From what I hear, you got right in. Everyone seems to like you, so I thought maybe you could put in a good word for me."

It didn't surprise me in the least that he'd been black-listed. I doubted there was anything I could do about that even if I'd wanted to. Dave Shipley was the current president and there was no way he'd ever let Dwayne be a member. "I don't think that will help," I told him.

"You could at least try," he said. His whiny tone made him sound like a petulant two-year-old.

"I'll think about it."

"What's there to think about? All you have to do is talk to Shipley and whoever else makes these decisions."

"Why is it so important to you?" Jake asked.

"It's not," Dwayne said. "It's just that it would sound good when I'm telling people about my beer. And I feel left out. Like I'm not part of the community."

I looked at Jake and he nodded. He seemed to know what I was thinking.

"I'll tell you what," I said. "I'll mention it to Dave if you do something for me."

"Like 'you scratch my back and I'll scratch yours'?" His grin was more like a leer.

Ew. I felt Jake tense beside me. "No," I said. "I just need you to answer a question or two."

"That's it? No problem." He drained his glass and pushed it aside. "Shoot."

I leaned my elbows on the bar. "Why didn't you mention that Reginald Mobley was your brother-in-law?"

If Dwayne's jaw dropped any lower, he'd have to pick it up from the floor. "What? How did you . . . How do you know that?"

It was nice to see him almost speechless. "It wasn't that hard to find out. I don't understand why it was a big secret."

"I had my reasons," Dwayne said.

"Which were?"

"It's none of your business."

"I guess you don't want me to talk to Dave about your membership, then."

He picked up a paper napkin that was on the bar in front of him. "I do want you to talk to him. None of this has anything to do with Reggie's death, if that's what you're thinking." Whatever his reason, it was making him nervous. He was tearing the napkin into tiny pieces.

"How do I know that if you won't talk to me?"

Dwayne tossed what was left of the napkin onto the bar and hopped off his stool. "Sorry. No can do. Forget I even asked about the Brewers Association. I don't even want to belong anymore." He headed for the door and turned around when he reached it. "By the way, your lager stinks."

"That went well," I said to Jake after the door closed behind Dwayne. "We didn't learn anything."

"Not true," Jake said. "Something spooked him—enough for him to tell you to forget about something as important to him as talking to Dave about his membership."

I went around the bar and took a seat on one of the stools. "I hoped to learn more than that. I wanted to ask him about his brother-in-law's finances."

"There are other ways to do that. You'll figure it out. Give it some time."

Jake was a lot more patient than I was. I turned around when I heard the door open. Vincent Falk entered, holding a folded piece of paper in his hand. He was accompanied by two uniformed officers.

Things seemed to have gone from bad to worse. First Dwayne and now my least favorite detective. It wasn't a good sign that he wasn't alone. I slid off the stool and looked at Jake. "What was that you said about giving it some time? It may have run out."

CHAPTER ELEVEN

ake came around the bar and stood beside me as Vince headed our way. The uniforms parked themselves by the door. The customers at the lone occupied table watched in fascination, no doubt torn between staying to see what was going on and getting up and leaving.

I took a deep breath and relaxed my clenched fists before I was tempted to use them on Vinnie the Viper. "Detective Falk," I said with false cheerfulness. "What can I do for you? Would you like a table? We have a delicious—"

"No," he said. "I'm not here to eat." He snapped open the paper he was holding, which was as stiff as the starched white shirt he wore. "I have a warrant to confiscate all your bottled water."

A sense of relief went through me. I had thought it would

be worse. With two uniformed officers accompanying him, I had expected it to be an arrest warrant. I took the paper from him. Jake and I read it together; then I handed it back to him.

"Why confiscate the water?" Jake asked.

Vince folded the warrant and slid it into the pocket of his suit coat. "You don't need to know that."

"Yes, we do," Jake said.

Vince stepped toward Jake until they were almost nose to nose. "If I had my way, this would be a full-blown search warrant or, better yet, an arrest warrant. I know you killed that critic and I still mean to prove it."

Jake's whole body was tense. I touched his arm, but he didn't relax. Before he did something he'd live to regret, I said, "Jake, why don't you take those two officers back to the storeroom and show them where we keep the bottled water."

He stared the detective down for a few more seconds, then took a step back. "Sure." He waved to the patrolmen, who then followed him to the storeroom.

I hadn't realized I'd been holding my breath until I let it out.

"Is that the only place you keep bottled water?" Vince asked.

I showed him where we had some behind the bar. "I still don't understand why you need these," I said as I pulled bottles from the small refrigerator behind the bar.

"Maybe you should ask Daddy."

I set one of the plastic bottles down on the bar top much

harder than necessary. "What do you mean by that? My father doesn't talk about his cases with me." Not much, anyway.

"Right."

"I'm going to ask again," I said. I measured each word carefully, trying to keep my anger in check. "Why do you need these bottles? I have a right to know the reason."

He was silent for a moment and I thought he wasn't going to answer. "We're looking for cyanide."

"What?" I said. I knew Mobley had died from cyanide poisoning, but taking our bottled water made no sense to me.

"Cyanide was found in the victim's water bottle. Until we find where that bottle came from, we're taking all the bottles from anyone who had contact with him."

"Shouldn't you only confiscate bottles of the same brand? We don't carry the same kind they had at the festival."

"You could have changed the label."

I had to bite my tongue to keep from telling him that was the dumbest thing I'd ever heard. I settled for "That's ridiculous."

"We're done here," he said. "That's all I'm going to say."

After the police cleared out with five cases of bottled water—Vince wasn't happy that I demanded a receipt for them—I went back to my office. Jake headed for the kitchen to check on prep for the dinner rush. I paced back and forth trying to get my anger in check but hadn't succeeded by the time Jake came in, carrying two plates holding chicken salad sandwiches. I'd forgotten all about eating lunch.

He put them down on the desk. "You're going to wear a hole in the floor if you keep that up."

"I'm just so mad, I can't sit still." Jake pulled me into his arms and I rested my head on his chest. I was still angry, but this was definitely better than pacing. "I guess we can't stay like this for the rest of the day."

He kissed the top of my head. "Nope."

We reluctantly separated and sat down at the desk. I didn't think I was hungry until I bit into the sandwich. I devoured it in minutes.

Jake grinned. "That's what I like to see. A girl with a healthy appetite."

I balled up my napkin and threw it at him. "A bottle of water would hit the spot about now, but we don't have any."

"Forget about that jerk."

I leaned back in my chair. "I wish I could. For the life of me, I can't figure out why he'd confiscate all that water. He couldn't possibly think there's cyanide in any of them. It's not even the same brand. If someone put it in Mobley's bottle, it was put there for him—and only him."

"It could be a random poisoning, like that Tylenol thing years ago," Jake said.

"I don't think so. Someone wouldn't put it in only one bottle. There would be more victims." That was a horrible thought. We went back and forth with some other ideas, none of which made sense. The only person who might be able to shed some light on this was my dad. At this point I was still angry and I really didn't care if Vince thought I was tattling.

I'd had enough of him. I got Dad's voice mail and asked him to call me when he got a chance.

Dad hadn't returned my call by the time I left for the Brewers Association meeting. I was beginning to worry a little thinking about what Candy had said—that maybe my father was being forced out. I didn't want to think it could be true. Dad was exactly what a cop should be—the complete opposite of Vincent Falk. By the time I reached Fourth Base, Dave's brewpub on the North Shore, I'd convinced myself that my dad was just busy and he'd call me when he had a chance. After all, I hadn't told him what I wanted to talk about. For all he knew, I was calling only to chat.

There was a Pirates game at PNC Park, so parking was at a premium. I drove around the block three times hoping for a spot on the street with no luck. I even resorted to the Saint Anthony lost-and-found prayer I had learned when I was a kid. I finally managed to find what had to be the last space in one of the parking garages. Whether it was Saint Anthony or just dumb luck was up for interpretation. I thanked the saint just in case. Needless to say, I was almost late for the meeting.

Other than good beer, Fourth Base didn't have much in common with the Allegheny Brew House. Where I'd kept vintage touches and exposed brick, Dave had opted for the modern sports bar look. Because of its location between PNC Park and Heinz Field, most of its patrons were sports enthusiasts, so it worked. The place was packed and assorted ball games were on six large-screen televisions positioned around the room. I crossed the black-and-white tile floor to an industrial-looking steel staircase that led up to the banquet room on the second floor.

I was a little envious that Dave had a banquet room, although I don't know how much use one would get in my brewpub. I planned to add a rathskeller in the basement eventually, but that was a couple of years down the road.

This was the first time I'd been upstairs at Fourth Base and when I opened the door to the room where the meeting was held, I was immediately struck by the view. The room had an entire wall of windows that showcased the downtown Pittsburgh skyline. The rest of the room was typical of one for large gatherings, with round tables, a bar, and a parquet dance floor. It would be a beautiful spot for a wedding. I imagined wearing a white dress, dancing with Jake in this room, the lights of the city reflecting off the river. I pushed the thought out of my mind before I got carried away and heard wedding bells.

A dozen or so of my fellow brewers were gathered around the bar, so I headed that way. Dave stood behind the bar, pouring beer from a half-gallon glass growler, and he passed a glass to me. One of the cool things about these meetings was that whoever was hosting usually came up with a new specialty brew without telling the others what it was, and we played Stump the Brewer. Attendees tried to guess the ingredient that made it so special. There were no prizes, but it was fun.

"You'll never guess this one, Max," Dave said. "So far, no one's gotten it."

I smiled. "I'll give it my best shot." I held the glass up to the light. It was definitely a light-colored lager, but it had a slight blue or purple tinge to it. I put the glass under my chin and used my other hand to wave the aroma toward my face, like I'd learned to do in Germany.

Cory Dixon laughed. "Hey, Max, that ain't some fancy wine."

Another brewer—I didn't remember his name—said, "And your nose is a little higher on your face."

I stuck my tongue out at both of them. Very adult of me, I know. I closed my eyes and breathed in. "Some kind of berry," I said.

"Berries?" Randy Gregory said. "You're making fruity beer now?"

"Hey, if you can make pumpkin beer, I can make fruity beer," Dave said. "Max is right—it's a berry. The big question is, what kind of berry?"

I studied it some more. Sniffed it again and tasted it a couple of times. It definitely wasn't strawberry or raspberry. I finally settled on blueberry.

"You are so close," Dave said. "But it's not blueberry."

"How about blackberry?" I said.

Dave shook his head. "And you only get one guess."

"Drat," I said. "It's good, whatever it is."

"Don't keep us in suspense," Cory said. "What's in it?"

Dave grinned. "Huckleberry!"

The room erupted in laughter and comments ranged from "What the hell's a huckleberry?" to "You mean like the dog in the old cartoons?" Finally everyone settled down and Dave called the meeting to order.

Dave went over the minutes from the last meeting and we discussed some changes in the liquor law that the state legislature had recently passed. It wasn't long before the discussion moved on to the festival and the murder. Everyone had his own theory on who killed Reginald Mobley. I kept quiet, not only because I wasn't sure how much I wanted to share about the little I knew, but I wanted to listen in case one of them revealed something important. None of them mentioned having their bottled water confiscated, which puzzled me. Vince had said that he was confiscating water from anyone who'd had contact with Mobley. Granted, most of them ran breweries and not brewpubs, but Dave's son had been in the burger competition and had contact with the critic.

Randy Gregory noticed I wasn't participating in the conversation. "So what's your take on all this, Max? What's your pop saying?"

"Not much," I said. "He doesn't talk about active cases."

"I'm sure you have some kind of theory," Randy said. "We all know you were the one who figured out who killed your assistant. You must know something."

I didn't say anything.

Randy wouldn't ease up. "Come on. You know something. I can tell."

I was becoming uncomfortable with his persistence. Why did he want to know so badly? Was he just being a neb-nose? Or was it more than that?

"Knock it off, dude," Dave said sharply. "If Max knew anything important, she'd tell us."

"Sheesh. Lighten up. I don't mean anything by it. I'm just

wondering, that's all." Randy got up from his chair. "I gotta get going anyway. See yinz guys the weekend."

After that, the others left one by one until only Dave and I were left. "Sorry about Randy," Dave said.

"You don't need to apologize for him," I said.

"You know I didn't have any love for that jackass Mobley, but Randy and Cory practically foam at the mouth when anyone mentions him. Cory keeps saying someone did the world a favor when they offed the guy. I'm not exactly sad he's dead, but . . ."

"They're going overboard."

"Yeah." He screwed the cap onto a half-gallon growler that still had some beer left in it.

"Why do they hate him so much?" I asked.

Dave shrugged. "I don't know. Neither Butler Brewing or the South Side Brew Works are brewpubs, so Mobley wouldn't have reviewed either one of them. I had more reason to hate the guy than they do. Unless . . ."

"What?"

"It may be nothing, but Cory applied for a brewpub license about a year ago and got turned down."

"Mobley was a food and beverage writer," I said. "He didn't work for the state."

"No, but maybe he knew someone who did." Dave picked up an empty growler.

"That's a stretch, don't you think?" I followed him to the adjacent kitchen.

Dave turned on the water at the sink. "Probably. It's all I can think of, though." He rinsed out the glass bottle and placed it on the counter.

I hated to ask my next question, but I had to. "Is there a chance that either Cory or Randy could have killed Mobley?" I half expected Dave to immediately come to their defense, but instead he seemed to consider my question.

He rubbed his bearded chin. "I'd like to say no, but to tell you the truth, I don't know. I don't think they did it, but that's not the same thing, is it?"

"No, it's not." Unfortunately.

𝕴 would have kicked myself if I hadn't been driving. I was almost to the Fortieth Street Bridge when I realized I'd forgotten to tell Dave about Dwayne's visit that afternoon, or about Dwayne's relationship with Melody. It wasn't that I wanted to do Dwayne any favors, but he had worked for Dave. It was likely Dave knew more about him than his penchant for recipe theft. Then I remembered Dwayne had also worked for Cory at South Side Brew Works. I hadn't had much of a chance to talk to Cory at the meeting. Maybe if I had time tomorrow, I could head to the South Side again. Not only would it be a good opportunity to ask about Dwayne, but I could try to find out why Cory hated Mobley so much. If only I'd known about Dwayne and Melody before I'd gone to the funeral home, I could have stopped by his brewery then. Of course, if I made another trip, I could check out the new shoe store on Carson I'd heard about.

While I was at the meeting, I'd gotten a voice mail from my dad, telling me he was returning my call and he'd be home all evening. Instead of taking the Fortieth Street Bridge to Lawrenceville, I stayed on Route 28 and took the

Highland Park Bridge to my parents' house. I parked on the street in front of the house. Despite Dad's insistence that I keep the door locked at my apartment, he didn't practice what he preached. The interior door was open and the screen door was unlocked. His excuse was always that it let a nice breeze through. If I had done the same, I'd never hear the end of it.

In the living room, Mom was sitting in one of the blue striped wing chairs reading a Nora Roberts novel and Dad was stretched out on the blue couch flipping through channels with the remote. Dad spotted me and he kind of looked like how my brother Patrick used to when he got caught sneaking into the house after curfew. It was hard to believe Pat was a cop in Richmond now after some of his youthful shenanigans. Dad quickly hit the off button on the remote.

I laughed. "You're allowed to watch TV, Dad."

Mom looked up and closed her book with a smile. "I keep telling him that."

"There's nothing on, anyway."

"You're not working tonight?" Mom asked.

I took a seat in the other striped chair. "I went to a brewers' meeting." I told them about the visit to the funeral home and talking to Linda Mobley.

Dad sighed. "I know you mean well, honey, but you really shouldn't be going around talking to these people— especially anyone who might be a potential suspect."

"I have to do something. I'm not going to sit by while your partner tries to railroad Jake."

"That's not going to happen."

"I'm not so sure about that. Your partner stopped at the

pub again today with a warrant to confiscate all our bottled water. He told Jake he still planned to prove that he killed Mobley."

"Vince isn't going to do that, but I'll have another talk with him," he said.

I didn't understand why Dad seemed to be defending him. "What good will that do? It hasn't helped so far. Why are you giving him free rein to do anything he wants to?"

Dad swung his legs around and put his feet back on the floor. "Look. I know you don't think much of Vincent, but he really could be a good detective someday. Unfortunately, he has his mind set on doing things his own way right now. He needs to be steered in the right direction and that's the job I've been given. I'm trying to teach him that his way isn't necessarily the right way."

"He's obviously not paying attention, then," I said. "Confiscating that bottled water had to be his idea."

"It was," Dad said, the corners of his mouth turning up. Mom smiled, too, like she was in on a secret.

"Wait a minute." I looked from one to the other. "What aren't you telling me?"

Dad shrugged and leaned back on the couch, so I turned to my mother.

"Remember when you were about six or seven," Mom said, "and you insisted on running the Great Race with Sean even though he was twelve years older than you and you'd never done anything like that before?"

I felt the pink creeping into my face. "How could I forget it?" Sean had been a senior in high school and I'd just started first grade. The Great Race was a 10K that was held every

September. Sean ran cross-country in high school and he and a couple of his friends entered the race, and in my six-year-old mind, I figured I could run it, too. The problem was, while he and his friends ran every day, I played in the backyard or with my Barbie dolls. On the day of the race, I insisted on running with Sean. About halfway through, I wanted to quit. I cried for Sean to carry me, but he wouldn't. He told me if I wanted to run with him, I had to do exactly that. I gave him a lot of credit—still do—for staying beside me and not running off with his friends. Anyway, I finished the race and learned three lessons that day. One—you finish what you start and don't quit. Two—let people make mistakes and learn from them. And three—I hate running.

I didn't think Vince's lesson was one or three. "I get it now." I grinned at my parents. "You're teaching Vince the power of learning from his mistakes."

CHAPTER TWELVE

"You could say that," Dad said. "I wasn't going to tell you about any of this, but your mother convinced me you should know." He winked at her. "As usual, she's right."

"Why were you keeping quiet?" I asked. "I was beginning to worry about you and what was going on. Candy had me convinced the powers that be were trying to force you out."

"It's nothing like that." Dad leaned forward. "Promise me you'll keep this to yourself."

I nodded. "Of course."

"Vincent happens to be the governor's nephew, so there's a lot of politics at play here. I'm not going to get into the whole thing, but suffice it to say, the mayor and the chief were convinced to accept Vincent's transfer from across the state. And they figured I was the perfect guy to keep him in line and show him the ropes."

"And the mayor is still your friend?"

Dad chuckled. "He is. Anyway, Vincent isn't a bad cop when he forgets about trying to make a name for himself and he stops thinking he's right all the time. He's ambitious and unfortunately he thinks he's made the big time with this case. So far, just about everything I tell him goes in one ear and out the other. I finally decided to give him—as your mother so eloquently puts it—the freedom to make his own mistakes."

I wasn't sure that was a good idea. "But won't that make him come after Jake with a vengeance?"

Dad shook his head. "He's not stupid. He knows he can't make an arrest without the proper evidence. And while he's looking in all the wrong places, I'm following up on everything else. Sooner or later, he'll get back on track and see he's going in the wrong direction."

I hoped he was right. We chatted awhile and I filled him in on what I'd discovered. He was aware of most of it, and he was already looking into Mobley's financials. One thing he hadn't known was that Dwayne was Melody's brother. He planned on paying Dwayne a call first thing in the morning. I wished I could be a fly on the wall for that interview.

I got up earlier than usual the next morning and headed to the brewery before six. The stout and the IPA that I had in the fermenters would need to be kegged today or tomorrow. Since tomorrow would be filled with setting up for the second and final weekend of the festival, I decided on today. I still wanted to pay a visit to South Side Brew Works and talk to Cory if I got the kegging finished today.

When I drove into the lot, I was surprised to see Jake getting out of his truck. We'd talked on the phone last night, and he'd offered to help with the kegging. I'd told him it wasn't necessary, but I was happy he'd decided it was. His hair still looked wet from the shower, and when he smiled at me, my stomach did a little flip.

"Morning, gorgeous," Jake said, pulling me to him when I got out of my car.

He kissed me and the little flip became an acrobatic extravaganza. We parted when the driver of a passing car honked his horn and hollered "Woo-hoo!" out his open window. We were laughing as we walked hand in hand to the front door. Jake unlocked the door and once we were inside, I disarmed the security system. My pulse had almost returned to normal by then.

While Jake went to make coffee, I tossed my purse onto the desk in my office, then went into the brewery and checked the gauges on all the tanks. Everything was in order. I began moving some of the stainless steel half-barrel kegs that had already been cleaned and sterilized over to the tank. When Jake came through the swinging door with coffee, I took my mug and we sat on the metal steps beside the mash tun, drinking our coffee.

"I should come in early more often," he said. "This is nice."

"Yes. It's so quiet and peaceful."

"It is, but I meant sitting here with you."

I smiled at him. "Yeah. That, too."

"Don't sound so enthusiastic, O'Hara."

"You know what I mean."

"Do I?"

We'd never talked much about how we felt about each other, and this wasn't really the time and place to do it. "I mean I wouldn't want to be anywhere else," I said. "I like being here with you. I'm glad you came in."

"I can't imagine being anywhere else. One of the best decisions I ever made was moving back here."

I rested my head on his shoulder. "I'm glad you did."

We sat like that until our cups were empty; then Jake set them aside. "Enough goldbricking," he said. He pulled me to my feet. "So, where do we start, boss?"

Transferring beer from a pressurized tank to a keg is what I'd call a "hurry up and wait" process. The keg is pressurized with CO_2 as well. A tube with a valve is attached to the top of the keg so that the CO_2 can "gas off" as the keg fills with beer. Eventually the valve releases foam, and then beer, which means the half barrel is full. I've learned to do something else while keeping an eye on the valve.

Jake had returned to the kitchen an hour before we opened for the day to supervise the staff and get things rolling there. When Nicole came in, she helped me finish and did some of the perpetual cleaning and sanitizing. She stayed until she was needed in the pub. By midafternoon everything was spic-and-span, so I took that opportunity to head back to the South Side.

I took the same route I had when I went to the funeral home—up Fortieth Street, over the Bloomfield Bridge, and through Oakland. Traffic in Oakland was never light because of the hospitals and the University of Pittsburgh, but it was better than usual since many of the students were home for the summer. I hit the most traffic on Bates Street, but I was soon sailing over the Hot Metal Bridge and into the South Side.

I had no trouble finding the South Side Brew Works, even though I'd been there only once. I figured Cory would wonder why I decided to visit all of a sudden, so on the way over I tried to come up with an excuse. I settled on telling him I was in the neighborhood to check out a new shoe store. Not the best reason in the world, but it was the best I could do. Cory's brewery was in a plain concrete-block building with few windows and a metal entry door. The tiny parking lot had room for four cars, and I pulled into the last open one.

Cory had three brewers working for him, but I knew only one of them. Fortunately Tom Wilkins was the one who greeted me. Tom was what could be considered an old-school brewer. He had worked for the former Steel City Brewing before they were bought out. He didn't particularly care for some of the fancier craft brews, but as long as he was allowed to brew what he called "real beer," he was happy. Frankly, I thought Cory was lucky to have him. Tom was extremely knowledgeable and kept Cory—who was known to think up some rather wild concoctions—on the straight and narrow. Whenever Cory came up with one of his more adventurous brews, Tom's question to him was always, "Will it sell?" Often the answer was no. Cory still experimented more than some of us, but not as much as he would without Tom.

"How ya doing, darlin'?" Tom said. He called everyone *darlin'*—every female, that is. "Long time no see."

"Nice to see you again, Tom." I shook his outstretched hand.

"How's that brewery of yours?" Tom asked. "Franny said the place is really hopping." His face lit up when he said her name.

I'd introduced him to the woman who was putting the brewing museum together. Her father had worked at Steel City even before Prohibition, and she had a treasure trove of artifacts and photos of the brewing history of Pittsburgh. Fran didn't want to take credit for it, but her knowledge of the brewery during the Prohibition era had led me to finding the person who'd killed Kurt. She and Tom had a lot in common and they'd hit it off right away. Tom was in his late sixties and only a few years younger than Fran, and I suspected there might be a little romance blooming between them.

"We've been busy, which is a good thing," I said.

"That's because you got some good beer." Tom looked around before he continued. "You could teach Cory a thing or two. I can't even talk about his latest idea."

I laughed. "Just because it's different doesn't mean it's bad."

"Oh, I know that, darlin'. But sometimes that boy doesn't have any sense. None at all."

"Speaking of that boy," I said, "is he around?" Tom pointed toward the room where the tanks were located, and I headed that way.

I found Cory standing beside a metal table that was covered with small plastic containers filled with assorted grains, hops, and a few things I couldn't identify. He was writing on a legal pad and when I got closer, it appeared he was doing some math calculations. He pushed the tablet aside when he spotted me.

"Well, this is a surprise," he said. "What brings you to my end of town?"

"I'm going to check out a new shoe store that opened over here and I thought I'd stop and say hello."

He gave me a look that told me he didn't believe it for a minute, then laughed. "You're investigating, aren't you?"

"Why would you think that?" I felt heat rising in my cheeks.

"One, you're a lousy liar. Two, your face is all red."

"Guilty as charged," I said with a grin. "In my defense, I went to twelve years of Catholic school and my brother's a priest."

"Not to mention your dad's a cop." Cory pulled a couple of beat-up stools from under the table. "Have a seat."

I probably should have thought this out more, because I wasn't sure where to start with questions. It turned out I didn't have to ask much, because Cory did most of the talking.

"First," he said, "I'm only doing this because I like you, Max. I wouldn't give most people the time of day. It's none of their business."

"You don't even know what I want to ask you."

"It ain't that hard to figure out. You want to know if I killed Reginald Mobley."

"Did you?" I blurted out.

Cory laughed again. "No. Did I want to? Hell, yes. I'm glad someone took him out. That man did more damage to those of us in the food and beverage industry than anyone realizes."

He slid off his stool. "Wait here. I have something to show you." He went through a doorway into what appeared to be an office and returned moments later carrying a red folder. He slid it toward me as he sat back down. "Take a look," he said.

Inside the folder I found papers with the familiar crest of the Commonwealth of Pennsylvania at the top. Some of the paperwork was familiar in other ways, too—like the application for a license to operate a brewpub. I already knew Cory had been turned down, so it wasn't a surprise to see a letter saying as much. There was no reason given in the letter. "They didn't tell you why they turned you down?" I asked.

"Not until I pressed the point. And hired a lawyer. I met every single one of the qualifications. I didn't think they could legally turn me down, and neither did my lawyer." He pointed to the papers. "Keep reading."

I skimmed a few pages full of legalese, which to me was

harder to understand than an advanced biochemistry text-book. I finally reached a copy of a letter from Reginald Mobley that was addressed to the high-ranking official in charge. In reading it, I understood Cory's hatred of the man. It was full of inaccuracies regarding the business, including that he had "proof" that Cory had stolen recipes from an-other brewer. Mobley didn't say it, but it was obvious to me that he was in cahoots with Dwayne. "Wow," I said.

Cory nodded. "There's more that's not in writing. I know I should have let my lawyer handle it, but when I saw this, I confronted Mobley. It wasn't pretty. He threatened me, saying he could completely ruin me if I didn't back off. I'd already lost thousands of dollars that I didn't have over the whole thing. I couldn't afford to lose any more." He shrugged. "I convinced myself that I still had the brewery, so that would have to be enough."

"Did he do the same thing to Randy?" I asked.

"Yep. And he would have done it to Dave, too, if Dave hadn't already been established."

I still wasn't seeing the entire picture. I didn't know what was in it for Mobley. Why would he care if some brewers wanted to expand from just brewing to opening brewpubs? The only thing that made sense was that he and his brother-in-law thought the brewers would be too much competition. He hadn't blocked my application, though. He probably hadn't thought a female brewer was any kind of a threat.

I'd wanted to talk to Cory about Dwayne, so I asked him if he was aware of the relationship between Dwayne and Mobley.

He shook his head and uttered an expletive. "That explains an awful lot. That little weasel must have convinced Mobley that I stole his recipes and not the other way around."

"Dwayne came to see me yesterday to ask a favor. He wanted me to talk to Dave about letting him join the Brewers Association."

"That'll never happen. Especially not as long as Dave's in charge."

"That's what I figured. I came right out and asked Dwayne why he had never told anyone Mobley was his brother-in-law. He didn't deny hiding it and seemed afraid of something. He told me to forget about the association even though five minutes earlier he was practically begging me to talk to Dave."

"I wonder what he was afraid of."

"I was kind of hoping you might be able to give me an idea, since you worked with him," I said.

Cory thought for a moment. "I didn't think he was a bad guy at first. Maybe a little lazy, or maybe that he was one of those guys who had to be told exactly what to do. He asked a lot of questions. Like exactly how much of a certain malt or hops went into a brew. He even wrote everything down. I assumed he was anxious to learn brewing and didn't want to make any mistakes. By the time I realized what he was doing it was too late."

"I guess he never gave you any indication what his brother-in-law was planning, either?"

"I never had an inkling the two even knew each other, and I sure as hell didn't know they were related. Now that I know Dwayne was behind it, I'm not going to let him get away with it. Looks like I'm going to be getting my lawyer involved again." He pointed to the tablet he'd been using when I came in. "Maybe those numbers I've been crunching will come in handy after all."

"What do you mean?"

"I'm going to reapply now that Mobley's dead. I was trying to figure out whether I could afford it or not."

"Can I do anything to help?" I asked.

"Not at the moment, but thanks for asking. If I think of anything, I'll let you know."

I wished him luck. As I drove back to the pub, I replayed the conversation in my mind. After hearing Cory's entire story, I believed him when he said he hadn't killed Mobley. He certainly had a motive, but I couldn't see him doing it. Dad always said a good detective should trust his—or her, in my case—instincts as well as look at the evidence. My instinct said he wasn't a killer.

But what about Randy Gregory? I needed to hear his story as well. Unfortunately, his brewery was a good thirty to forty-five minutes away. It was too late in the day to pay him a visit and after the way he'd badgered me at the meeting last night, I wasn't sure I wanted to talk to him alone. He would be at the festival over the weekend. I'd just wait until then.

That evening, I was surprised to see Ginger Alvarado and her husband, Edward, waiting for a table. It was five o'clock and especially busy for some reason. Every seat was occupied, including those at the bar. Nicole was helping me at the taps when I spotted the Alvarados. I told her there was someone I needed to see and I'd be back as soon as I could.

"Take your time," she said. "I'll be fine."

"Welcome to the Allegheny Brew House," I said when I reached the couple.

"I'm sorry I haven't stopped in before this," Ginger said. "It looks fabulous." She introduced me to her husband. Edward was a few inches taller than Ginger's five foot six. His black hair was short and cut in a JFK style with an odd white streak in the front. He was dressed casually in khakis and a polo shirt like he'd just stepped off the golf course.

"It's nice to meet you," I said.

Edward shook my hand. "Likewise. I've never met a lady brewer before."

"I've never met a city councilman before, so I guess we're even."

He laughed. "Good point." His laugh was hearty, like I'd just told the best joke in the world.

"Your wife is doing a great job with the festival."

"Yes, she is." He put an arm around her shoulders. "As she does with most things."

Ginger smiled at her husband. It was clear that they adored each other. "You give me too much credit. There are dozens of people who have pitched in to make it a success."

By this time a table had opened up and I bussed it myself, then grabbed two menus and led them to their seats. I told them about the specials and the beer and said their server would be right with them. After they'd placed their orders, Ginger waved me over and asked me to sit for a moment.

"I wanted to fill you in on a couple of things for this weekend," she said.

"Nothing bad, I hope."

Ginger shook her head. "On the contrary. It's great news. We'll have three judges again and the burger competition final will definitely proceed as planned."

"That is good news," I said. "Is it anyone I'm familiar with?"

"Actually, you met her last Friday. It's Phoebe Atwell."

CHAPTER THIRTEEN

"That's a surprise," I said. "She was willing to come back after what happened to her replacement?"

"More than willing. Phoebe called me yesterday and offered her services again," Ginger said. "It took me by surprise, too. I had planned to just make do with two judges." She smiled at her husband. "Edward offered to be number three, but he knows nothing about food."

He laughed. "I know plenty about eating food—just not how to cook it. I would have been a great judge."

She patted his arm. "It wouldn't have looked right having my husband as a judge." She returned to the subject at hand. "Anyway, I asked Phoebe about the emergency that made her bow out last weekend and she assured me it had all been taken care of. Frankly, it's a relief she's coming back."

I agreed. I didn't know all that much about Phoebe, but the most important thing was that she wasn't anything like Reginald Mobley. I'd read a few of her articles and reviews when I began preparing for the festival, and she seemed fair. And having three judges instead of two would make for a better competition—especially in case of a tie between two contestants.

Ginger continued. "It will be good for the future of the festival to be able to put last weekend's incident behind us."

As much as I liked Ginger, her statement was a little off-putting. It seemed a bit euphemistic to call a murder an *incident*, almost as if it were in the same category as a purse snatching. I didn't like the next thought that popped into my head. The publicity hadn't hurt the attendance at the festival one bit. As a matter of fact, the turnout after the murder had far exceeded everyone's expectations. What was the saying? "There's no such thing as bad publicity"? It looked like my suspect list had just grown a little longer.

Edward interrupted my thoughts. "Ginger tells me that young detective has been harassing you."

His statement took me by surprise and I paused before answering. "Not exactly. I don't think he likes me much, though."

"I can talk to some people and have him removed from the case."

"That's not necessary." If he'd said that before I talked to Dad last night, I might have taken him up on it. With Dad in control, I didn't need Edward's help. I doubted that a lone city councilman had that kind of power anyway—especially since the detective was related to the governor.

"I imagine it's difficult for your father," he said.

"Not really."

"It must be frustrating for him, then."

I was glad that Cassie, their server, brought their meals just then so I didn't have to listen to any more of Edward's assumptions. I excused myself and told them to enjoy their meals. Nicole had things under control at the bar, so I went back to my office and closed the door. I needed to think.

The conversation had made a definite awkward turn. From Ginger downplaying that a murder had occurred by calling it an "incident," to her husband asking about Vince and my dad. It seemed like he was fishing for information, but I didn't know why. And why would he care if Vince was harassing me? If Ginger told him Vince was harassing her, I could see why he'd care about that. But me? It didn't make any sense. Unless . . .

Ginger certainly had the opportunity to kill Mobley. No one would think twice, or even notice, if she had been the one to place the poisoned bottle of water at Mobley's spot. She had every reason to be there. Come to think of it, when Mobley bellowed for water, Ginger was the one who picked up the bottle by his chair and handed it to him. But what about a motive—or her husband's if he was involved as well? Ginger wanted the festival to succeed. In order to make it an annual event and recoup the cost of planning and executing it, she'd need a large turnout. There would have been no guarantee that murdering Mobley would increase attendance. If anything, it could have done the opposite. The festival could have been a huge flop. And what about Edward Alvarado? I couldn't think of any reason why he'd be involved in murder. But he could be protecting his wife. His fishing expedition could be to find out what my dad knew.

I didn't quite buy that Ginger would kill someone on the off chance it would boost the festival. If she murdered the critic—and I wasn't convinced she did—there had to be more to it than that. I needed to find out whether she'd known Mobley before the festival.

There was a knock on my door and Cassie poked her head in and told me the Alvarados were ready to leave and wanted to say good-bye. I pushed my suspicions aside for the moment and headed back out to the pub.

I had planned on skipping our monthly book club meeting and making an early night of it, since I'd been at the brew house since six that morning, but I was still full of energy by seven o'clock. Jake had gone home earlier. Since his mom was spending the evening with her old bridge club, he and Mike had taken Jake's dad to the Pirates game. I was invited to both, but begged off, thinking I'd be too tired. Plus, I had no idea how to play bridge, and it would be a nice men's night out for the guys. Since I wasn't tired, I grabbed the book I'd made it only halfway through and headed to the library.

I'd always liked to read but had gotten sidetracked when I went to grad school. I joined the book club thinking I'd have more time since I didn't have textbooks to study, but the only book I'd managed to read all the way through was the one I'd chosen last month. And I kind of cheated because I'd chosen *To Kill a Mockingbird*, which I'd read several times over the years.

Kristie looked up in surprise when I walked into the conference room where we held our meetings. "Max! I didn't think you were coming tonight."

"I didn't, either," I said.

"I told you she'd be here," Elmer said. "Max has a sense of duty. She's a paratrooper at heart."

Candy snorted. "Hardly. Max is afraid of heights. And she'd have too much sense to jump out of a perfectly good airplane."

I felt like my smile went from ear to ear. It seemed like forever since I'd seen my friends, even though it had been only days. I took a seat beside Amanda, who was the children's librarian here at the Lawrenceville branch. This month's book—one of the latest young adult novels—had been her choice.

"I'm glad you came," Amanda whispered to me. "Elmer has already said he hated the book." Elmer griped about most of the books we read unless it was one he picked. We were used to it by now.

I noticed Kristie's mother was absent tonight. "Pearl couldn't make it?" I said to Kristie.

"She wanted to, but she has a bit of a cold and didn't want to pass it on to anyone," she said.

We chitchatted for a few minutes, then discussed the book. It wasn't long, however, before the conversation veered to the investigation into Reginald Mobley's murder. Candy had already told Kristie about the funeral home visit, but she repeated it for Amanda's sake.

"Oh my," Amanda said. "The wife really pushed the ex-wife into a vase of flowers? It's just like a soap opera."

"That's not all, either," Candy said. "Max talked to the ex and got an earful."

I told them about meeting with Linda Mobley.

Kristie shook her head. "So that Dwayne guy and Melody are brother and sister. Throw Mobley in the mix and it kind of makes sense in a weird sort of way."

"How do you figure?" Elmer asked.

"They're all the same type," she said. "And that type sticks together."

Elmer made a face. "And how would you know that, missy?"

"I see all kinds of people in the coffee shop. I can tell the type of person just by how they order their java and how they treat the baristas. I have a hunch those three would order something off-the-wall just to trip me up and then berate me if I didn't get it right."

"You might have something there," Candy said.

The wheels were turning in my head. In addition to being a great barista, Kristie actually had a master's in psychology. She could read behavior as well as—or better than—some practicing psychologists. Actually, being a barista, or even a bartender, wasn't all that different from being a psychologist. The venue was different. And the pay scale, of course. I told them about the brewers' meeting and how Randy wouldn't let up with the questions, my visit to Cory's brewery, and this evening with the Alvarados. I asked Kristie what she thought.

"I think you have a boatload of suspects," she said. "Melody, Dwayne, the ex-wife, those brewers, Ginger and her husband. I'd have to see them in action to give you any more than that."

"My money's on that politician," Elmer said. "Can't trust any of them."

Candy shook her head. "It's not him. No motive. He was just being nosy. Don't forget—he's planning on running for county executive, so he's collecting information he might be able to use later to his advantage. The killer has to be someone with a personal connection, like Melody."

"Or Dwayne," I added.

Candy gave me a look for interrupting, then continued. "Melody seems to think she's the center of the universe. She wants all the attention, which was pretty apparent at the funeral home. She didn't like it when Mobley's ex-wife showed up and the focus moved away from her."

"Yes!" Kristie sounded excited. "That's exactly it. Maybe you should have been a psychologist."

I had no doubt that Candy had used a lot of psychology in whatever her former career had been. I kept going back and forth between some kind of law enforcement or government work. Right now I was thinking profiler. I wondered if she'd ever tell me. Probably not. She enjoyed keeping me guessing too much.

"My career choice is not the topic right now," Candy said.

Or maybe she'd been a teacher. She had that correctional voice down pat.

"As I was saying, Melody wants the focus on her. What if, for some reason, she felt like her husband was overshadowing her? You put two narcissists together like that and something's got to give. Both of them can't come out on top."

"How does Dwayne fit into that picture?" I asked.

Amanda had been silent, but finally spoke up. "Maybe he's in love with his sister."

We all stared at her. I couldn't believe the idea had come out of the mouth of a children's librarian. "That's really creepy," I said.

Candy said, "Creepy or not, we should consider it."

Elmer agreed. "You can't get much creepier than poisoning a guy in front of hundreds of people. Those two could be in it together."

We tossed some more ideas back and forth, but didn't come up with anything concrete. Melody and Dwayne were at the top of my suspect list. If Ginger had killed Mobley, there had to have been more to it than publicity for the festival. I moved her—and Cory, too—to the bottom of my mental list. For now, I'd focus on the two I would see at the festival this weekend—Dwayne and Randy—and somehow find a way to talk to Melody. I was more glad than ever I had decided to show up for book club. Sometimes brainstorming with Candy, Elmer, and Kristie was more frustrating than helpful, but tonight it left me energized. And hopeful I'd figure it all out.

W hen I got home, I fed Hops, then fixed a sandwich for myself. I retrieved my laptop from my bedroom, then settled on the sofa and ate my very late dinner while the computer booted up. Hops soon joined me, but she seemed more interested in the chipped ham on my sandwich than anything else. I gave her a small piece and after she gobbled it down, she circled a few times, then snuggled up beside me.

I wasn't sure what I was even looking for, but I hoped Google would lead me in the right direction. I had too many suspects and I didn't want to make the mistake of being sure a certain person was the killer when it was someone else entirely. Been there, done that. There was also a little voice in my head telling me I should just forget the whole thing and let the police handle it. If Vincent Falk hadn't been involved, I would do just that. I knew my dad said he had everything under control, but it couldn't hurt if I helped him out a little. With the second weekend of the festival coming up, I worried about the possibility the killer would strike again. If Mobley had truly been the target, I knew that would be unlikely. Maybe my curiosity had just gotten the best of me, but I couldn't stop now.

I began my search with the obvious—Reginald Mobley. I scanned some of his reviews and was sickened by his vitriol. I didn't understand how someone could possibly hate everything and everybody. Supposedly everyone had some redeeming quality, but in his case there didn't seem to be one. I couldn't find anything that showed his financial status. There was also nothing to show a connection to any high-ranking state officials, but that wasn't altogether surprising. If there was something shady going on, neither party would want it made public.

Hops opened one eye when I said aloud, "Next up is the

wife." I typed *Melody Mobley*. I felt a bit like a ghoul when the first item listed was her husband's obituary. There wasn't much information on her other than some mentions at a few charity events around Pittsburgh. I tried her maiden name next and hit the jackpot—so to speak. Apparently Melody Tunstall had been a frequent visitor to the North Shore Casino, evidenced by the number of photos she'd taken of herself and posted online. Her selfies weren't at slot machines, either. She seemed to have an affinity for certain table games. The kind where you can win—or most likely lose—a lot of money.

"So Melody likes to gamble," I said.

Hops opened both eyes this time. "Murp."

I took that to mean she agreed with me. Either that or she was telling me to be quiet. I stared at the wall and stroked Hops on her head while I thought about what I'd found. If Melody had gambled a lot before she married Mobley, had she kept it up? She hadn't posted any pictures under her married name, but that didn't necessarily mean anything. If she was losing money, it might have made her husband angry. He demanded she stop going to the casino, so she killed him. It was possible, but I wasn't all that thrilled with the theory. That alone didn't seem like a strong enough motive. They could have just split up. Unless Mobley had her sign a prenuptial agreement, that is. From the little I knew about him, I was sure he would have left her with nothing, which gave her a much stronger motive for murder. But what about her brother?

I yawned and glanced at the clock on the wall. Eleven o'clock. I'd do one more search, then go to bed. I typed in

Dwayne's name. I half expected to find pictures of him at the casino, but there weren't any. I found a few mentions of his brewery and was glad most of them weren't very complimentary. I yawned again. Any more searching would have to wait. I closed my laptop, picked up the kitten, and headed to bed.

If it hadn't been for the steady rain and the fact that we all seemed to know what we were doing, Friday morning would have been a repeat from the previous week. By the time Jake and I got our canopy up, we were both soaked. And of course, as soon as we were under cover, the rain stopped and the sun came out. A typical July day in Pittsburgh.

While we'd been putting up the tent, I started to fill Jake in on everything he'd missed the previous day. By the time we'd finished setting up, I'd gotten only as far as telling him about the Alvarados when I spotted Ginger heading our way with Phoebe Atwell. I nudged Jake. "Better brace yourself. Look who's back."

He grinned. "Jealous?"

"Only if your type is feral cat." Or blond and gorgeous.

He pulled me close and kissed the top of my head. "I prefer petite black-haired beauties who brew beer."

"That's good to know. Nice alliteration, by the way."

"Thanks. Besides, I can handle Phoebe's type."

He didn't have to say it was because he'd been engaged to someone much like how Phoebe appeared to be. I could imagine Phoebe trying to run his life the way Victoria had. His ex-fiancée had wanted a famous hockey player man-about-town for a husband and dumped him when he didn't live up to her expectations. Jake preferred old T-shirts and jeans, not the tuxedos and expensive suits Victoria had wanted him to wear. Thank goodness.

"You remember Max and Jake, don't you, Phoebe?" Ginger said when the duo reached us.

Phoebe's reaction was much the same as it had been last week. Even though Jake's arm was around my shoulders, she ignored me and gave Jake a very slow once-over. "Oh, I remember all right," she said. "How could I forget?"

"It's nice to see you again," Jake said. "I'm sure you re-member Max."

"Of course." She gave me a quick glance before focusing on Jake again. "I heard your burger is as delicious as you are." The feral-cat comment I'd made before wasn't far off. She practically purred.

Jake shrugged. "It's nothing fancy."

"I'll be the judge of that," Phoebe said.

Ginger rolled her eyes behind Phoebe's back and took her by the elbow. "Shall we? We have a lot of people to talk to yet."

Phoebe sighed. "Duty calls. Too bad."

When they were out of earshot, I said, "If Phoebe has any say in the matter, you can probably declare yourself the winner of the burger competition. We can just skip the whole thing and go home."

"That wouldn't be any fun. Where's your sense of ad-venture?"

"I seem to have misplaced it for the moment."

Dwayne Tunstall had pulled his van up to his spot while we talked, and he got out and stalked over to us. "This is your doing, isn't it?" he said. "What is that woman doing back here?"

CHAPTER FOURTEEN

"What are you talking about?" I said. "Why would we have anything to do with Phoebe coming back?"

Dwayne shoved his hands into the front pockets of his white baggy pants. He must be going for the eighties *Miami Vice* look today. "Because you two hate me," he said. "You did it to make sure I lose."

"You're way off," Jake said. "Phoebe told Ginger she wanted to come back."

"Why should I believe you?"

"You can ask Ginger if you don't believe us," Jake said.

"Maybe I will."

"What do you have against Phoebe?" I asked. "She seems like she'll be a fair judge."

"Fair?" Dwayne snorted. "She wouldn't know fair if she tripped over it. All she cares about is her next conquest."

I couldn't help myself. "Like you, Dwayne?"

"I'm not even going to answer that."

I took that to mean she wouldn't give him the time of day. At least Phoebe had good taste. "How do you know she won't be fair? I've read some of her articles. They're a lot more reasonable than the things your brother-in-law wrote."

"Leave Reggie out of it."

"That's a little hard to do considering everything that's happened," I said. "Why is it such a big secret that he was married to your sister?"

"I'd kind of like to know that, too," Jake said. "It makes it seem like you're hiding something."

"It's not a secret. Not that it's any of your business. I didn't broadcast it because I didn't want anyone to think I had an unfair advantage. That's all."

I didn't believe that was the reason why he didn't say anything. He certainly had an unfair advantage with his brother-in-law judging the contest. If Ginger had known, Dwayne probably would have been disqualified. And he'd definitely been afraid for some reason when he stopped at the brew house. "That's not the impression I got," I said.

"Well, your impression is wrong."

He couldn't or wouldn't look me in the eye. I wasn't sure if it was because he was lying or because he didn't want to show that he had been afraid of anyone discovering the relationship. "If it wasn't a secret, why weren't you at the funeral home to support your sister? Why wasn't your name mentioned in the obituary? Come to think of it, it didn't even mention your sister's maiden name. What are you two hiding?" I was on a roll and would have kept going, but Jake put his hand on my arm. I clamped my mouth shut before I accused him of murder.

"For your information, Little Miss Neb-Nose," Dwayne said, "I was at the funeral home, just not when you and your weirdo friends were there." My surprise must have shown on my face, because he said, "Yeah, I know all about your visit. Melody is sharper than most people give her credit for. She knew who you were, but she's a pretty good actress."

He obviously didn't realize it, but he'd just given me more reason than ever to suspect that Melody had killed her husband.

"Why all the secrecy, then?" Jake asked.

Any fear Dwayne had shown earlier had disappeared. He clenched his fists. "I told you why. If the public knew Reggie was my brother-in-law, I'd never get the respect I deserve. That's all. I suggest you both mind your own business from now on." He started to walk away, then turned around and pointed his index finger at me. "Your father, too. I'm sure you're the one who squealed to him. Just butt out and leave me alone."

When he was gone, I turned to Jake. "I still think he's hiding something."

"Yep. I wonder if your dad got anything from him."

"I hope he did," I said. "It's hard to tell a cop to mind his own business." We walked over to Jake's truck and began unloading the half barrels while we continued the discussion. I told Jake about my conversation with Cory Dixon and how Mobley had sent a letter that put a halt to Cory's brewpub application.

Jake shook his head. "It's hard to believe that guy had that much influence. There's some money changing hands somewhere."

"Either that or there were more objections than Cory knew about. I have a feeling Dwayne and Melody had something to do with it, too." I told him what I'd found in my search the previous night. "I can't help but wonder if it's connected to Melody's gambling."

"I can see her marrying a rich guy so she'd have the money to pursue it, but how would her problem tie into a rejected brewpub application?" Jake opened a bag of ice and dumped it over one of the kegs.

"I have no idea."

He tossed the empty plastic bag into the crate we were using as a makeshift recycle bin. "If we do this again next year, I'm buying a portable refrigeration setup."

I didn't want Jake to use his own money for something that should come out of pub funds, but I let it slide for the moment. We could discuss it later. I opened another bag of ice and passed it to Jake. "Here's an idea. What if Melody found something out about one of the officials gambling?"

"Maybe," Jake said. "But that's not enough for blackmail—if that's what the Mobleys were doing."

"What if he was using state money to do it? Or what if he was in so much debt he was stealing from department funds?"

"That would do it. And considering how some state officials have been caught doing just that over the last few years, it's not a stretch to think there would be another one."

We finished setting up well before the festival's planned opening at eleven. I watched for Randy Gregory to arrive. He finally made it at ten minutes before eleven. Nothing like cutting it close. Jake hollered over to see if he needed any help.

"All I can get," he yelled.

We crossed the gravel aisle to Randy's spot. "I was starting to wonder if you were coming today," I said as the three of us easily popped open his canopy.

"We had a little emergency at the brewery," he said. "Stuck mash."

"Oh no." Grains and hot water stuck in the mash tun didn't happen often, but it was a mess to deal with when it did.

"We had to open the door and let it drain that way, and most of it ended up on the floor. It took all morning to clean up and get it unclogged."

"Anything we can do?" Jake asked.

"Nah," Randy said. "We're fine now. Thanks for your help with this."

The gates opened a few minutes later, so I went back to our space, while Jake stayed with Randy to help him get set up. More than a few attendees had taken an early lunch hour, but most still took the time to chat, saying they'd be back sometime over the weekend to sample more. When Jake came back from helping Randy, he filled me in on what they'd talked about.

Randy had tried to pry information out of Jake just like

he had done with me at the brewers' meeting. Jake played dumb and told him he didn't know anything. "But I was able to get some information from him," Jake said. "I told Randy you had talked to Cory and he told you about Mobley's interference with the brewpub application."

"And?" I said.

"You were right. The same thing happened to Randy, and he had even stronger words than Cory had about Mobley. The last time I heard that kind of language was in a locker room."

"Did you tell him Cory is thinking of reapplying?"

Jake shook his head. "That wasn't my place. I figured I'd leave that up to Cory. If he wants Randy to know, he'll tell him."

Good call. "Anything else?"

"He mentioned something about Mobley that didn't really make any sense to me."

"What did he say?"

"That Mobley finally got what was coming to him."

"That's nothing new," I said. "He's said that before."

"Yeah, I know. But this time he added something like 'I hope in his last moments he thought about the other ones.'"

"What is that supposed to mean?" I asked.

"I told you it didn't make any sense."

"You didn't ask him what he meant?"

"I didn't have a chance. He changed the subject and the opportunity never came up again."

I rose from my seat when a couple who appeared to be tourists headed toward our booth. "It sounds to me like we need to move Randy to the top of the suspect list."

* * *

Jake returned to the pub a half hour later to check on a new kitchen employee who was starting that afternoon. He trusted the kitchen staff, but he genuinely liked being hands-on. He wanted to make sure the new hire got off on the right foot.

In between talking to festivalgoers about my brews, I tried to figure out what Randy had meant by "the other ones." I finally came to the conclusion it must mean others who had applied for brewpub licenses and were turned down. It just seemed like a strange way to put it.

The three judges—Leonard Wilson, Marshall Babcock, and Phoebe Atwell—made their rounds again at one o'clock to taste the beers. One of the things they were judging was consistency. We were to serve the same three beers as the previous week and we'd be judged on whether they tasted the same as they had last week. They carried their clipboards— Phoebe had a tablet computer—with last week's scores. I wasn't quite sure how Phoebe could score the consistency category since she hadn't been here last week. Even with their scorecards, I didn't know how they would remember what last week's beers had tasted like. When Leonard and Marshall crossed the gravel to our tent, Phoebe stayed behind to flirt with Randy. He seemed to like her attention. I didn't think I'd ever seen him smile so much.

I shouldn't have been, but I was more nervous than I'd been last week when I poured their samples. Winning the competition would be nice, but I wouldn't be devastated if I didn't win. There were many excellent brewers here who had been making beer long before I had. I told myself to just relax and enjoy the process. Easier said than done.

Just like on the previous weekend, Leonard and Marshall both tasted their samples from light to dark.

"This ale is exactly how I remember it from last week," Marshall said. "The citrus notes up front are spectacular." He took another sip. "And the hops give it just enough bite without being overwhelming."

"Agreed," Leonard said.

Both thought the IPA was average, which I was okay with. You can't hit them all out of the park. Leonard especially liked the stout, as he had the previous week, but Marshall thought the malt was a little too roasted for his taste.

When Phoebe joined them a few minutes later, she shocked me by her attention to the tasting, because I'd been invisible to her up until then. Maybe she finally noticed my presence because Jake wasn't there to distract her. And he was definitely distracting. In a good way, of course.

She smiled at me when she finished. "These are quite good," she said.

I could have fainted. "Thanks."

"You shouldn't be surprised, Phoebe," Leonard said. "Max knows what she's doing."

"I'm happy to hear that," she said. "I'd like to hear more about your brewery sometime. Maybe I'll stop by when the festival is over."

Dumbfounded, I watched the three of them move on to Dwayne's tent. I'd never seen anyone do a complete turnaround like that. Weird. Definitely weird.

*　*　*

Since Jake was at the pub, I'd enlisted Mom and Kate and put them to work. They were more than happy to oblige and they arrived around two. Kate had left Maira and Fiona with her husband, which was a nice change, since Mike was usually the one helping me out.

"Was Mike okay with babysitting?" I asked Kate once I'd instructed her on the procedure I'd been using.

Kate grinned. "He was thrilled. Although I'll probably have a mess of laundry to do. They're going out for ice cream."

She wore white shorts and a baby blue tank top, and with her hair in a ponytail she looked like she could be sixteen instead of thirty. It reminded me to tell her to ask for ID before serving anyone who might be underage. I'd gotten into the habit of asking mostly everyone regardless of how old they looked. I came close to being the new best friend to several women who were well past the age of twenty-one.

"We'll be fine, sweetie," Mom said. "Why don't you take a little break? We'll call if we need anything."

I hesitated.

"Go." Mom made a shooing motion with her hands.

I told them I wouldn't be long. A quick trip to the restroom would be all I'd need. I'd already eaten the peanut butter and jelly sandwich I'd brought with me, so I didn't need to find food anywhere. Not exactly a gourmet meal, but it would tide me over until dinner. Jake's parents were looking forward to stopping at the festival later, and Dot had insisted on bringing dinner.

After using the facilities, I walked around and talked to a few other brewers. I ran into Dave at a booth where he was discussing flavored beers with a brewer from New York named Nancy. She gave me a sample of a shandy she'd created with another New York brewery. Instead of the traditional beer and lemonade combination, Nancy used strawberry lemonade. It was delicious. She gave me her card and said if I was ever interested in collaborating on a brew, to give her a call. It was an interesting proposition, and I told her I'd keep it in mind.

"How did that shandy compare with my huckleberry ale?" Dave asked as we left Nancy's booth.

"Hard to say," I said. "They're not the same thing." Dave's ale was all beer brewed with huckleberries, while the shandy was only half beer. "I liked them both."

Dave laughed. "You could never be a judge for one of these things. Everyone would be a winner."

I laughed along with him. He was right. "I would definitely have a hard time choosing."

"What do you think about Phoebe Atwell coming back?" Dave asked. "I was surprised."

"So was I when I first heard. I was more surprised that she was friendly to me this afternoon."

"She seems like she'll be good."

He wanted to know if I'd talked to Cory and Randy, so I told him what I'd found out. I also told him about Dwayne coming to see me at the pub, and about Dwayne and Melody's relationship.

"You're kidding me," Dave said.

"Nope. I was as surprised as you are. When Dwayne

came to see me, I brought it up and asked why it was such a big secret. He did a complete one-eighty from wanting me to ask you about him getting into the Brewers Association to telling me to forget it. He seemed like he was afraid of something. I just can't figure out what it could be."

"Me neither." Dave shook his head. "I still can't believe they're related. That kind of explains a lot, though—like why Mobley seemed to like, or at least pretended to like, Dwayne."

"Pretended is more like it." I was just about to ask him if he had any idea what else Dwayne could be hiding when my phone buzzed.

It was Kate. "Sorry to bother you," she said almost in a whisper, "but are you on your way back yet?"

"I can be. Is there a problem?"

"Sort of."

I heard a commotion in the background. "What's going on?"

"I can't say, but you need to come back. Pronto."

CHAPTER FIFTEEN

I hurried up the aisle with Dave at my heels. A visibly intoxicated Melody Mobley stood—or rather wobbled—in
front of the booth. She wore one of those stretchy tube tops
that were popular years ago and Daisy Dukes that came close
to showing what most people liked to keep covered. Her sandals with the four-inch heels weren't helping her balance any.

"Please tell me where she is." Melody's speech was
slurred, all the syllables running together.

I assumed she was talking about me. "I'm here. Is there
a problem?" I'd come up behind her and she spun around.
Dave caught her by the elbow before she toppled over.

"I've been looking for you," Melody said. "Those two"—
she pointed to Mom and Kate, who were behind the table

under the canopy—"wouldn't tell me where you were. And they wouldn't give me anything to drink."

"Maybe you've had enough to drink for a while," Dave said.

Melody squinted at him. "Who are you?"

"Just a friend," he said.

"You're no friend of mine, so mind your own business." She turned back to me. "What are you going to do about it?"

"About what?" She could be talking about any number of things—her husband's murder, for one.

Melody rolled her eyes. "Not what. Who."

"Okay. Who." I felt like I was in the middle of an Abbott and Costello routine.

She swayed again when she raised her arm and pointed at Mom and Kate. "Them!"

"Maybe you'd like to sit down," I said.

Kate brought one of our camp chairs over and Melody plopped into it. I glanced over at Dwayne's booth, but it was empty. It seemed odd that he'd leave without someone watching over his equipment. Anyone could walk up and help himself.

Dave must have noticed, too. "I'm going to see if I can find Dwayne."

I nodded. A crowd had gathered around us, but there wasn't much I could do about it. Someone asked if we needed any help and I told him we had everything under control. I hoped I was right. I turned my attention back to Melody.

"Dwayne told me you're a troublemaker," she said. "About how you're sticking your nose into nothing that concerns you. But I'm not sure I believe him. He's not a bad brother, you know. He's not a bad person." It sounded like she was trying to convince herself instead of me.

"I never said he was." Thought it, yes. Said it, no.

There was a lot I wanted to talk to her about, but now wasn't the time. She was definitely drunk and I shouldn't take advantage of that fact, even though it was tempting. I'd have to wait until she was sober. She hadn't yet said why she had wanted to talk to me, so I asked her.

She blinked a couple of times, then stared at me for a moment. "I . . . I don't remember. Why was I looking for you?"

I spotted Dwayne jogging toward us. Dave was behind him, walking at a more leisurely pace. Dwayne was winded when he reached us.

"Melody, what the hell do you think you're doing?" he snapped.

I would've thought he'd be worried, but it sure didn't sound like he was.

"You were supposed to be watching my stuff. I should have known I couldn't rely on you."

She started to cry. "I didn't do anything. I just came over here to talk to . . ." She looked up at me. "What's your name again?"

Dwayne took her by the arm and roughly pulled her out of the chair. "You shouldn't be talking to anyone. Especially these people. Time to go."

Melody leaned on his arm as he led her away. The show was over for now, and bystanders went back to enjoying their afternoon. When those who had been waiting for samples began asking questions, Mom, Kate, and I played dumb, which wasn't too much of a stretch.

In between customers, Mom asked me what that was all about.

I shook my head. "Frankly, I'm not sure. That was Melody Mobley."

"The widow?"

"Yes."

"So the man with the funny haircut is the brother you told your dad and me about."

"Yes."

"She was really upset that you weren't here," Kate said.

I got out some more plastic cups, then put the remainder back in the box I used for carrying items. "I can't figure out why she wanted to talk to me. Why would she be here at all? Would you go to the place where your husband was murdered? And only a week later?" I didn't wait for an answer. "Something's not right."

"I feel sorry for that poor girl," Mom said. "Maybe it's a comfort for her to be here."

I glanced over to Dwayne's tent. I couldn't hear the conversation, but he was gesturing like he was still mad at her. Melody leaned forward in her chair with her head in her hands. "It doesn't look like it's much of a comfort right now."

Mom and Kate turned to see what I'd meant. My mother's cheeks reddened. "I should go over there and give him a piece of my mind. I don't care if he's upset she didn't stay there and babysit his beer. That's no way to treat anyone, especially someone who's just suffered a loss like she had."

"That's not a good idea." I told them what I'd discovered about both Melody and Dwayne.

"You really think she's a murderer?" Kate asked. "She doesn't look like one."

I checked the ice around one of the kegs. I loved Kate like she was my own sister, but that comment annoyed me, especially after my own previous encounter with a murderer. "You can't tell what someone's capable of just by looking at them."

Kate blushed and then I felt bad for snapping at her. I apologized and we moved on to more pleasant subjects.

At four o'clock, I was just about to tap another keg when there was a loud crack of thunder accompanied by a bright flash of lightning. Seconds later the sky opened up and it began pouring. It appeared the rain from that morning had returned with a vengeance. Festivalgoers scattered, looking for shelter. Most ran for the parking lot. It wasn't long before Ginger's voice came over the loudspeaker and announced that, due to the dangerous thunder and lightning, the festival would be closing for the day. She invited everyone to come back the following day and if they showed their ticket for today, admission would be free.

I called Jake and told him and he said he'd be here shortly. Mom, Kate, and I packed everything up and when Jake arrived, we loaded the kegs into the truck. I waited under the tent while he dropped Mom and Kate off at their car; then he swung back and picked me up.

On our way back to the pub to put everything away, I filled Jake in on what had happened with Melody. I couldn't stop thinking about her. The big looming question that I couldn't get out of my mind was, why had Melody wanted to see me? I didn't have an answer to that.

Because of the rainout, I had had plenty of time to shower and feed Hops before going over to Jake's house for the dinner that his mother had planned to bring to us at the festival. She had made an incredible meal of old-fashioned meat loaf, mashed potatoes, and sweet-and-sour green beans.

Bob Lambert leaned back in his seat and patted his stomach when we had finished eating. "You outdid yourself again, Dot." He looked across the table at me. "This is why I can't lose the twenty pounds the doc keeps telling me to lose. Dot's the best cook in the world."

We were seated in the dining room of the Lamberts' house. When Jake's parents had moved to Florida, they'd taken their furniture with them with the exception of the dining room set. Their condo didn't have a dining room. The fifties style didn't fit Jake at all, but he was reluctant to part with it, much the same as I had been with my grandmother's furniture. It didn't matter, because he rarely used the dining room. He'd furnished the rest of the house in a comfortable, casual style. He hadn't replaced the beige Berber carpeting, but he'd painted the rooms in neutral colors. The first time I came here with Jake, I'd expected there to be hockey memorabilia all over the place and the rooms decorated in early locker room. I was happy to discover I was wrong. The only trace of his former life was a small cabinet with glass doors in the family room in the basement.

"Dinner was delicious," I said to Jake's mother. "If we served that meat loaf at the brew house, we'd have people waiting in line for days."

Dot smiled. "I'm so glad you liked it."

Jake stood and began clearing dishes. He bent and kissed his mother on the cheek as he passed her. "You outdid yourself. But don't even think about taking my job."

"Never," Dot said. "I don't think your Max would consider hiring an old lady who only knows how to make fried chicken, meat loaf, and apple pie anyway."

I liked how she said *your Max*. "I'm sure you can make a lot more than that. I'd hire you in a minute. Maybe we should add those three things to the menu and your mom can be the new head chef. What do you think, Jake?"

"I think you're trying to get rid of me," he said. "Maybe I'll see if Dave needs a chef."

Dot looked horrified. "Oh no! You can't!"

Jake and I laughed and Bob grinned and shook his head.

She realized we were teasing her and she swatted Jake on the arm. "You're just like your father. You'd think I'd have learned that by now."

I got up and helped Jake clear the table; then we all moved to the living room. I sank into the leather sofa and considered never getting out of it.

"Jake said you had some excitement at the festival today," Bob said. "That man's wife made a scene."

"I'm still not sure what it was all about and what she

wanted. I'm not even sure anything she said was the truth. Her brother said she was a good actress."

Jake sat beside me and took my hand. I always got a thrill when he did that. "The whole thing could have been for show."

"Why would she do that?" Dot asked.

Jake's thumb drawing circles on the back of my hand was making it hard to concentrate. "Maybe for attention."

Bob pulled a throw pillow out from behind him. "That's better." He put the pillow on the floor. "Why would she want attention—especially if you two think she might have killed her husband?"

"Oh dear." Dot shuddered.

"She was also intoxicated," I said. "It's possible that she wouldn't have behaved like she had if she had been sober."

"And her brother was there, too?" Bob asked. "How does he figure into it?"

Jake and I took turns filling them in on the whole story. Bob was intrigued. Dot was horrified. When she got up and went to the kitchen to serve up dessert, I followed to help.

"You have a much stronger constitution than I do," she said as she cut into an apple pie. "I can't even watch crime shows on television."

I smiled at her. "There's nothing wrong with that. I'm kind of used to it, since Dad's a cop. I grew up with it." I added a scoop of vanilla ice cream to the slice of pie on the plate she passed to me.

"Just promise me you'll be careful."

"I will." There would be no more showdowns with killers for me. Once was more than enough as far as I was concerned. As soon as I knew who had poisoned Mobley, I'd pass the information off to Dad. Or Vincent. That was an even better idea. I'd kind of like to see the look on his face.

She handed another plate to me. "This is the first time I've gotten to talk to you alone. I want you to know I'm so glad—Bob, too—that Jake found you. I always knew you were the girl for him."

"Really?"

Dot patted my arm. "Really. I saw all those adoring looks you sent his way over the years."

I felt my face redden.

"And Jake was completely oblivious to them," she went on. "Although I do think that when you went overseas, it bothered him more than he wanted to admit."

I wasn't sure I believed that. By the time I was out of grad school, Jake had had his own life playing professional hockey. The only time I'd seen him during those years was when Mike and Kate got married.

Dot placed the pie server and the knife in the sink and returned the ice cream to the freezer. "He used to ask about you all the time."

"Why didn't he ever say anything to me?"

Jake barged into the kitchen. "Dad wants to know how long it takes to cut four pieces of pie."

I shoved two plates at him, hoping he didn't notice my pink cheeks. "Here you go." I took another plate from Dot and followed Jake back to the living room. The pie was delicious and we chatted about nothing in particular for a while until I had to call it a night.

The rain had stopped by this time. Jake walked me to my car and put his arms around me. "I think they liked having you here tonight as much as I did," he said.

"I loved spending some time with them." I rested my head on his chest. "I've missed this."

"What? Standing on the sidewalk by your car?"

I laughed and lifted my head. Before I could swat him on the arm for being a smart aleck, he leaned down and kissed me. I'd definitely missed this.

"Ahem."

We stopped kissing, but Jake kept his arm around me. "You have really rotten timing, Dad," he said.

Bob had a big grin on his face. "I'm sorry to break up the romantic interlude, but I remembered something."

"And it couldn't wait until I came back in?" Jake asked.

"Max might want to hear it, too."

I couldn't imagine what was so important he had to rush out of the house to tell us.

"That night we had dinner at the brew house, we were talking about the man who was murdered," Bob said. "I told you that when I saw his picture on TV, I thought I recognized him, but the guy I knew wasn't named Mobley."

I only vaguely recalled the conversation.

"Lots of people look alike," Jake said.

Bob shook his head. "Sure they do, but that's not the case this time. As soon as you two walked outside, I picked up the newspaper and the headline on one of the articles jogged my memory. I definitely knew the dead man, but like I said before, when I knew him, his name wasn't Reginald Mobley. He owned a restaurant I used to go to."

CHAPTER SIXTEEN

We moved back to the front porch so we could hear Bob's story.

"It was about fifteen years ago when I was working downtown. Me and a couple of coworkers used to eat lunch once in a while at this place on Fifth Avenue." Bob gave us a little smile. "Not too often, though. It was a swanky place and a bit pricey. The owner, Ronald Moore, was a nice enough guy, although a little standoffish."

I wished he would get to the point.

"Anyway," he continued, "he didn't just own the place. He also did a lot of the cooking. Some of the stuff I didn't care much for. I'd never even heard of some of the things that were on the menu. I'm a meat-and-potatoes kind of guy, so I usually just ordered a steak or chicken."

"Dad, what does this have to do with Mobley?" Jake asked.

"You'll see in a minute. One day, three or four of us went out to lunch. We hadn't gone to this place in a while, so we decided to go there. When we arrived, we were surprised it was all closed up and there was a notice from the health department taped to the door. The place never opened up again."

"Dad—"

Bob put up his hand. "Before you ask me again, the guy you knew as Reginald Mobley is Ronald Moore—the guy who owned Le Meilleur. I'm sure of it."

I didn't want to doubt him, but it seemed a little far-fetched to me. "Why would he change his name? And his profession?"

"That I can't tell you," Bob said. "I didn't think all that much of it back then. Restaurants come and go all the time. We figured the health inspector found roaches or mice or something like that and the owner decided to call it quits and move on. I never gave it another thought until I saw that article in the paper about a restaurant shut down for health violations. Then it all clicked. It was driving me crazy that I couldn't remember where I'd seen him before."

After Bob went inside, Jake walked me back out to my car. "What do you think about what your dad told us?" I asked.

Jake put his arms around me. "I don't know. I'd like to believe it, but why would a guy who was probably making a decent living running a restaurant drop everything like that? Why wouldn't he just fix whatever issues the health department found and reopen it? Instead, he not only disappeared—he changed his name. It doesn't make sense."

"Exactly."

The next morning I told Candy about Melody's behavior at the festival. Mary Louise had the day off and my friend was working the bakery counter with a high school girl who worked part-time. I'd just bought one of my favorite apple cinnamon muffins and planned to go across the street for an iced mocha. I needed the sugar and caffeine fix this morning. I'd tossed and turned most of the night, even though I was exhausted. Plus, every time I rolled over, Hops thought it was playtime. I finally managed to sleep three solid hours and only dragged myself out of bed at seven.

"Do you think Dwayne was telling the truth the other day when he told me Melody was a good actress and she knew who we were at the funeral home?" I asked Candy.

She shook her head. "She might be a good actress, but not that good. You saw the look on her face. She was trying to figure out if she knew us or not. If she was acting, she wouldn't have looked so confused. And from what you said happened yesterday, that wasn't an act, either. She seems to have some real problems."

"Dwayne got her away from me awfully quick, too. I think he was afraid she was going to say something she shouldn't," I said. "Maybe even admit that they killed her husband."

"It's possible." Candy looked over at her helper. "Think you can handle the store while I go get a cup of coffee?"

The girl told her she'd be fine, so we walked across the street to Jump, Jive & Java. We were greeted by the soothing voice of Frank Sinatra singing "I'll Never Smile Again."

Candy sighed. "That voice just makes me want to swoon."

Kristie was at the counter. "Don't you dare do that. My insurance rates are high enough." She grinned. "The usual?"

"Extra whipped cream on mine," I said.

"Late night with Jake?" Kristie asked. "Now, that man is definitely swoon-worthy."

"Not exactly," I said. "I mean he definitely is, but I was with Jake and his parents. His mom made dinner."

The coffee shop wasn't busy, so after she prepared our drinks, Kristie joined us at our usual table under the movie poster of *Casablanca*. I brought her up to speed on what Candy and I had already discussed.

Kristie shook her head. "I kind of feel sorry for her. If she didn't kill her husband, that is."

I filled them in on some other things that I hadn't talked to either of them about up until now, like Melody's casino photos, and Cory's and Randy's brewpub license issues.

"If it's true that Mobley had a hand in that somehow, he was even more of a creep than I thought," Candy said.

"But is that enough motive for someone to kill him?" I asked. "I don't think Cory did, but I'm not so sure about Randy. But with the way Melody and Dwayne acted yesterday, I'm leaning toward one—or both—of them. There's definitely something going on there."

Candy tapped her black-and-gold-polished fingernails on the table. "We need to get Melody alone somehow and talk to her."

"Do you think she'll be at the festival today?" Kristie asked.

"I don't know. Dwayne might try to keep her away."

"Kristie and I are both planning on coming down later," Candy said. "We can keep an eye out for her. If she doesn't show, we'll think of another way."

I brought up what Jake's dad had told us last night. Candy and Kristie didn't seem to think it was as far-fetched as Jake and I had. Candy offered to do a little research on Ronald Moore and his restaurant, Le Meilleur. If anyone could get the scoop, she could.

Just when I thought Vincent Falk was going to leave us alone, he proved me wrong. He was standing on the sidewalk in front of the brew house when Candy and I left the coffee shop.

"Is that who I think it is?" Candy asked.

"The one and only. Come on, I'll introduce you."

"Oh, goody," she said. "I can't wait." She sounded like she meant it.

We jaywalked across the street like any good Pittsburgher would do. I highly doubted Vince would lower himself to actually write a ticket. Besides, if cops in the city gave out citations for jaywalking, they'd never get anything else done. No one used crosswalks if it meant walking another ten feet. It was a hard habit to break.

I plastered a pleasant smile on my face. "Good morning, Detective."

He gave the briefest of nods. "Miss O'Hara."

Candy launched herself forward and grabbed his right hand. "Oh, another friend of our darling Max! How thrilling!" She pulled him into a hug. "Isn't she the best?"

Poor Vince didn't know what to do and I had a hard time keeping a straight face.

"Um, yeah," he managed to mutter while attempting to extricate himself from Candy's grasp.

She finally took pity on him, released him from the hug, but kept her hand on his arm. "You must be that nice detective that Max told me so much about. She just goes on and on about how diligent and thorough you are." She squeezed his arm. "That killer doesn't stand a chance with you on the case."

I coughed to disguise the chortle that threatened to escape.

Vince's face had turned as red as his tie. He worked his mouth, but nothing came out. I was sure he'd never run into anyone like Candy before. I decided I'd better rescue him before she had him cowering in a corner.

"What can I do for you, Detective?" I asked as I unlocked the door to the pub. Vince, with Candy still attached to his arm, followed me inside and I deactivated the alarm.

He regained his composure. At least as much as he could with Candy beside him. "I need to speak to you."

"Have a seat." I pointed to the nearest table. I didn't offer to make coffee this time. I'd already had mine and if he hadn't, he could go across the street.

The three of us pulled out chairs and Vince looked at Candy. "In private," he said.

Candy waved a hand and plunked herself down in a chair. "Don't pay any attention to me. Pretend I'm not even here."

His gaze moved to me and I shrugged. "It's best to indulge her," I said. "She has a way of finding out everything that goes on anyway." I took the seat across the table from Vince and made proper introductions. I could tell he wasn't happy that he didn't get his way. Candy, however, was loving every minute of this.

"You planned it this way, didn't you?" he said.

"Planned what?"

"Having your friend here so we can't talk in private."

"You're the one who came to see me, not the other way around," I said. "I can't help it if I'm with a friend when you show up unannounced. Maybe the next time you should call first."

I was pretty sure he didn't believe that I hadn't planned anything of the sort, but he didn't pursue it. "I came to tell you that we tested all your water bottles and none of them showed any trace of poison."

I could have told him that. "It's too bad you wasted your time with that instead of going after the real killer."

Candy butted in. "It wasn't a waste. The good detective was just using the process of elimination. Now he knows for sure that you and Jake had nothing to do with the murder."

"I know nothing of the kind," Vince sputtered.

He should have stopped with *nothing*.

"Just because those bottles were clean doesn't mean you didn't slip the victim a poisoned one." He glared at me. "And

I want you to keep away from Mobley's widow. I received a voice mail that you were harassing her yesterday."

"What? Who told you that?"

"He didn't leave his name."

Figures. "I didn't harass her. For the record, she came looking for me. If you want to talk harassment, maybe you should talk to her brother. He really gave her a hard time when he found out she was talking to me."

"What do you mean by that?" Vince said. "Melody Mobley doesn't have a brother."

It was so hard not to smile or gloat. Or both. It was obvious he hadn't read any of my dad's reports. But why read when you already think you know everything? "Of course she does."

Vince sat up straighter in his chair. "If she had a brother, I would certainly know about it. I've talked to her extensively."

"Did you ever ask her what her maiden name was during any of your conversations?"

"No, I didn't. I asked questions that were pertinent to the investigation."

More than anything, I wanted to tell him that Dwayne was her brother, but I stopped myself. He'd only deny it and tell me I was making it all up. I'd let him figure it out for himself. "Interesting," I said. "You may want to ask her about it the next time."

He scowled at me. "Don't tell me what to do. I know my job. You're trying to throw me off track here by bringing up something that has nothing to do with the investigation." He pushed his chair back and stood. "I came to tell you to leave the widow alone. If I find out you so much as sneeze in her direction, I'll cite you for harassment. You and your boyfriend aren't off the hook yet. Not by a long shot."

"Charming," Candy said drily after he was gone.

"Isn't he?" I finally let loose the smile I'd been holding back. "Your performance was award-worthy. The look on his face when you hugged him was priceless. Well worth all the aggravation he's caused me."

Candy pushed herself up from the table. "Maybe he'll call first the next time." She gave me an evil grin. "And if he does, be sure to let me know. The poor boy may need another hug."

I laughed. "You can count on it."

"I'm sorry I missed it," Jake said when I told him about it later. We were setting up at the festival once again. "The first time I met Candy is etched in my memory. It's not something you forget easily."

When I'd introduced her to Jake, I thought she was going to faint. She didn't hold it against him that he'd played hockey for the New York Rangers and not the Penguins. He was still a hometown boy and that's all that mattered. Although I'm sure she would have been even more ecstatic if he'd worn the black and gold. "Hopefully Vince won't forget it, either," I said.

We were pros at setting up by now, although it helped that we'd left the tent and table here overnight. Everything was still a little damp, but it was bright and sunny, so it wouldn't be long before it was all dry. It was ten thirty and the gates—rope in this case—were to open at eleven. There was already a long line of people waiting to get in, which meant a busy day. Mike planned to come at four with a few more kegs and relieve us so we could get some dinner. Jake and I would spell each other during the afternoon if needed.

Despite the warning from Vince Falk to leave Melody alone, I hoped she would be here today. I was sure that Dwayne was the one who'd told him I'd been harassing her. He didn't want her talking to me and that made me more curious than ever.

Dwayne showed up at only ten minutes to eleven, and he was alone. I wasn't going to let that deter me. "I think I'm going to see if Dwayne needs any help," I said.

"Aren't you supposed to leave him alone?" Jake asked.

"Not Dwayne. His sister. Besides, when have I ever let anything like that stop me?"

Jake laughed and shook his head. "I'm not bailing you out if you get arrested."

I stuck my tongue out at him.

"But only because I think you'd look really cute in those red scrubs they'd make you wear in the county jail."

"Gee, thanks," I said. "Remind me again why I like you."

"I'll make a list."

I rolled my eyes and headed for Dwayne's booth.

He was bending over tapping a keg when I reached him. He straightened. "What do you want?"

"I thought you might need some help."

"I'm fine. I don't need any help." He went back to the keg.

"Are you sure?"

"Of course I'm sure." He rolled the keg aside. "Why are you really here?"

"I wanted to see if your sister was okay. I don't think she was feeling all that well yesterday."

Dwayne crossed his arms over his chest. "That's really none of your business. And for the record, there's nothing wrong with her."

"She didn't seem like herself to me." I didn't want to come right out and say she was as drunk as a skunk. He had to know that. "She was a little confused."

"I told you there was nothing wrong with her. She just had a little too much to drink." He rolled another keg into place.

It was more than a little too much. "Is that why you were so mad at her?" I asked.

"I wasn't mad," he answered. "I was upset she was so unreliable."

"Because she left your booth unattended?"

He stopped what he was doing. "Well, wouldn't you be? I gave her a simple task and she couldn't even do that right."

"Maybe you should cut her some slack. She did just lose her husband. She probably has other things on her mind."

"That's beside the point."

I didn't think it was possible to dislike him any more than I already did. "No, Dwayne. That's exactly the point."

"You have no idea what you're talking about. Go away and leave us alone."

"Dwayne—"

"Go away!"

I took the hint.

"I take it he didn't want any help," Jake said when I got back.

I shook my head. "Not only that, he just about bit my head off when I asked about Melody."

"That shouldn't surprise you."

I sighed. "It doesn't. Not really."

Jake put an arm around me and pulled me close. "You can't fix everyone's problems, Max."

I leaned into him. "I know." I would have liked to stay in his arms for the rest of the day, but the first group of festivalgoers descended upon us. We spent the next couple of hours serving and discussing our selections with craft beer enthusiasts. There was a lull around two o'clock. Jake took a short break and as soon as he returned, I took mine.

Dwayne was alone and he ignored me when I waved to him. Dave, on the other hand, hollered a hello when I passed, and his wife and son, who were helping him out, waved enthusiastically. I continued down the aisle and spotted Phoebe Atwell sitting on a bench concentrating on her phone screen.

"Hi, Phoebe," I said. "All by yourself today? Where are your cohorts?"

She looked up from her phone. "Oh, they're probably around somewhere. Looks like it's going to be a busy day."

"It's been that way so far."

"Good," she said. "I'm looking forward to the burger competition final tomorrow."

A flash of turquoise and blond hair caught my eye, so I quickly told Phoebe good-bye and hurried to catch Melody.

She was headed in the opposite direction of Dwayne's booth and I suspected he didn't know she was here. Once again I wondered why she had wanted to talk to me yesterday. And why Dwayne had been so angry at her. Well, I was going to find out.

CHAPTER SEVENTEEN

"Melody!" I called. I half expected her to run away, but she stopped and turned around just outside the large tent that had been set up as the prep area for the burger competition. The tent was empty today except for a few festivalgoers who were taking advantage of the shade it provided.

"I'm not supposed to talk to you," she said. She was dressed better than she'd been yesterday, wearing modest white Bermuda shorts and a turquoise tank top. Her hair and makeup were perfect. If she was hungover, it didn't show.

"Then why are you?" I asked.

She shrugged. "Maybe I don't like being told what to do."

I noticed a makeshift bench fashioned out of two-by-fours on top of cinder blocks and suggested we sit.

Melody inspected the bench and brushed off an invisible something or other before she took a seat. "What can I do for you?" she asked, sounding as formal as if she were interviewing me for a job.

"I appreciate you talking to me," I said.

"I really shouldn't be."

"Why not?" I asked. "Who told you not to?"

She stared at her white sandals.

"Was it your brother?" Her cheeks reddened. She didn't have to answer the question. That was all the confirmation I needed. "Why doesn't Dwayne want you to talk to me?"

She sighed. "I'm so tired. Tired of the charade. Tired of all the lies."

Was she about to confess to killing her husband? "I'm a good listener," I said. "If you don't want to talk here, we can go somewhere else." I'd have to let Jake know and call someone to cover for me, but I could work it out.

Melody shook her head. "I don't need to go anywhere. And I don't care anymore if Dwayne sees me." There was a flash of anger in her eyes. "He's been trying to run my life for far too long. I wanted to see you yesterday, but it didn't work out that way."

I had to tread carefully here. "Because you'd been drinking?"

"Partly." She blushed again. "I thought I'd only had two drinks, but I guess it was more than that. They hit me all of a sudden. I never had that happen before. And then Dwayne dragged me away. I'm sorry about that."

"That's all right." There was no way she'd had only two drinks. Even if she'd downed them all at once, she wouldn't have been falling-down drunk and not have remembered why she wanted to see me. A terrible thought came to me. What if there was more than alcohol in her drinks? There were drugs that would enhance the effects of alcohol. If Dwayne had dropped something in Melody's drink to keep her from talking to me, he was more despicable than I'd ever imagined.

"It's such a relief to get to talk about this," she said.

I gave her what I hoped was an encouraging smile. "You really haven't told me anything yet."

"I'm not sure where to start."

"Why don't you begin with how you met your husband?"

"I know you'll find this hard to believe, but I did care for Reggie."

She was right. It was definitely hard to believe.

"I met him at the North Shore Casino a little over a year ago. I was a hostess there at the time. A lot of the tips I got were in the form of chips, so I played some of the games once in a while."

That explained the photos she had posted online.

"Anyway, Reggie was a regular at the blackjack table." She smiled. "He could be quite the charmer when he put his mind to it."

His ex-wife Linda had said the same thing. It was probably better that I didn't mention that to Melody—especially after the incident at the funeral home.

"He was nice enough, but I had no interest in dating him," Melody continued. "I mean, you saw him. He wasn't exactly my type. I was a foot taller than he was, and he certainly wasn't good-looking. But there was something about him."

As vicious as some of Mobley's reviews had been, I couldn't reconcile what seemed like two different aspects to his personality. I didn't know which one was the real Reginald Mobley. I mentioned this to Melody.

"It's true," she said. "He could be very harsh in his reviews. I asked him about it once and he said it was his job to be mean. People didn't want to read good reviews, so even if he liked a place, he trashed it anyway. He said the restaurants got more business from bad reviews than good ones."

I didn't think that was true. People paid attention to reviews. Bad ones, especially those written by her husband, had caused more than one restaurant to close. He'd obviously told her what she wanted to hear. I kept that to myself. I wasn't going to antagonize her now.

Melody returned to her story. "Reggie asked me out several times, but I told him I wasn't interested."

"Why did you change your mind?"

"Dwayne talked me into it."

Why was I not surprised to hear that?

"Dwayne stopped at the casino one night when I was working. I was serving a drink to Reggie at the blackjack table and he was flirting with me like he usually did. Dwayne recognized him right away. Later on, he told me I was crazy for not going out with Reggie, about how influential he was. He went on and on about how Reggie could advance his career. I started to see him a little differently after that and the next time he asked me out, I accepted."

"What was Dwayne's relationship like with him?" I asked.

Melody examined her French manicure before she answered. "I always thought it was good, but lately . . . Reggie was avoiding him. If Dwayne came over for dinner, Reggie would be out. If Dwayne called to talk to him, I had to tell my brother he wasn't home. Things like that." She took a deep breath and continued. "Since Reggie died, Dwayne has been overbearing. I can't leave the house without him asking me where I'm going, who I'm seeing, you name it."

"And that's unusual?"

There was a flash of anger in her eyes again. "You bet it is. I made the mistake of letting him stay in our guest room because he said he was only looking out for me. Well, I found out that's not true. He's been lying to me all along."

My heart beat a little faster. This was what I'd been waiting for. "What did you find out?"

"I went looking for him yesterday morning. I thought he was still at my house, so I knocked and went into his room. It's my guest room, in my house, so I had the right to go in there." She sounded like she had to defend herself. "The room was a mess. Dwayne has always been a bit of a slob. He doesn't think twice about dropping things wherever he feels like. I started straightening up and noticed his checkbook was on the bedside table. I couldn't help myself." Her cheeks reddened again. "I had to look at it."

My phone chimed with a text message. It was Jake. "Hold that thought," I told her. Jake wanted to know where I was and if everything was okay. I responded that I was fine, I was talking to Melody, and I'd fill him in as soon as I got back. I apologized to Melody for the interruption and asked her to continue.

"There were a lot of entries of deposits in my brother's account from Reggie over the past year. I didn't take the time to add them all up, but it had to come to more than ten thousand dollars." She squeezed her eyes closed. "I don't know what it means, but I don't think it's good. Otherwise Reggie would have told me."

"Did you ask Dwayne about it?"

"No. I didn't want him to know I was snooping," she said. "But I came down here with him yesterday to help him out and all he could talk about was you, and how you thought Reggie's death was your business just because you solved another . . . murder." She shuddered. "I hate that word. I hate to think someone really killed my Reggie."

I was beginning to see Melody in a new light. Unless this was all a big act—which I didn't think it was—she really did love her husband.

She went on. "Dwayne warned me to stay far away from you. To never talk to you." She gave me a slight smile. "Which made me think that you were exactly who I needed to talk to."

"And that's why you came looking for me yesterday."

"Yes. I'm sorry about that. I don't understand what happened."

I had a good idea what had transpired, and Dwayne had better have a good answer when I asked him about it.

I wanted to get back to the entries in Dwayne's checkbook. I remembered someone mentioning they'd been business partners. "Is it possible those deposits in Dwayne's account were because your husband was just helping him out? Maybe an interest in his business?"

Melody shook her head. "No. Because of Reggie's position, he couldn't play favorites. Dwayne wanted him to be a partner in his brewery and Reggie told him flat-out no, that he couldn't be involved in anything to do with the restaurant business."

We talked for a few more minutes, but Melody didn't have any idea why her husband had been giving money to Dwayne. As I headed back to my booth, I was sure I knew the reason. Dwayne had been blackmailing Reginald Mobley. And I thought I might know why.

The line at our booth was long when I got back. Jake seemed to be enjoying himself, but I could tell he was glad to get some help. Thirty minutes later, the line became a trickle and I finally got the chance to tell him about Melody.

Jake's expression was grim. "I should have a little talk with her scumbag brother. If he really drugged his sister—hell, if he drugged anybody at all—someone needs to do something."

"And someone will. We can't let him know we suspect anything—especially if he killed his brother-in-law. I'll talk to my dad and tell him the whole story. In the meantime, we'll just keep an eye on him."

Mike arrived at four as promised and he brought reinforcements with him. I was surprised and happy to see both

Mom and Dad. I was even more pleased that my brother Sean was with them.

"Hey, Maxie," he said, kissing me on the cheek. Sean was the only person I permitted to call me that. "How's my baby sister?"

"Glad to see you, big brother," I said. "No Mass tonight?"

He grinned. "Well, there is, but I'm not saying it."

I smacked him on the arm. "Very funny."

He told us the parish was hosting a visiting priest from Kenya and the deacon was assisting him tonight, giving him the evening off.

Mike interrupted. "Hey, bro. Enough with the chitchat. I thought you were going to help me pour these samples."

"I will." Then to me he said, "I'm going to help Mike while you, Jake, Mom, and Dad go get some dinner."

I protested, but both of my brothers insisted that they'd been planning this for days and we were to get out of their hair.

"They're not going to take no for an answer," Dad said. "We may as well go eat."

We walked up the street to Primanti's, famous for putting fries and coleslaw on the sandwich instead of beside it. We only had to wait fifteen minutes for a table and as soon as we'd placed our orders, I told my parents about my talk with Melody today.

Mom shook her head. "That poor girl."

"I'll have to talk to both of them again," Dad said. "I'll see about a subpoena to get Tunstall's bank records. Mobley's records showed some cash withdrawals, so we'll have to see if they line up."

"There's more," Jake said. He told them about his father's revelation that Reginald Mobley had been Ronald Moore.

Our food arrived then and between bites I told them what I had been thinking. "I think Dwayne knew about what had happened with the restaurant. He knew Mobley's former name and identity, so I'll bet he was blackmailing his brother-in-law to keep quiet. And neither one of them wanted Melody to know about any of it."

"That's not a bad theory," Dad said. "It would explain the payments to Tunstall."

"There could be another explanation," Jake said.

Mom wiped her mouth with her napkin. "Like what?"

Jake brought up the letters that Mobley had written that had led to Cory's and Randy's brewpub-application denials. I'd totally forgotten about them. If Dwayne knew about it, that could be another reason for him to blackmail Mobley. This was getting entirely too complicated.

Dad had a plan, though. He would interview Dwayne again and ask him about the payments. I worried it would give Melody away, but he assured me he wouldn't mention the fact that she had seen his checkbook. He could make it sound like the evidence was in Mobley's bank records.

We ordered a couple of sandwiches to take back for Mike and Sean, then took a leisurely stroll up Smallman Street and back to the festival. Fortunately my brothers had done a great job holding down the fort, even though the line was long. The aisles were packed with people and it looked like everyone had long lines. I glanced over to Dwayne's booth and was shocked to see that Melody was helping him out. I had assumed she'd go home after our talk, or at the very least avoid her brother.

Jake and I moved out from under the tent to talk to the people waiting in line while the rest of the family poured. I found it interesting that more than a few of those we talked to were from out of town and visiting the city. There had been a time when no one would have pegged Pittsburgh for a vacation destination. Things had certainly changed over the last few years. I'd just introduced myself to a man from Texas when a bloodcurdling yell for help cut through the air.

It sounded like Dwayne.

CHAPTER EIGHTEEN

Jake and I pushed our way through the crowd, reaching Dwayne's tent in seconds. Dad was right behind us. Dwayne was kneeling beside Melody, who lay on the ground. There was a plastic water bottle on the ground beside her. "Do something!" he cried. "Someone do something!"

He turned and I was able to get a better look at his sister. The sandwich I'd just eaten became a brick in my stomach. Melody's skin was cherry red and her lips were blue, just as her husband's had been. Dad felt her neck for a pulse, then shook his head. There was nothing anyone could do for her. Jake's arms went around me and pulled me close.

The next few minutes were a blur. I heard Dad on his phone, Sean praying, and Dwayne sobbing. Paramedics had arrived within seconds of the call and they attempted to revive her, but it was fruitless. The off-duty cops who were working the festival cordoned off the area. Mom took Dwayne by the arm and guided him to one of the camp chairs that Mike had placed just outside our canopy.

Sean came over to Jake and me and asked if we were all right. I wiped a tear away that I hadn't realized I'd shed until I'd felt the wetness on my cheek. "I'm okay," I said. "Dwayne might need you, though." I tried to smile but couldn't quite pull it off. "Some day off, huh?"

"You should know by now that priests and police officers are never really off duty." He squeezed my arm. "I'll go and talk to him."

"We should go over there, too," I said to Jake.

"I don't think that's a good idea right now." He sounded angry.

"Why not?" I looked up at him.

"Because I'll be tempted to beat the crap out of that lowlife."

It suddenly hit me why he felt that way. "You don't think . . ."

"Who else?" Jake said. "His sister conveniently dies drinking poisoned water in his tent hours after she talks to you when he ordered her not to. We already think he slipped her something yesterday. It's not a stretch to think he killed her."

Oh my God. That hadn't even crossed my mind. I looked over to where Dwayne was sitting. He leaned forward in the chair with his head in his hands. My mother had a hand on his shoulder. I watched as Sean stooped down and talked to him. Dwayne nodded at whatever Sean said. I turned back to Jake. "He seems so devastated. Do you think it's all an act?"

"It has to be. It's the only thing that fits. Who else would want to kill Melody?"

I glanced back at Dwayne. It was possible, but I wasn't convinced Jake was right. "You can stay here if you want, but I'm going over to talk to him."

"Are you sure you want to do that?"

"Not really, but I need to. I owe that much to Melody."

Jake nodded and kissed me on the forehead. "Be careful."

I avoided looking toward Dwayne's booth as I passed. I'd have enough trouble getting the image of Melody lying on the ground out of my mind. I wanted to remember the beautiful woman she'd been earlier and not how she was in death.

Dwayne was still leaning forward in his seat when I reached him. Mom and Sean stood talking a few feet away. Now that I was here, I wasn't sure what to say to him. "I'm sorry for your loss" didn't seem like the right thing. I took a deep breath. "Dwayne?"

He raised his head. "It's all my fault."

Was this a confession? "Why do you say that?"

"I warned her to stay away. She wouldn't listen to me. If she had, she wouldn't be . . ." He swallowed hard. "Oh God. I can't even say it."

"I talked to Melody this morning," I said.

Dwayne leaned back and blew out air. His eyes were bloodshot from crying. "I know."

"You know?"

"She told me. She never was very good at keeping secrets.

That's why I was trying to protect her. I tried so hard to protect her."

He wasn't making any sense. "Protect her from what?"

"From that." He pointed to his booth. "If she would have stayed home like I told her to, she'd be alive. I'd be the one lying over there, not her."

I was more confused than ever. "I don't understand."

"Melody would be alive and I would be dead because that water bottle was left there for me."

"You don't know that, Dwayne."

"Yes, I do. It was for me."

He sounded so sure of himself.

Dwayne's gaze went past me. "We'll have to talk more later."

I turned around to see what he was looking at. Dad and Vince were heading this way. I had hoped Dad's partner had better things to do, but he was probably thrilled to have another murder to investigate. And would probably try to find a way to blame me and Jake.

Dwayne grabbed my arm. "Don't say anything about what I just told you. They can't find out. Not yet."

I didn't get the chance to say I couldn't make any promises before Dad and Vince reached us. Dad told Dwayne they needed to ask him some questions, so I made my leave. Vince didn't say a word, but it was apparent he was playing second fiddle to Dad and wasn't happy about it. I noticed Ginger standing in the aisle not too far from Dave's tent, so I headed that way, ignoring questions from bystanders asking what was going on. I was surprised that vendors farther down the aisle were still serving beer. I had assumed everything would be shut down, especially with a second murder.

"You're not closing the festival?" I asked Ginger when I reached her.

She shook her head. "I thought it was better to proceed as normal. There's nothing to gain by sending all these people home. I'm telling them someone had a medical emergency and it's nothing to worry about."

It took me a few seconds to find my voice. "Nothing to worry about? A woman is dead, probably killed by the same person who killed her husband, and you say that's nothing to worry about?"

Ginger had the good grace to blush. "I meant there's nothing for the festival attendees to worry about. They're perfectly safe."

"What if they're not?" I said. "You're selling bottled water, aren't you? What if there are other poisoned bottles out there?"

"That's ridiculous. There's nothing wrong with ours."

"You can't possibly know that." Unless she was the one who'd poisoned the water. But why would she do that? I didn't know what her motive could be, or why she would take the chance of ruining something she'd worked so hard to get off the ground.

"The truth is," she said, "I can't afford to send anyone away. When Reginald was killed and we closed early that day, plus the rainout yesterday, I had to refund a lot of money to a lot of irate people. I can't do it again. Even though we're charging admission, I put a good portion of my own resources into this and I can't lose any more. I just can't."

"I see," I said, although I really didn't. In her eyes, the cash was more important than any lives lost.

A man came over just then and asked Ginger if she was the one in charge, then wanted to know what was going on. She plastered a smile on her face and began her "medical emergency" spiel. As I walked away, Dave waved me over.

"She shutting us down?" he asked. I told him what she'd said and he shook his head. "What happened exactly? I know Mobley's wife died, but that's it."

"Melody was poisoned, just like her husband had been." I didn't care what Ginger was telling everyone—I wasn't going to sugarcoat it.

"Man, that's a shame," he said. "How's Dwayne taking it?"

"As well as can be expected. He's pretty broken up."

"Poor guy," Dave said.

"I thought you didn't like him."

"I don't, but that doesn't mean I can't feel bad for the little weasel."

That was an interesting perspective. "My dad is interviewing him now."

The medical examiner's van pulled up behind Dwayne's booth. I couldn't help but wonder how Ginger was going to explain that one away. Dave and I watched until they took Melody's body away. Dave turned back to me. "You don't think Dwayne could be the killer, do you?"

I wasn't sure what to say. I didn't want to reveal anything that Melody had told me yesterday, or that Jake and I thought she might have been drugged. "I honestly don't know what to think," I said. "That was Jake's first thought, but Dwayne's reaction doesn't seem like an act to me. I guess we'll have to wait and see what my dad finds out."

"And what you find out." The corners of his mouth turned up. "You won't be able to help yourself."

I would have protested, but he was right. I was in too deep. Even though Jake and I couldn't possibly be considered suspects any longer—even to Vince—I couldn't stop now. I had to know what happened to Melody. And I was determined to find out.

"I can't believe it," Candy said when I told her what was going on. She and Kristie had arrived shortly after I returned to my station. Jake was helping Mike at our makeshift counter, and Sean had just left to take Mom home. The festival was scheduled to run until nine and while the police activity had scared some people away, it was still crowded for the most part. Dwayne's tent was one of the few empty ones. It hadn't taken the crime scene techs long to gather any evidence and the area was forlornly void of people.

Candy, Kristie, and I stood off to the side of my booth, out of earshot of the crowd. "I can't, either," I said. I finished telling them everything that Melody had said when I spoke to her earlier that day.

"You told your dad all this, right?" Kristie said.

I nodded. "I filled him in when we went to dinner. He planned to ask Dwayne about the deposits."

"It sounds like blackmail to me," Candy said. "I looked into that closure of the restaurant owned by Ronald Moore. It was much more than a mere shutdown by the health department. There had been a serious case of food poisoning. Ten people were affected and one woman died. Ronald Moore was officially cleared of any wrongdoing, but the woman's family still blamed him. If Moore and Mobley are the same person, Dwayne must have found out about it and blackmailed him to keep it a secret, and killed his sister because she'd discovered it."

"How do we find out if Moore changed his name?" I asked. "Wouldn't it be a matter of public record?"

"If he changed it legally, yes," Candy said. "But if the dead woman's family filed suit against him, I doubt the court would let him change it. If he really didn't want to be known as Ronald Moore any longer, and didn't want anyone to know that had been his name, he probably didn't go through proper channels. But I'll check. For all we know, we're off base and Ronald Moore is still out there somewhere."

"Jake thinks Dwayne killed Melody, but I'm not so sure. I talked to Dwayne for a minute before Dad and Vince got to him. He was really broken up. He kept saying it was all his fault and he should have protected her better. That he should have been the one lying there because the poison was meant for him."

Kristie said, "What the heck is that supposed to mean?"

"I don't know. That's when my dad and Vince came over to ask him some questions. The last thing Dwayne said was to not tell anyone yet, which I took to mean the police. I'm not sure why."

Candy's gaze roamed the area. "Is Dwayne still here? We could talk to him."

"I haven't seen him since I left him with Dad."

"Maybe he arrested him," Kristie said. "I don't know the guy, but it's too hinky that his sister dies right after talking to you when he told her not to, and especially after what happened yesterday. I think he's playing you. He wants you to feel sorry for him."

"I guess that's possible," I said, "but if Dwayne isn't the killer and someone really is out to get him, he's in danger. I need to talk to him and find out why he thinks someone wants to kill him."

CHAPTER NINETEEN

𝕴 woke up at five a.m. wide-awake. There was a church not too far away that had a six o'clock Mass, so I decided since I was up, I might as well get an early start to the day. It was a quick service, with no singing and a two-minute homily. I was back in my car and headed to see Dwayne in less than thirty minutes.

The Mobley residence was located in Shadyside, one of the more upscale neighborhoods of the city. Even smaller houses sometimes sold for half a million dollars, which was well above average for Pittsburgh. The Mobleys' house, a large Victorian on South Negley Avenue, would probably be pushing the million-dollar mark. As I pulled up in front at a very early seven a.m., I remembered Linda Mobley telling me her ex had been well-off. She had also mentioned that she didn't know where he'd gotten his money. And now I wondered about that again.

If Reginald Mobley really was Ronald Moore, how did his fortune fit into that scenario? An owner of a small restaurant, no matter how overpriced the food, wasn't going to accumulate a fortune in a few short years, even if he invested wisely. The timing of everything was a little fuzzy in my mind, so I tried to figure it out. Ronald's restaurant, Le Meilleur, closed fifteen years ago. Linda had been married to Reginald ten years and they had a ten-year-old son. He'd been a food writer for the newspaper at that time. That made a gap between the restaurant closure and their marriage. But Linda said he'd already had money when they married. If he was Ronald Moore, was he already well-off when he owned the restaurant? Maybe that's why he was able to disappear and possibly reinvent himself.

I suddenly had another thought that turned my stomach. With both Melody and her husband gone, Linda's son would likely inherit the estate. To my mind, that was a mighty big motive. She hated Melody and blamed her for Reginald's no longer paying the medical bills. I hadn't seen her at the festival this weekend, but that didn't mean she hadn't been there. If she put poison in the bottle of water, though, how would she know who was going to drink it? She would have had no way of knowing that Melody would be the one. If she had planned to kill Melody, it would have made more sense to do it another way. Not that killing ever made sense, but still.

That brought me back to Dwayne saying he was the one who was targeted, which was the reason I was here. I hadn't talked to my dad last night—or his partner, thank goodness—so I didn't know whether Dwayne was even here. It was an assumption on my part that he would still be staying at his sister's house if he wasn't in jail.

Fortunately my assumption was correct. Dwayne answered the door after I'd rung the doorbell twice, and I was pretty sure I'd woken him up. I doubted he was an early riser on the best of days. The hair on top of his mullet went in five different directions, and one side was flat and the other stuck out. I wished I'd brought scissors. He stared at me in a way that made me think he was going to slam the door in my face, but instead he opened it wider and let me in.

The interior of the Mobley residence wasn't the typical Victorian layout. Not at all. They must have completely gutted it and started over. Instead of the usual small distinct rooms, this one took open concept to the extreme. An architectural historian would have had a stroke. There were no walls anywhere, only some Grecian columns that I imagined were hiding some heavy-duty support posts. At least I hoped something was supporting the upper floors. The walls were all white and the hardwood floor was a bleached color somewhere between white and gray. The only thing original to the house was the staircase, but all that gorgeous wood had been painted white. There was some color in the room, however—the sofa and chairs were upholstered in a bloodred velvet.

"I'm sorry if I woke you," I said.

"I had to get up anyway. The cops kept me late last night," he said. "I'll make some coffee."

I followed him across the room to the kitchen at the rear

of the house. The cabinets were white like everything else, and the marble counters matched the bleached floor. I watched while Dwayne struggled with the high-end coffee-maker. He finally got it working and we took seats at the island.

Dwayne waved his hand in a swooping motion that encompassed the room. "Pretty impressive, isn't it?"

"I guess you could say that." I couldn't come up with anything nicer. I didn't want to tell him I hated it.

"Reggie designed it himself after he dumped his second wife," Dwayne said. "She had a conniption when she dropped the kid off one weekend after it was done. Went on a rant about how he ruined the house."

I would have to agree with that. "I bet Melody liked it, though."

"She loved it." He shook his head. "I still can't believe she's gone. I keep thinking I'm going to wake up from a bad dream."

I wasn't used to Dwayne not being confrontational with me. It was almost like having a normal conversation. There was an awkward pause before I figured out what to say. "You said the cops kept you late last night?"

"Yeah. Your dad's a nice guy. He tried to play bad cop to that other loser's good cop, but I saw right through them. They should have reversed roles."

I tried not to smile. That was a pretty accurate assessment. "They let you go, though."

The coffeemaker beeped, so Dwayne got up and poured two cups. He retrieved a container of cream from the stainless steel refrigerator, which was bigger than my kitchen. "You take sugar?" he asked.

I nodded and he brought over a sugar bowl from the counter beside the coffeemaker.

He put a splash of cream into his coffee and sat back down. "They asked a lot of questions, but they couldn't arrest me, because I didn't do anything."

"What did you mean yesterday when you said that water bottle was meant for you?"

"It's obvious, isn't it? I've been working the festival alone. No one knew Melody was going to be there. I didn't even know that. I told her to stay home—especially after that fiasco the night before. I can't believe she got so drunk she could hardly walk."

"She told me she only had two drinks."

Dwayne snorted. "Right. It was way more than that. It had to be. It was unlike her, though. She wasn't a big drinker."

"Is it possible she was drugged?" I studied his expression to see if I could catch him in a lie when he answered.

"Why would you think that?" He looked puzzled and not like he was hiding anything.

"It would explain her condition if she really only had two drinks, plus the fact she couldn't remember why she wanted to talk to me."

Dwayne's face lost the little bit of color it had and his hand shook when he raised his cup to take a drink. "Oh no." He put his cup down abruptly and some coffee splashed onto the countertop. "Why didn't I see that? I didn't believe her when she told me she hadn't had that much. I just assumed . . . Oh God. It really is all my fault."

"You said that yesterday. Why is it your fault?"

"Because it is." He stood and began pacing.

"I don't understand," I said. "You're going to have to do better than that, Dwayne."

"It's a long story and I'm sure you don't want to hear it."

I gave him a look Candy would be proud of.

Dwayne stopped pacing. "Fine, but don't say I didn't warn you. I have to show you something. I'll be right back."

While I waited, I sipped my coffee. I resisted the urge to snoop and see what was in the fridge and the cabinets, but only because I didn't know how long it would take Dwayne to return. It was a good thing I stayed put—he was back in a few minutes, holding a checkbook and some sheets of paper.

He sat at the counter again. "I don't know why I'm going to tell you any of this. I know you're friends with Shipley and the others, and none of them want to have anything to do with me."

For good reason, too.

"And maybe I deserve it. But I didn't steal their recipes. If they didn't want anyone else to have them, then they shouldn't have shown me how to brew them."

"That doesn't make it right for you to brew the same thing and call it your own. Did you ever think that maybe if you'd asked Dave or Cory, they'd have given you permission to use their recipes? And why wouldn't you put your own twist on them, anyway? One little change would have made all the difference."

Dwayne stared at the counter. "It doesn't matter. No one takes me seriously anyway."

"Maybe you should talk to Dave and Cory. An apology would go a long way."

He shook his head. "It's too late for that. They won't listen to me."

"You won't know that unless you try." When he didn't respond, I said, "I guess we're back to why you even want to talk to me."

"Because you're not like the others. You at least listen to me, even if you think I'm wrong." He slid the checkbook over to me. "I'm sure this is part of the reason someone is out to get me."

He was aware that Melody had talked to me, but I didn't know if she'd told him she knew about the checkbook, so I played dumb. "Why would anyone care about this?"

"Melody said she told you about Reggie giving me money."

So she had told him. "She did. She was understandably upset. She had no idea he was doing it." I flipped through the entries quickly, doing the math in my head. "Twelve thousand dollars over the past year or so? That's a lot of money."

Dwayne fidgeted in his seat. "If I thought even once that it would get him and my sister killed, I never would have taken the money."

"Why did you?"

"Like I said before, it's a long story."

"I'd like to hear it," I said.

There was a pause while he seemed to be gathering his

thoughts. "I knew Reggie a long time ago. Way before he met my sister. He owned a little restaurant downtown called Le Meilleur."

Jake's dad had been right.

"Le Meilleur means 'the best,' and it really was. It was a great place. I was between jobs and working part-time as a busboy. He was really easy to get along with back then— not the guy everyone knows now. He was friendly and outgoing and always smiling."

I couldn't wrap my mind around that. He had been such a bitter and nasty man that I couldn't even picture him smiling.

"The customers liked him and he loved cooking and dreaming up new dishes. His pastries were the best I ever tasted. Even better than your friend's."

"So what happened?"

"I don't know exactly how, but a day after he served one of his brand-new dishes—I don't even remember what it was—eel something or other, I think—a bunch of people got really sick. The health department came in and shut down the place and there were all kinds of accusations against Reggie, especially after one woman died."

"That's terrible," I said.

Dwayne nodded. "He was devastated. He took it so hard, some of the staff worried that he might kill himself. He never went back to cooking. He closed up the restaurant permanently. He even moved out of town for a while and changed his name because he was getting threats."

Although I already knew, I asked him what Reggie's name had been.

"Ronald Moore."

"Were any of the accusations proven?"

Dwayne shook his head. "No. It was definitely food poisoning, but no one could prove it was Reggie's fault. All the lawsuits were thrown out of court. He was meticulously clean. There was no way he did anything wrong."

"Then why were you blackmailing him?"

"It wasn't like that," he said. "When I recognized Reggie at the casino, I called him Ronnie and he about had a fit. There were a lot of people around and he was afraid someone would hear it. And I guess someone did, because not long after that, he started getting threats again." He took a drink of his now-cold coffee and made a face. "He thought they were from me, even though I told him time and again that they weren't. That's when he started giving me money. I told him I didn't want it, but he kept it up."

"Let me get this straight," I said. "He thought you were threatening him, he was giving you large sums of cash, and he still married your sister."

"Weird, huh?" Dwayne smiled slightly. "They really loved each other. I promised to keep Melody in the dark. She knew nothing about his past and we wanted to keep it that way. It was only in the last three or four weeks he realized I wasn't the one sending the notes when I started getting them, too. These are the ones I've been getting."

He passed the papers to me that he had been holding. There were three pages in a very generic-looking Courier font. The first two read, "You're as much at fault as he is. Your silence makes you an accomplice. Keep looking over your shoulder." The third was different and a chill went through me when I saw it. It was in the same font but in all caps and read, "YOU'RE NEXT."

He explained the third note had come a few days after his brother-in-law was murdered. "Whoever killed Reggie is after me now, and killed my sister."

I asked him if he had any idea who was sending the notes.

He sighed. "I wish I did. All I know is that it has to have something to do with Reggie's former restaurant. Someone at the casino heard us talking and put two and two together."

I pushed the papers back across the countertop. "You need to tell the police everything you've told me."

"I can't do that. They'll think I was blackmailing Reggie."

"But you weren't. Not technically, anyway," I said. "And even if you were, it's not going to matter now. He's dead. He can't accuse you."

"I don't know."

I stood. "Dwayne, you have to tell my dad. You're still in danger and I don't think this person is going to stop at killing your sister."

He picked up the papers and the checkbook. "I'll think about it."

That would have to do. For now.

CHAPTER TWENTY

nlike Dwayne, I didn't have to think about it. I called my dad's cell phone as soon as I got in the car. His voice mail picked up, so I left a message that I had some important information for him. It was likely Dwayne would be angry with me, but so be it. Before I left him, I tried to convince him to skip the festival today. It was the last day and he'd only be putting himself in danger. Despite everything that had happened, he refused to miss it. He was still determined to win the Golden Stein. I'd practically forgotten about it. He could have it as far as I was concerned.

Even though it was Sunday and the brew house was closed, I headed there anyway. I liked to check the tanks at least daily and the brewery was a good place to think. I could let my mind wander, and more than once, I'd come to conclusions about things that I hadn't considered before.

After depositing my purse and keys in my office, I went to the storeroom and lugged the ingredients for a brown ale into the brewery. It was only eight thirty, and since Nicole and Jake were going to open up our booth when the festival began, I had just enough time to start a new batch. I would head down to the festival this afternoon and take over for Jake so he could get ready for the burger competition final. The scent of malt grain and hot water coming together in the mash tun was just what I needed to organize my thoughts.

I'd learned an awful lot that morning—not only that Reginald Mobley was indeed Ronald Moore, but someone besides Dwayne knew it and had targeted him. The big question was why. From one of the notes Dwayne had received, it definitely had something to do with what had happened at Mobley's restaurant fifteen years ago. Someone still blamed him for the food poisoning death of the woman who'd eaten there. My guess was that it was a close relative or friend. Maybe even the woman's husband.

As soon as I transferred the wort to the brew kettle and added the hops, I called Candy and told her about my visit with Dwayne.

"You've had a busy morning already," she said. "Do you think he was telling the truth that he wasn't blackmailing his brother-in-law?"

"I didn't until he showed me the threats he'd received. They're the reason he was so frightened every time I asked him why he hadn't wanted anyone to know that Melody was his sister."

"I hope Dwayne has enough sense to stay away from the festival today."

I sighed. "He doesn't. I tried to talk him into staying home, but he has his heart set on winning the competition. I'll just have to keep an eye on him." Maybe if I didn't let him out of my sight, the killer wouldn't attempt anything.

Candy told me she was going to call a friend of hers who worked at the paper and have her search the archives for any articles about Ronald Moore and his restaurant, and she'd meet me at the festival later. When we were finished talking, I went back to my office and booted up my computer.

Dwayne had said he thought someone at the casino had overheard him call Mobley by his former name, because the threats began shortly after that. I typed in *Melody Tunstall* like I had earlier and began looking through the dozens of photos she had posted. The background images were blurry in most of them, so I wasn't able to make out many faces. I didn't recognize any of the people who weren't blurry. I thought I spotted the back of Reginald Mobley in one, but I couldn't be sure. It had been a long shot that I'd find the killer this way, but I was disappointed anyway. After that, I Googled Ronald Moore, but there were too many people with that name, and I didn't have time to scroll through everything. I'd have to rely on what Candy came up with.

Nicole came in as I headed back to the brewery to move the wort from the kettle to the fermentation tank. "Are you sure you don't mind working on your day off?" I asked her.

"Are you kidding?" Her light brown hair was in a ponytail and it swayed back and forth as she shook her head. "You're paying me to hang out at a festival all day talking to people about beer. That's not exactly work to me." She followed me through the swinging door into the brewery. "You started a new batch?"

"Yep. I figured I had time. It's a brown ale."

"I don't think I've seen you brew one of those yet," she said. "Can I help? Or at least watch what you do?"

"Of course." The process is more complicated than most people think. You don't just pump the wort to the tank. The liquids have to be separated from any solids, which is done by pumping the wort out and then forcing it back in through a jet nozzle. The hops and any other solids will move to the center and the liquid is drained out. Then it must be cooled quickly, the yeast is added, and the specific gravity is measured. It will be measured again later, which is what determines the ABV, or alcohol by volume. It also tells us when to stop fermentation.

Since Nicole was a chemistry major, I let her figure the specific gravity. "Too bad some of my chem classes aren't this much fun. If they had a brewing class, they'd have to turn people away. Everyone would want to take it. You should teach one."

I laughed. "I think I'll settle for leading brewery tours." That was something I planned on doing eventually once the brew house was well established.

"So, since this is an ale, it ferments for about two weeks. Right?" Nicole asked.

Before I could see if she remembered at what temperature ale fermented, Jake breezed through the door. "Just what I like to see," he said. "My two favorite ladies hard at work." He crossed the room and kissed me on the forehead.

"Don't let your mother hear you say she's not your favorite," I said, grinning.

He made a face. "My favorites after her, of course."

I helped them load the kegs onto Jake's truck, then headed back inside to tackle every brewer's least favorite job—the cleanup.

Candy met me at the festival entrance at a little after noon. The Steelers logo on the folder she was carrying matched the logo on her sequined ball cap, without the sequins, of course. She was an equal-opportunity sports fan today. The Steelers cap was accompanied by yellow pants with the Pirates logo, and a commemorative Penguins T-shirt from their last Stanley Cup victory. I didn't question it.

I had a little time to spare before I had to get to my booth and relieve Jake, so Candy and I searched for a place to sit where we could go over what she'd found. We ended up at one of the makeshift cinder block and wood benches. Not exactly comfortable, but it would have to do. She put the folder down between us and opened it.

The first article had the headline POSSIBLE FOOD POISONING AT LOCAL RESTAURANT. It was only a paragraph long and just said that several people were sickened and ended up in the emergency room a few hours after eating dinner at Le Meilleur. None of the victims' names were listed.

The second article was dated three days later. DEATH OF PERRYSVILLE WOMAN BLAMED ON FOOD POISONING AT DOWNTOWN RESTAURANT. This article had much more information than the first one did. It identified the dead woman as Darlene Nichols, forty-five years old. It stated her teenage daughter had been at the restaurant with her but hadn't eaten the same meal. I scanned the rest of the article for the daughter's name, but it was never mentioned. There was only an old, grainy photo of the two of them together. "That's disappointing," I said. "I hoped there'd be more to go on."

Candy picked up the next article. "Maybe this one will be better. It's about a wrongful-death lawsuit brought on behalf of the minor daughter." She skimmed the page. "It still doesn't mention the daughter's name—only the name of the law firm—Anson, Gregory and Powell. Maybe we can contact the lawyers."

"That's a possibility," I said, "but it doesn't help find the killer now. There's no way of knowing if it's even one of Darlene Nichols's family members. I could be way off and the murders have nothing to do with her."

"Nothing else fits. And we know the last name is Nichols, so that should help."

"Except the daughter is an adult now. She could have married. She might not even live in this area anymore."

Candy stared at me. "I've never known you to be so contrary about anything. What gives?"

"Nothing." I paused. "It's just that this is the final day of the festival and Dwayne could be in real danger. Plus, there's no telling what else this person has planned and is going to do. Maybe others here are targets, too."

She patted me on the leg. "Max, you're doing your best. That's all you can do. Keep your eyes open, and I'll do the same. Call your dad again. Call that cute little Vince if you have to."

I couldn't help smiling at her calling the detective cute. "Maybe you want to call him. I'm sure he'd be thrilled to hear from you."

She pushed herself up. "I'm sure. Tell him I said hello when you talk to him. In the meantime, read through these articles again and I'm going to make the rounds and see what I can find out." She smiled. "All in the guise of talking up my bakery, of course."

"Oh, of course."

"Are you nervous?" I asked Jake fifteen minutes later.

He shrugged. "A little maybe. It's not like playing for the Stanley Cup."

I put my arm around his waist and gave him a little hip bump. "I know. You can't check anyone into the boards."

"Very funny, O'Hara."

"You'll do fine. You're a great cook." I slipped my other arm around him. "You'll always be in first place to me."

"Good to know."

I tilted my head up and Jake leaned down and kissed me.

Nicole cleared her throat and we separated. She was grinning.

Jake grabbed his cooler and cooking supplies and headed to the kitchen tent.

The festival wasn't as busy as it had been the day before, so Nicole and I had plenty of time to talk. I'd spoken to my dad after Candy and I parted, and both he and his partner planned on being here today. I hadn't seen either of them yet, but I was sure they'd be watching the burger tasting very carefully. I still worried that whoever the killer was would attempt to get to Dwayne today. I kept glancing over at him, but so far, nothing was amiss.

When I finished telling Nicole about my visit to Dwayne's that morning, she asked, "Do you really think the killer will go after him today?"

I told her I did. "Especially if it's someone who has been here both weekends. I just wish there was a way to find out. The only ones we know for sure are the vendors, the judges, and the others working here."

"Maybe that's where you should start, then," Nicole said.

"You're right." I'd already considered some of them and it wouldn't hurt to do it again in light of everything I'd found out. "Let's start with what I know so far. Whoever killed Mobley and Melody, and is now after Dwayne, most likely knew his previous identity. And is probably related to the woman who died fifteen years ago—possibly her daughter."

Nicole nodded. "That makes sense."

"The daughter was sixteen or seventeen when her mother died. That would put her in her early thirties now."

"Which is probably half of the women working here. Not to mention a good portion of the attendees."

"But it seems to eliminate one of my suspects—Ginger Alvarado. She's in her fifties."

We stopped to pour samples to a group of three couples and answer their questions. They liked our offerings and promised to stop in to the brew house soon.

"Back to what we were talking about," Nicole began. "What if it's not the daughter? Ginger could still be in the running. She could be the woman's sister."

"I didn't think of that. Maybe you should become a detective instead of a chemist."

Nicole smiled. "You mean future brewer. I think I've found my niche."

"I'm so glad to hear that." I wouldn't have to look anywhere else for the assistant that I was going to need soon. She was right in front of me. I gave her a hug. "This is great news. But you'd better finish school first."

"I plan to. Don't worry," she said. "Is Ginger a possibility?"

"If it turns out she's related to the dead woman, yes."

Another group came over and we had to end the discussion. We hadn't had a chance to talk about my other suspects—Dave, Randy, and Cory. After we served this group, it was time for me to leave for the burger competition. I'd be gone only about an hour, but I asked Nicole if she'd be all right alone. She said she would.

I stopped to check on Dwayne, since I had to pass that way. He told me everything was fine. I hoped it stayed that way. "If you need to take a break later, let me know," I told him. "I can keep an eye on things."

"I appreciate it," Dwayne said. "Cory is coming over in a bit to do that." He shook his head. "Everyone is being so nice to me. I can't get used to it."

I liked the change in his attitude, but I couldn't help wondering how long it would last.

When I reached the area where the competition had been set up, I spotted my dad talking to a uniformed officer. There was a much larger police presence than there had been last week. When they were finished talking and the officer left him, I wandered over.

"Hi, sweetie," Dad said, kissing me on the cheek. "All's well so far."

"It would be nice if it stayed that way. Where's your shadow?"

"He's watching the chefs."

"Great." I felt my blood pressure rising.

Dad knew what I was thinking. "Don't worry. I spoke to Jake. He knows Vincent will be watching over his shoulder."

"That's just what Jake needs. How is he supposed to cook with that jerk breathing down his neck? Can't you call him off?"

Dad put his arm around my shoulder. "No can do. Besides, that's the best place for him. We had a little talk and went over everything, including what you told me earlier. Vincent knows he was on the wrong track. He just doesn't want to admit it. I think he's trying to save face right now by keeping his eye on Jake. Just in case."

"He should be watching Dwayne instead to make sure nothing happens to him."

"I got it covered. There are some plainclothes officers patrolling the grounds."

Just then, Ginger's voice came over the loudspeaker announcing the competitors were ready to plate their creations and bring them to the judges. Dad squeezed my shoulder and said he'd talk to me later. He moved to the rear of the crowd as Marshall Babcock, Phoebe Atwell, and Leonard Wilson came forward and took their seats. I noticed each of them carried reusable water bottles that I imagined they'd brought from home. There were no disposable bottles anywhere.

I had butterflies in my stomach as the finalists came forward and put their plates on a table in front of the food critics. Jake looked much calmer than I felt. I realized my fists were clenched because my fingers started cramping. I shook them out. Vince had followed the finalists out and he moved to stand behind the judges. With his dark sunglasses, starched white shirt, and tie, he could be mistaken for a Secret Service agent. Maybe I could suggest that to him.

One by one the judges examined the offerings and gave their opinions on the presentation and appearance of each. I was disappointed that both Leonard and Marshall declared Jake's "average." Phoebe gave him a higher score, but I wasn't sure if it was for the plate or for him personally.

Jake's burger was the second to last to be tasted. Marshall was impressed. "You've upped your game a bit since last week," he said. "You added some jalapeños this time." I crossed my fingers as the other two tasted it. Leonard liked it, but not as much as the previous contestant's. Phoebe declared it should be called the "Almost Better Than Sex Burger" to the hoots and hollers of the observers. When they'd finished, the judges left to compare notes and decide on the winner. The results of the burger competition, as well as the beer competition, would be declared at an awards ceremony that was planned for after the close of the festival. The vendors would be breaking down their booths and packing up at five, and the ceremony was scheduled for six.

Jake and the other contestants went back to the kitchen area to pose for photos and be interviewed. While I waited outside the tent for them to finish, Vince found me. "I'm sure you're happy your boyfriend is in the clear," he said.

"And I'm sure you're happy he's not."

He removed his sunglasses. "Miss O'Hara, going after a guilty party does not make me happy. It's my job. It's what I do. The investigation has gone in another direction, and that's the one I'll follow now." He dropped his sunglasses into his shirt pocket and walked away.

I picked my jaw up off the ground. It wasn't exactly an apology, but I'd take it. Dad had been right. There was hope for him yet.

CHAPTER TWENTY-ONE

After Jake finished in the kitchen tent, we headed back to our booth. I sent Nicole to enjoy the rest of the festival. She said she'd be back to hear the announcement of the contest winner. My mom was bringing Jake's parents down shortly so they could be here if Jake won. Everything was calm and even Dwayne seemed more relaxed when we stopped to check on him on our way back.

And the fact that everything seemed so normal made me nervous. Jake and I were discussing this when Dave stopped by a few minutes later.

"How did the competition go?" he asked. "I figure since my kid was knocked out of it last week, I should probably root for you."

"Thanks a lot, pal," Jake said with a laugh. "I think I did okay."

Dave tilted his head toward Dwayne's tent. "Any word about that?"

"A little bit," I said. "You've been around the restaurant scene for a lot of years—"

"Are you calling me old?" He grinned.

"Maybe." I returned his grin. "Did you ever hear of a place downtown called Le Meilleur? It closed about fifteen years ago."

Dave scratched his beard. "It sounds really familiar."

I picked up the folder that Candy had given me earlier and passed it to him. I waited while he scanned the articles.

"I remember it now," Dave said. "There was a lot of talk back then of what happened. Some people thought this Moore guy should've been charged with murder, and the rest thought he'd gotten a bum rap. Personally I was in the latter camp. He had no way of knowing the eel he'd bought was tainted. What's this have to do with what happened here? I thought Mobley and his wife died from cyanide poisoning, not food poisoning."

"They did," I said. I went on to explain what Dwayne had told me that morning.

"You're kidding," Dave said when I'd finished. "No wonder Mobley was such a mean son of a gun. He couldn't cook anymore, so he hated anyone who did. Makes a lot of sense now."

"And now Dwayne is in danger because he kept Mobley's secret." I pointed to the grainy newspaper photo of Darlene

Nichols and her daughter on the page he was holding. "Do you recognize either one of them?"

Dave studied the picture. "I don't think so, but this was fifteen years ago. And Le Meilleur wasn't exactly my kind of place." He flipped to the last article about the wrongful-death suit. "Hey, I know that law firm," he said. "That Gregory in Anson, Gregory and Powell is Randy's dad."

"Seriously?" Jake said.

Something clicked in my brain. Randy fishing for information at the Brewers Association meeting. A comment Randy had made to Jake. Something like Mobley got what was coming to him, and he hoped he felt like the other ones. The "other ones" comment hadn't made any sense at the time, but I thought it might now. They were the diners who'd suffered from food poisoning. But how did Randy know that Mobley was Moore?

"Yeah," Dave said. "Randy's dad was a lawyer. He died a couple of years ago."

That meant I couldn't talk to him. But I could see what Randy knew. It seemed like he knew a lot. I glanced across the aisle to Randy's booth. He was already beginning to pack up. "I'm going to talk to Randy."

"Not by yourself, you're not," Jake said.

I rolled my eyes. "It's just across the way. You can see everything from here."

Dave said, "I can go with you."

I shook my head and took the folder back from him. "I'll be fine. I'm just going to talk to him."

I could see Jake wanted to come up with a good reason

for me not to go, but without going into full protection mode like my dad and brothers would, he had little choice in the matter. He relented. "Be careful. I'll be watching the whole time. If he gives you any trouble at all . . ."

I didn't wait for him to finish. I wanted to race across the gravel, but forced my pace down to a casual stroll. Randy saw me coming and waved.

"How did Jake do in the contest?" he asked.

"We'll know soon enough."

"That was a shame about Mobley's wife. What's your dad saying about it? Any idea who did it yet?"

"We have a pretty good lead. It's just a matter of time." I watched him closely.

He showed no reaction other than taking a great interest in his shoes. "Really? That's good news."

"Yes, it is."

"So, who is it? My money's on Dwayne. He's a total loser. It would be just like him to do something like that."

"Oh, it's not Dwayne." Maybe it wasn't the smartest thing to do, but that comment ticked me off. Dwayne might be a lot of things, but a killer wasn't one of them.

Randy raised his head. "Who is it, then?"

I didn't want to come right out and accuse him. So far, that approach hadn't worked out all that well for me. Something must have shown on my face, though.

"You're thinking it's me, aren't you?" When I didn't answer, he said, "That's ridiculous." He laughed shakily. "That's a pretty good joke."

I opened the folder and pulled out the page that mentioned his father's law firm. "That's your dad, isn't it?"

"Yeah. So what?"

I showed him the articles about Le Meilleur. "You knew Reginald Mobley was Ronald Moore."

He shoved the papers back at me. "Like I said, so what? The guy was scum. Instead of facing up to what he did, he ran away. You can't get much lower than that. That poor girl grew up without a mother. Even though that suit was dismissed, my dad spent half his life trying to track him down. He was right under our noses the whole time."

A few people passed closely by the tent, so the discussion was put on hold until they left. When they were out of earshot, Randy said, "I'll never admit I'm not glad he died, but I didn't kill him."

"Then tell me the whole story. If you didn't kill Mobley and Melody, you must know who did. That would make you an accessory."

His face turned pale. "But I don't know who it is."

I pulled my cell phone from my shorts pocket. "Then you don't mind if I call my dad."

"Wait." He ran a hand through his hair in exasperation.

I put my phone back.

A couple came up to the booth and Randy lied and told them he was out of beer. As soon as they were gone, I asked him how he knew Mobley's identity.

"I was at the casino the same night Dwayne ran into him. The table games were way out of my league, but I saw Dwayne standing by a table and I slowed down as I was passing. I wanted to know what he was doing there. I heard him call the guy sitting there 'Ronnie,' and the guy went ballistic. It seemed weird to me, so I followed them when they left the table, and I listened in on their conversation. That's when I knew."

"Who did you tell about it?" I asked.

"No one. At least not at first. I didn't even think about it until I got that letter from the state turning down my brewpub license. Cory told me Mobley was behind it. I didn't have the money to fight it. I could have gone to my dad's firm, but I was too embarrassed. He always wanted me to follow in his footsteps and was disappointed in my choice. That's when I decided to dig into some things and find a way to expose him for what he really was." He paused and drew himself a beer from the sole keg that was still tapped. "Want one?"

I shook my head. "I only want to hear the rest of your story."

He took a long drink and wiped his mouth with the back of his hand. "I went through some of my dad's files that he had at home. I found a current address for the daughter and wrote her a note. After that, we started exchanging e-mails and we've been friends ever since. She's not interested in revenge. She doesn't want the notoriety that opening this up would bring."

Regardless of whether any of his story was true or not, I wanted to know the daughter's name. I asked him what it was.

"Mary Patrice Nichols," he said.

It didn't sound even vaguely familiar. I'd expected it to be someone involved with the festival. Maybe I was on the wrong track.

"But you know her by a different name," he added. "She goes by Phoebe Atwell now."

CHAPTER TWENTY-TWO

"Phoebe?" My voice came out as a squeak. "Phoebe is the dead woman's daughter?"

"That's what I said." Randy looked at me like I was an idiot.

"And you didn't think it was a little strange she'd suggest the man who caused her mother's death to be her substitute when she got called away on her so-called emergency?" Everything was beginning to make sense now and fall into place. As soon as Phoebe found out Reginald Mobley was Ronald Moore, she planned his demise, despite what she had told Randy. Getting called away was just a ruse to get Mobley installed as judge and murder him in front of hundreds of people.

"Wait just a minute," Randy said. "You can't possibly

think Phoebe had anything to do with the murders. She's a kind, gentle, fun-loving woman. She would never even consider killing someone. Besides, she wasn't even here when that poor excuse for a critic was killed."

"I'm sorry, Randy, but it's too much of a coincidence that her emergency just happened to resolve itself in time for her to come back after Mobley's death. She came back to finish the job on Dwayne but killed Melody instead."

He shook his head. "You'll never get me to believe that."

"It's the only thing that fits. Think about it."

"You don't know her like I do. She's not like that. She's not."

Even as he said that, I could see the doubt in his eyes. He was in love with her and didn't want to believe it even though everything I said made perfect sense. His doubt would soon turn to hurt, then betrayal. I'd seen the same look when a friend of mine learned her beloved was a cold-blooded killer. I felt terrible for Randy, but I couldn't do anything to help him right now. I needed to find Phoebe.

I ran back across the aisle. "We need to find Phoebe," I said to Jake and Dave.

"Why?" Jake asked. "What's going on?"

I told them what I'd found out from Randy.

"I can't believe it," Dave said when I'd finished. "I'm going to go over and stay with Randy. I'll make sure he's okay and that he doesn't do anything stupid, like giving Phoebe a heads-up."

While Jake started packing up our stuff, I called my dad and filled him in.

"You're sure about this?" he said.

"Absolutely."

He didn't pause for more than a few seconds, but it seemed like a lifetime to me. "Here's what we're going to do. I want you and Jake to act like nothing has happened. Let everything proceed as normal."

"You can't be serious," I said.

"Let me finish. If Miss Atwell isn't aware that anyone suspects her, we can take her into custody when the judges appear to announce the winners of the contests. That will be the safest way to get to her. In the meantime, I'll notify all the officers here to be on the lookout for her and I'll send someone to talk to Randy Gregory."

I wasn't sure it was a good idea to wait. What if Phoebe got to Dwayne before then, or Randy was somehow able to contact her? "I don't like not knowing where she is," I said to Jake after I was done talking to my dad. "Maybe we should finish packing up and look for her."

Jake agreed with me. I called Mom and told her we'd meet them at the small stage they were setting up near the kitchen. As soon as we had the truck loaded, we headed toward the other end of the festival grounds. Dwayne's booth was unattended when we passed it and that worried me. I hadn't seen Phoebe anywhere near it, but that didn't mean she hadn't lured him away somehow. I offered up a quick prayer for his safety.

While we walked, I called Candy and told her what had happened.

"Of course!" she said. "I should have suspected her all along, but in my defense, she played it brilliantly. She never went anywhere and was in the perfect position to commit murder. I'll keep my eyes open and if I spot her, I'll call my favorite detective."

When we reached the other end of the festival grounds, Ginger was near the stage, directing workers on where to place a few chairs and a podium. Jake and I headed that way. She waved when she saw me and gave us a big smile. "Are you excited?" she asked. "I know I am. I can't wait to see who wins."

Neither one of us answered her question. Instead I asked if she'd seen Phoebe anywhere.

"No, I haven't. I saw Marshall and Leonard a little while ago. They were looking for her, too."

I hoped that wasn't a bad sign.

Ginger's gaze moved from me to Jake and back again. "Is there something going on I should know about?"

Anything we said would take too long to explain and I had no doubt she'd have a million questions. It was better to keep mum. "Nothing you need to worry about."

Jake added, "We just wanted to talk to Phoebe."

For the next half hour we circled the entire perimeter of the festival without seeing Phoebe or Dwayne anywhere. Most of the brewers had taken down their booths and packed them up by this time. Except for all the people milling about, there was a clear view of almost the entire area.

"I don't like this," I said.

Jake squeezed my hand. "We'll find her. Maybe your dad is right and she'll show up for the ceremony. Or maybe they've taken her into custody already."

"Or maybe she killed Dwayne already and is long gone and they'll never find her."

"There are plenty of cops here and your dad is not going to let anything happen to Dwayne. Even if she's taken off, they know who she is. They'll find her."

It was almost six o'clock, so we returned to the stage area. Ginger's voice came over the loudspeaker, welcoming everyone and telling them it was almost time for the awards to be given out.

We moved closer to the stage. I looked for Mom and Jake's parents, but the crowd was thick. I spotted Candy standing with Nicole on the opposite side of the crowd. I pointed them out to Jake.

"That's good," he said. "We have both sides covered, plus all the police. Phoebe won't get away with anything."

I wished I could be as sure as he seemed to be. I had a terrible feeling everything was about to go wrong.

Marshall and Leonard took the stage beside Ginger. No Phoebe. While Ginger droned on about the festival and her plans for next year, I stood on tiptoe and scanned the crowd for Phoebe and Dwayne. Neither one of them was anywhere in sight.

"And now without further ado," Ginger said, "I'd like all ten finalists in the burger competition to take the stage."

"Crap," Jake said. "I didn't know they were going to do that. I can't go up there now."

"Yes, you can." When he looked hesitant, I added, "You'll have a better view of the crowd from the stage."

He squeezed my hand. "Don't go anywhere." I heard his

dad whooping from somewhere in the middle of the crowd when Jake got to the stage.

Ginger introduced the finalists, then said that there would be four runners-up and the big winner. She announced the fourth runner-up. I kept watching the throng while she continued. Where in the world was Phoebe? If she was still around, she should be onstage with the other judges. I paid closer attention to the activity on the stage when it came down to Jake and the only woman in the group.

Ginger opened the final envelope as dramatically as if she were the emcee at a beauty pageant. "And first runner-up is . . ." She paused. "Jake Lambert. That makes the winner of the check for one thousand . . ."

I tuned out the rest. Until now I hadn't realized how much I'd wanted Jake to win. He'd been very cavalier about the whole thing, but I saw the disappointment on his face. First runner-up was nice, but it wasn't enough. I made my way to the steps at the side of the stage and met him as he came down. I put my arms around his waist. "I'm sorry you didn't win."

He kissed me on the forehead. "It's no big deal. There's always next year."

"And now it's time to announce the winner of the Golden Stein, our new prestigious designation of the best in craft beer," Ginger's voice rang out. "And thanks to our generous donors, the winner will also receive a check for one thousand dollars."

"Maybe you'll make up for my loss," Jake said.

I made a face. "Not likely."

Since she couldn't call all fifty brewers onto the stage, Ginger began with the fourth runner-up, the woman from New York who had talked to me about doing a collaboration. I applauded when Brandon Long was named next. "And second runner-up is Max O'Hara, from the Allegheny Brew House."

I froze and glanced at Jake.

He smiled. "Get up there."

He had to give me a nudge to get moving. I shook Ginger's hand and took my place beside Brandon. I spotted my mother with Jake's parents and she gave me a big smile. I scanned the crowd, but I still didn't see Phoebe anywhere. I began to relax a little. Maybe she was far from the festival. The police would pick her up and everything would be all right.

"The first runner-up is Cory Dixon, from the South Side Brew Works."

"Yeah!" He pumped both fists as he bounded onstage. He grinned at me. "Hey, Max. Nice to see you here."

"Likewise."

Ginger rattled a sealed envelope. "And now for the big winner. She slid her thumb under the flap and opened the envelope. "The winner of the Golden Stein and a check for one thousand dollars, voted as best craft beer by festival attendees and our three judges, is . . ." She paused dramatically and pulled a card from the envelope. "Dwayne Tunstall, from Lazy River Brewing!"

There was a collective gasp from the brewers onstage and those in the audience. Marshall and Leonard had puzzled expressions on their faces like they couldn't believe it, either. Dwayne suddenly appeared from behind a nearby Porta-John and ran onto the stage. If I hadn't been so worried for him, I would have laughed. He shook Ginger's hand, then leaned into the microphone. "Thanks, yinz guys! You're the best!"

"Fixed," Cory grumbled beside me. "It had to be fixed."

"And now the presentation of the Golden Stein to our winner," Ginger announced.

I expected one of the festival volunteers to carry it to the stage, but instead Phoebe was crossing the stage, carrying something that looked more like a goblet than a stein. My stomach tightened and I looked around for police officers. There were a few guys in plain clothes moving slowly toward the stage. Dad was one of them.

Ginger frowned as Phoebe gave Dwayne a dazzling smile. "I hope our gracious hostess doesn't mind, but I'd like to start a new tradition for the winner."

I could see that Ginger had no idea what Phoebe was doing, but she played along. "I would be honored," she said. "I love to start new traditions. That's one reason we're having this festival."

I glanced back at the audience. If Phoebe pulled something now, the officers were still too far away. So was Jake— he was inching up the steps at the side of the stage.

Phoebe passed the stein to Dwayne. "I took the liberty of filling the stein with your best brew."

Oh no. She was going to murder him in plain sight of all these people. I wasn't about to let that happen.

She put her hand under his and prompted him to raise it to his lips. "Drink it down, my prince."

"No!" I charged forward and knocked the stein from his hand. It clattered to the floor, the contents spilling onto the stage.

Phoebe leaped from the back of the stage and took off running. I did the same. I heard officers yelling at people to move out of the way. Phoebe's legs were longer than mine and the gap between us widened. But I had the advantage of wearing sneakers as opposed to her heels, and I narrowed the gap when she slowed to kick off her shoes. I heard sirens as we reached the stairs that led up to the David McCullough Bridge. I was about fifty feet away when she scrambled up onto the railing near the center of the bridge.

"Don't come any closer," she said. She sat on the rail and swung her legs over the side. "I'll jump."

I stopped in my tracks. "You don't want to do that, Phoebe."

She laughed. "Why not? I don't have anything to lose at this point."

"That's not true. You have everything to lose."

"I lost everything fifteen years ago when that man killed my mother."

"From what I've heard about Ronald Moore, he never meant for anything like that to happen. It was a tragic accident." I didn't know what to say to her. I wasn't trained for anything like this. All I knew was that I needed to keep her talking until real help arrived.

"It doesn't matter whether he meant to or not," she said. "I don't care what the court said. He never should have served something like that. He killed my mother and he had to pay for it."

"What about Melody? She shouldn't have died."

"That was a mistake," Phoebe said. "It was meant for Dwayne."

In her mind it seemed to be all right for her to make a mistake and cause a death, but it hadn't been for Ronald Moore. I noticed that traffic on the bridge had stopped. I hoped that meant the police were on scene. I looked back and saw squad cars blocking both ends of the bridge. My dad and Vince, as well as Jake and Randy, were slowly walking toward us.

Maybe Randy could help talk her down. I told her he was here.

Tears ran down her face. "I can't talk to him. I never should have let him get close to me. He probably hates me now."

"He loves you, Phoebe. When I talked to him, he refused to believe anything bad about you."

Just then, Randy called her name and stepped forward.

"Stay away, Randy," she yelled.

He came closer. "No, Phoebe. Please let me help you. We'll make it right. My dad's partners can help you."

"Go away! I don't want your help! I don't want anyone's help!" Suddenly she pushed off from the railing.

I stood frozen at the sickening splash as she hit the water below. There was a flash of movement beside me. I turned my head in time to see Vince sail over the railing after her. I held my breath until he surfaced. He was holding on to Phoebe.

River Rescue had been notified as soon as Phoebe took to the railing, and they were already on their way. They arrived in less than a minute. Dad and Jake stood beside me as the crew pulled Phoebe onto the boat first, and then Vince. He gave us the thumbs-up.

Dad let out a breath. "It's a good thing he survived that jump," he said. "Because I'm going to kill him."

CHAPTER TWENTY-THREE

Dad and a soaking-wet Vince had taken Phoebe into custody. They were transporting her to one of the local hospitals to be checked and it was likely she'd end up in Western Psych for an evaluation. Randy went with them and by now had probably arranged for someone from his father's former law firm to represent Phoebe.

Most of the festivalgoers had gone by the time Jake and I returned. Ginger stood with her husband, Leonard, and Marshall. When they spotted us, they headed toward the stage, where Mom, Jake's parents, Nicole, and Candy were gathered around Dwayne. He was sitting with Dave and Cory on the edge of the stage. Everyone except Dwayne started talking at once, wanting a full accounting of what had transpired.

I put up a hand. "In a minute." I touched Dwayne on the arm. "Are you all right?"

His face was pale and his hand shook when he put it over mine. "Thanks to you, I am. I will never be able to repay you for saving my life. Dave told me how you figured it all out."

"I didn't figure it out on my own. I had lots of help. It was just a matter of putting all the pieces together."

Ginger was almost as pale as Dwayne. "I still can't quite believe it was Phoebe who killed Reginald and his wife. She seemed so . . . normal. I'm going to have to think long and hard about doing this again next year."

"Don't keep us in suspense any longer," Candy said. "What happened after you took off after Phoebe?"

"Yes," Nicole added.

There wasn't a whole lot to tell. I related how I'd chased her to the bridge and tried to keep her talking until help arrived, and how Randy had tried to talk to her. I told them how she jumped into the river and Vince dove in and rescued her. My voice cracked at the end of my tale, and Jake put his arm around me. The adrenaline was finally wearing off and now I felt teary and exhausted.

Mom came over and hugged the both of us. Jake's parents did the same.

"I'm so glad you're okay," Mom said with a smile. "You are definitely your father's daughter. I hope you're not planning a career change."

I smiled back. "Not a chance."

Jake ruffled my hair. "It's only because she knows I'd ruin the beer."

"Yeah, he'd much rather drink the stuff," Bob Lambert said.

Dwayne got to his feet. "Speaking of beer, I have a few things I want to say."

Everyone turned to look his way.

"First, it goes without saying that I want to thank Max for saving my life. And thanks to everyone who helped."

"Hear, hear," Bob said.

Dwayne hooked his thumbs on his pockets. "I don't feel like I've earned the prize that was given to me today. It really belongs to those two." He nodded his head toward Dave and Cory. "I want to publicly apologize to them and say that I shouldn't have used their recipes. I wanted to brew beer—really good beer—so bad and thought that was the only way to do it. It was wrong of me and I won't use them again. I'm really sorry."

When Dwayne reached out his hand, Dave shook it. Cory hesitated a moment, then did the same. It looked like the long-standing feud was over.

I was surprised at the turnout at Dwayne's party a few weeks later. He'd had a definite change of heart after coming so close to death, not once, but twice. I didn't know if it was permanent, but so far it seemed to be. He'd apologized to Cory and Dave numerous times since the festival and vowed never to use their recipes again. The funny thing was, the ones he came up with on his own were pretty good. He'd also admitted he had been the one who sent the letters to the state in Mobley's name to put a stop to the brewpub applications.

Even Vince was in a better mood these days. He was on somewhat better terms with Dad now, even if he did still think he knew everything. It didn't help that he'd earned a commendation for saving Phoebe's life and liked to let everyone know it.

Candy had done some more research and discovered that Ronald Moore's finances hadn't been as good as everyone seemed to think. He had lost more than he'd won at the table games, and any winnings and inheritance he'd had were gone. He'd been mortgaged to the hilt and there was nothing left in the estate. The only inheritance his son got was a fifty-thousand-dollar life insurance payout. Linda hadn't been happy about that.

Jake and I sat at a folding table that Dwayne had set up in his brewery. He had just poured everyone his latest brew. He tapped on a glass to get everyone's attention.

"I'm so glad yinz guys were able to come tonight," he said. "You don't know how much it means to me." He held up his glass. "This is the recipe I came up with just before all this happened. I'd like to propose a toast to my sister, Melody. May she rest in peace."

"To Melody!" Everyone raised their glass and took a sip.

I coughed and almost spit it out. It tasted like a Jolly Rancher on steroids. I looked around the room and everyone seemed to have the same reaction.

Even Dwayne made a face after he'd tasted it. "I guess it needs some work."

Dave went over and patted him on the back. "I know just what it needs."

I smiled as I watched them head to a chalkboard on the other side of the room. "For some reason that made me think of the end of the movie *Casablanca*," I said to Jake.

"Why is that?" he asked.

"It looks like the beginning of a beautiful friendship."

JAKE'S BREW BURGER

Makes four burgers.

1 lb. lean ground beef
2 tsp. Weber Gourmet Burger seasoning
1 12-oz. bottle of ale or other medium-bodied beer
1 green pepper, coarsely chopped
1 small sweet onion, coarsely chopped
½ cup sliced mushrooms
4 slices Swiss cheese
4 pretzel buns (or buns of your choice)

Place ground beef into a large bowl. Add the burger seasoning and ½ cup of ale and mix well. Refrigerate until ready to cook. Form into four patties and grill to desired doneness.

While burgers are cooking, spray a skillet with nonstick spray. Heat skillet on medium-high and when skillet is hot, turn the heat down to medium-low and add peppers, onions, and the remaining ale. When peppers begin to soften, add mushrooms and cook until the liquid has evaporated.

Place Swiss cheese slices on buns and then add a cooked burger to each. Top with the vegetable mixture and serve either plain or with your favorite condiments.

APPLE CINNAMON MUFFINS
Makes one dozen muffins.

1 egg
2/3 cup milk
¼ cup canola oil
1½ cups flour
1 tsp. salt
2 tsp. baking powder
¾ cup sugar
2 Tbsp. cinnamon
½ cup finely chopped apple

Preheat oven to 400 degrees. In a large mixing bowl, beat egg, then add milk and oil. In a separate bowl, mix the dry ingredients together, then add the dry mixture to the egg mixture. Mix only enough to moisten. The batter should still be lumpy. Gently fold in apple. If desired, sprinkle the top with streusel. Bake in a greased muffin pan (or use cupcake papers) for 15 to 20 minutes or until muffins test done with a cake tester or a toothpick.

STREUSEL TOPPING:

2 Tbsp. firm butter
¼ cup flour
¼ cup brown sugar
½ tsp. cinnamon

Mix with fork until crumbly.

CARAMEL PECAN BROWNIES
Makes approximately 48 brownies.

1 cup butter
1 12-oz. package semisweet chocolate chips
1⅓ cups sugar
2 tsp. vanilla
4 large eggs
1 cup flour

Preheat oven to 350 degrees. Line a cookie sheet or a mini-muffin pan with approximately 48 foil cups (2-inch size). Melt butter in large saucepan. Add chocolate chips and stir until melted. Add sugar and vanilla and mix thoroughly.

Remove from heat and add eggs one at a time, stirring thoroughly after each one. Stir in flour gradually until mixed well. Fill cups to approximately ¾ full. Bake for 25 minutes. Do not overbake.

CARAMEL TOPPING

25 pieces chewy soft caramel candies, unwrapped
1 Tbsp. water
1 tsp. vanilla
Chopped pecans (enough to sprinkle over tops of brownies)

Melt caramels and water in saucepan over low heat, stirring occasionally. Remove from heat and stir in vanilla.

Drizzle caramel over cooled brownies and sprinkle with chopped pecans.

TOMATO BASIL CHICKEN
Serves four.

4 boneless chicken breasts
1 28-oz. can crushed tomatoes
½ cup balsamic vinegar
1 Tbsp. olive oil
1 clove garlic, minced or pressed
¼ cup finely chopped fresh basil
Parmesan or Asiago cheese

Mix tomatoes, vinegar, oil, garlic, and basil. Pour over chicken breasts and marinate for at least 30 minutes.

Chicken can be either baked or grilled. If grilling, discard marinade and place on grill over low to medium heat, approximately 6 to 10 minutes each side depending on thickness of chicken. If baking, place chicken and marinade in pan sprayed with nonstick spray. Bake in a preheated oven at 375 degrees for 30 minutes or until juices run clear.

Sprinkle with Parmesan or Asiago cheese before serving.

Keep reading for a special preview of
Joyce Tremel's next Brewing Trouble Mystery,

A ROOM WITH A BREW

Coming soon from Berkley Prime Crime!

$\mathcal{J}$ slid onto an old piano stool as Daisy Hart placed the fall centerpiece she'd designed on the distressed wood counter in her flower shop, Beautiful Blooms.

"That looks great," I said. "It's exactly what I had in mind."

"When you said something for Oktoberfest," Daisy said, "I wasn't sure whether to go with autumn, beer, or Germany, so I looked it up and incorporated all of them."

"Well, it's perfect."

Daisy clapped her hands together, making her blond braids sway. Her choice of hairstyle made her look fifteen instead of early thirties. "I'm so glad."

It really was perfect. She'd used the traditional Oktoberfest colors of blue and white. The centerpiece consisted of creamy-colored mums and blue asters, and in the center was a miniature German beer stein. I'd ordered fourteen of them—enough to dress up all the tables in my brewpub. In two weeks, the Allegheny Brew House would be hosting its first Oktoberfest weekend.

Daisy came around the counter and took a seat on the other piano stool. "Explain one thing to me, Max. You're having this celebration in September. Shouldn't something called Oktoberfest happen in October?"

It was a common misconception. "The official Oktoberfest in Germany begins in mid-September and lasts for about two weeks. So it ends in October. Besides, Septemberfest doesn't have quite the same ring to it."

Daisy grinned. "No, it doesn't. How come you're wimping out and only having yours for a weekend?"

I laughed. "I'm having enough trouble coordinating everything for just the weekend. Do you know how hard it is to find an oompah band?"

"I never thought of that. But you did find one, right?"

"Yes," I said. "Candy, Kristie, and I are going to hear them play and make the final arrangements tonight. Why don't you come with us?"

"I don't know. . . ."

"It'll be fun. A Friday girls' night out." I didn't add that she needed to get out and do something besides work on flower arrangements. She'd gone through a rough patch last spring when the man she'd been in love with turned out to be . . . well . . . someone who didn't care for her at all. She'd been devastated and had even considered closing her shop and moving away. She was gradually becoming more like the old Daisy, but still had a little way to go.

She hesitated a moment, then said, "Maybe I will. It does sound like fun."

We talked a few more minutes and decided I'd pick her up at eight. I was glad she agreed to go with us.

And it would be fun. Candy and Kristie would be sure to bring Daisy out of her self-imposed shell. Candy Sczypinski owned the bakery—named Cupcakes N'at—that sat between the brewpub and Beautiful Blooms on Butler Street in the Lawrenceville neighborhood of Pittsburgh. Candy was a Pittsburgher—or Yinzer, as natives were sometimes called—through and through. I'd never seen her wear any colors but black and gold, and I always thought she looked like Mrs. Santa Claus in Steelers garb. Despite her age, she had more energy than a twenty-year-old. Kristie Brinkley was the owner and barista at Jump, Jive & Java, the coffee shop across the street. She bore no resemblance to the supermodel whose first name began with a *C*. Kristie looked more like Halle Berry, especially since she'd recently sheared off her dreadlocks and now had only a few streaks of purple in her hair. Purple this week, anyway. She changed color as often as some people changed their socks. I had a sneaking suspicion that her recent hairstyle change had something to do with her new love interest, which she denied having. Candy was on the case, though. If anyone could discover who it was, she could.

As I passed the bakery on the way back to the brew house, Candy's assistant, Mary Louise, waved to me and I returned her wave. I was tempted to stop in for a treat, but

I had a batch of stout in the brew kettle and it was time to get it ready for the fermentation tank. Inside the pub, my staff was preparing for the lunch rush, and delicious aromas emanated from the kitchen. Nicole Clark, my part-time manager, was stacking glasses behind the bar, so I stopped to see her.

"Everything okay?" I asked.

"Yep." She nodded her head toward the brewery. "Need any help in there?"

Nicole was studying for her master's in chemistry at the University of Pittsburgh and she'd taken a shine to the brewing process. She reminded me a lot of myself, although I'd been more interested in distilling when I earned my degree. That changed to brewing only when I made a trip to Germany.

"Sure, as long as I'm not taking you from anything else." Nicole followed me through the swinging door into the brewing area. The aroma of caramel malt was strong and I breathed in deeply.

Nicole had been assisting me with brewing more and more lately. As much as I liked having the brewery to myself most of the time, I appreciated the help. And it was fun being on the teaching end for a change. The next step in the process was to pump out the wort, then pump it back into the brew kettle through a nozzle that forced the solids and hops to move into the center, so when the tank was drained, the solids stayed. Then we cooled it quickly, added the yeast, and checked the initial specific gravity. It was lunchtime by then, so Nicole returned to the pub while I finished trans-ferring the stout to the fermentation tank. I set the temperature on the tank to sixty-eight degrees, where it would ferment for approximately two weeks.

My stomach was screaming for food by this time, so I decided to get something to eat before I tackled the cleanup. Cleaning and sterilizing all the equipment took time and I needed to be properly fortified. Besides, I hadn't seen Jake yet this morning.

The thought of seeing my chef brought a smile to my face. I'd known Jake Lambert practically all my life. He'd been my brother Mike's best friend and I'd had a crush on him for years. When my former chef, Kurt, had been killed four months ago, Jake had walked back into my life. He'd just retired from playing professional hockey and happened to be a certified chef. One thing led to another and we were now what my mother called "an item."

I crossed the pine-plank floor of the pub, stopping briefly to say hello to a few regulars. I liked that we had customers who kept coming back for the food as well as the beer. My stomach growled again as I went through the door to the kitchen. Two cooks plus Jake were in various stages of food preparation.

Jeannie Cross was assembling two grilled chicken salads and smiled when she noticed me. "Heads-up, everyone. The boss is on deck."

"Uh-oh," Kevin Bruno said without glancing up from where he was sautéing some vegetables while simultaneously grilling burgers. "She must be hungry."

Jake was elbow deep in kneading some kind of dough. He looked up and winked at me. It never failed to make my stomach do that little flip and I felt my cheeks grow warm. "Either that or she's here to fire your sorry behind," he said.

I laughed. I loved the camaraderie of my employees. They'd become my second family. "Don't worry, Kev. You're safe. As long as I get something to eat, that is."

Jake said, "Jeannie, fix Max one of those new turkey sandwiches we came up with." He held up his flour-covered arms. "I'd do it myself, but I'm a little indisposed."

"Coming right up." She put the finishing touch on the chicken salads by tossing a handful of French fries on top, which was a Pittsburgh tradition. I wasn't wild about it, but when customers kept asking for the fries, I gave in.

I followed Jeannie over to another stainless steel table, where she quickly assembled a sandwich on whole-grain bread with roasted turkey slices, a thick slice of cheddar, and baby spinach, and topped it with something that looked like a cranberry chutney or relish.

"Here you go, boss." She handed me the plate.

I took a bite. It was an interesting combination of flavors. The cheddar and turkey were familiar. The cranberry chutney was what made the sandwich. I tasted a hit of orange, and there was a little bit of heat to it as well.

"Well?" Jeannie said.

"I like it. Especially the cranberries. I like the combination of sweet, tart, and heat." I swallowed the second bite. "I'm not sure about the spinach on here, though."

Jeannie looked smug. "That's what I told Jake."

Jake pushed the dough aside and went to the sink. "I guess I'm outnumbered—unless Kevin is going to back me up."

Kevin raised a hand. "I'm staying out of it. I don't even like cranberries."

I took my lunch to my office and finished the sandwich

in record time, then buckled down to do some paperwork and make some calls. There was still a good bit that needed to be done for our Oktoberfest celebration. Jake had already come up with a special menu full of German food for that weekend—three kinds of wurst, schnitzel, sauerkraut, potato pancakes, and German potato salad. I made a note to pick up the menus at the print shop before the end of next week. I made a few phone calls and after I updated my to-do list, I headed back to the brewery to clean up. A brewer's work is never done.

The fire hall hosting the band I was hiring for our celebration was located just north of the city. Kristie drove, Candy rode shotgun, and Daisy and I white-knuckled it in the back. Kristie should have been a NASCAR driver. Thank goodness it was a short trip. I was tempted to make the sign of the cross when she screeched into the last empty parking space in the lot. I heard Daisy blow out air. She must have been holding her breath. Candy didn't seem to be fazed one bit by Kristie's driving. Then again, I'd been a passenger in Candy's car. She drove like the streets were an obstacle course.

The sound of accordion and horn music drifted across the lot when we got out of the car. "This is going to be so much fun," Candy said. Tonight she wore her best black-and-gold-sequined blouse, black pants, and gold ballet flats. "It's been years since I heard this kind of music. It really takes me back."

"Back where?" I asked.

"To my much younger days." She turned to Daisy. "I'm so glad you decided to come with us."

Daisy smiled. "I am, too."

By this time we were at the door. Two women were seated at a table with a steel cashbox and took our ten-dollar admission fees. There was a large sign welcoming us to their "Octoberfest." I decided it wouldn't be polite to point out that they were a little early, or that they'd misspelled it by using a *c* instead of a *k*. It gave me a bad feeling about the beer they'd be serving.

The hall was decorated with black, red, and yellow streamers that matched the tiny German flags on every table. Not exactly the traditional Oktoberfest colors. Daisy caught my eye and made a face. I smiled at her and shrugged.

Kristie pointed toward the far side of the hall. "There are some empty seats over there." We followed her across the room and sat at the end of a large banquet table. "I'm buying tonight," she hollered over the din. "What's everyone drinking?"

Daisy wanted only bottled water and Candy said she'd have the same. I offered to help Kristie and we headed to the bar. I was surprised at the assortment of beverages on hand, and especially that they had bottles of Oktoberfest beer from a local brewery. That moved them up a notch in my eyes. Despite the selection, Kristie and I also chose water for now.

It was too noisy in the hall for much conversation—especially with the band playing—so we sat and listened. The Deutschmen were very good and hearing them play again made me glad I'd decided to hire them. The four musicians played accordion, trumpet, keyboard, and sousaphone. I had to admit I'd never seen a sousaphone except in a marching band. I thought it an odd choice when a tuba would have worked just as well—or better. Plus it wouldn't have taken up half the stage.

There were only two couples on the dance floor until the band broke out in their version of the "Steelers Polka," which was sung to the tune of the "Pennsylvania Polka." A dozen people jumped to their feet, including Candy. She grabbed my hand. "Come on. You're dancing with me."

I tried to pull my hand back with no luck. "I don't know how to polka. I'm Irish. O'Haras don't polka."

"I won't hold that against you," she said. "It's easy. It's your basic one-two-three, one-two-three. Just follow me."

"Do I have any choice?" I asked as she practically dragged me across the room. Everyone in the hall except me seemed to know the words to the song, but I was too busy trying not to trip over my own feet to sing anyway. By the time the song ended, I could reasonably say I knew how to polka, or at least fake my way through one. We stayed on the dance floor for the "Beer Barrel Polka," but I drew the line when the band began playing the "Chicken Dance." I had my pride after all.

I collapsed onto my folding chair and guzzled half of my water.

"Nice work," Kristie said with a grin.

"I can't keep up with her." I pointed to where Candy was enthusiastically flapping her arms to the music. "I don't know where she gets the energy."

"I don't, either," Daisy said.

The Deutschmen finished the song and announced they

were taking a break and would be back shortly. A few minutes later, I went over to the bar, where the members of the quartet were quenching their thirst with cold beers. I'd talked to only one of them on the phone and had never met them in person, so I introduced myself.

The keyboard player shook my hand. "I'm Bruce Hoffman." He was in his mid to late fifties, with an obviously dyed crew cut that bordered on orange. He had a friendly smile that made up for his hair color faux pas. He introduced the others.

The trumpet player was Manny Levin, called "Toots" by his friends. Toots appeared to be in his sixties. He was bald and almost as wide as he was tall. The sousaphone player, Doodle Dowdy, was the youngest of the group—probably in his forties—with sandy hair that hadn't seen a barber in a while. The last member of the band, the accordion player, was Felix Holt. Felix appeared to be the oldest—close to seventy, or possibly even older. He had gray hair, gray eyes, and the deeply wrinkled skin of a smoker or a former smoker.

I invited them over to our table, where we discussed my upcoming event and made the final arrangements. While we talked, I noticed Felix kept staring at Candy. Finally he said to her, "You look very familiar. Have we met before?" He spoke with a slight accent.

Candy shook her head. "Absolutely not."

"I never forget a face," he said. "Especially one as lovely as yours."

I expected Candy to roll her eyes and make some smart remark. The man was obviously flirting with her. Instead of a witty comeback, she said, "You're mistaken."

"I don't think I am," Felix said. "I know you from some-where."

Daisy smiled at the man. "Maybe you've been to her bakery. It's the best one in Pittsburgh."

"Which bakery is that?" Felix asked.

"Cupcakes—"

Candy cut her off. "He's never been to my bakery."

"You're probably right. I'm sure I would remember the bakery," he said. "That's not it. I know you from somewhere else. I am sure of it. It will come to me."

"How many times do I have to tell you that you're mistaken? I don't know you, and you certainly don't know me." She rose quickly to her feet. "I need some air. I'll be outside."

ALSO AVAILABLE FROM

JOYCE TREMEL
To Brew or Not to Brew

A Brewing Trouble Mystery

The Allegheny Brew House is a dream come true for
Maxine "Max" O'Hara, who went all the way to
Germany for her brewmaster certification, and is now
preparing to open her own craft brew pub in a newly
revitalized section of Pittsburgh. But before she can
start pouring stouts and lagers to thirsty throngs,
there's trouble on tap. Suspicious acts of sabotage
culminate in Max finding her assistant brewmaster and
chef Kurt Schmidt strangled in one of the vats.

Between rescuing a stray gray tabby she names Hops
and considering a handsome ex-hockey player as her
new chef, Max doesn't have a lot of time to solve a
murder. But with a homicide detective for a dad, she
comes to criminal investigation naturally. And if
someone is desperate enough to kill to stop her from
opening, Max needs to act fast—before her brand-new
brew biz totally tanks...

INCLUDES RECIPES

Available wherever books are sold or at
penguin.com